MONTEREY MADNESS
MR. ONE POCKET

Wings Press, Inc.

L. C. Wright

Monterey Madness

In all the years of my existence, I believe there are very few things I can say are facts. One of them is that there isn't a man alive who truly understands women. It's a fact, and I'll be the first to admit I know less than most.

For example, I took the time while on break purely to do a good deed and go home to see if Jill was okay and if I could be there to support her. Many men would consider me a pussy for doing something like that. The rest would consider me stupid because it's a well-known fact that no good deed goes unpunished.

After a relaxing ride home, I didn't get the "Oh honey, it's so nice to see you" reward I admit I was hoping for. What I got was something considerably different.

Jill's greeting was, "Why would you let him do something like that?"

"I'm assuming you're talking about Tootie," I replied.

"Of course I'm talking about Tootie. And don't act so innocent with me. You let him take a dangerous job hunting down criminals and risking his life. You're allowing *my* father to risk his life... for what? Do you want him to get killed? Do you think I'll be more dependent on you if he's not around? Do you need to control me that bad? You're sick, Adam Shaw. You are sick and disgusting and I can't believe you would do this to me."

The thing about women that has always baffled me is their ability to change their minds on a dime and expect a man to understand. It's true they keep us guessing and sometimes it's even sorta cute...but damn—

MONTEREY MADNESS
MR. ONE POCKET

L. C. Wright

A Wings ePress, Inc.
Mystery Novel

Wings ePress, Inc.

Edited by: Jeanne Smith
Copy Edited by: Joan Powell
Senior Editor: Jeanne Smith
Executive Editor: Marilyn Kapp
Cover Artist: Richard Stroud

Wings ePress Books
http://www.wings-press.com

Copyright © 2010 by L. C. Wright
ISBN 978-1-61309-968-1

Published In the United States Of America

Wings ePress Inc.
3000 N. Rock Road
Newton, KS 67114

Dedication

There are many people that have offered support, advice and suggestions during the creation of this work. However, without the support (not to mention the constant prodding) of my wife Melissa, none of it would have happened. To her I give my most sincere thanks

Prologue

There were more shadows than light on the busy coastal town's street. The bars in the area were yelling for last call; the killer knew the window of opportunity would be small. There wasn't a need for dialogue, introductions or pleasantries—only action.

The target, like always at this hour, left the pool hall a bit too satisfied, a bit too sure of herself, a bit too drunk. It was her flaw, the only flaw of one of the city's most beautiful creatures and after tonight, it would be the death of her.

The killer knew where the woman was heading. Hell, she had practically taken out an ad in the coastal living section of the local paper announcing her intentions, but nobody paid her any attention. She was harmless, or... maybe nobody cared.

She was close now—moments away—the back door to the pool hall opened and someone—another girl—yells an obscenity her way and then they both laugh. *That's the problem with today's youth.* They didn't realize just how much words—even playful, obscene words—could hurt. They didn't understand that everything has meaning. Every word has a power unto itself. Everything—anything—could come back and bite you in the ass.

~ * ~

Standing above her, looking down at what used to be a beautiful albeit pretentious young lady, the killer checked one last time to make sure the eyes didn't open, the feet didn't move, the heart, once again, didn't start beating.

She wouldn't be coming back to haunt. The dead couldn't hurt you.

The living, on the other hand, could screw you royally.

One

"I've been known to make a mistake or two," I told the review board. "However, those times are usually alcohol related, and I don't see what they have to do with the matter at hand." Of course, it became quite clear—when they told me I was suspended—that they didn't appreciate my sense of humor. And now I have the next ninety days to "Get my act together" or, they made it very clear, the ninety days would be extended permanently.

When I was in the first grade, I thought my teacher said I was a disturbing elephant. Later, I found out that she meant disrupting element. Apparently, I hadn't changed much and my bosses had gotten tired of my lack of respect and underwhelming social skills.

Ah...what the hell. I haven't really liked being a cop for the last couple years anyway. Maybe it's time for me to do something else. I always wanted to try fishing for a living. Or maybe get my pilot's license and run a little charter business flying the California coast and telling strangers about the wonders of the Golden State.

Who am I kidding? I've been a cop for over twenty years; investigating crime is what and who I am. Taking down bad guys can be such a rush. The only problems I have are the friggin' bureaucrats and politicians. For whatever reason, they are of the opinion that they know more about how to bring down criminals than I do. Anyone who knows me will tell you how stupid that assumption is.

Oh, by the way, my name is Adam Shaw. Most everyone knows me as Samson and it isn't because of my biblical qualities. Rather, at six-six and two hundred thirty pounds—not to mention long reddish-blond hair to the middle of my back—most people don't know anyone bigger.

I live on a small "gentleman's farm" in Carmel Valley, California, which consists of a garage that could be used for overhauling an eighteen-wheeler—but no truck—and a three-stall horse barn with no horses. The only animals I own are a cat with no manners and a black lab that can't decide if he's a dog, cat or human.

I do have two loves in my life. The first is my wife, Jill. She's a brazen southern belle from Texas who *will not* put up with my shit. Not that she ever has to deal with anything from me. For her, I only offer the best. But just in case she would at some time in the future ever have to deal with such behavior, she reminds me on occasion that size doesn't matter and small packages pack a powerful punch. She's a tough woman with a heart the size of her home state.

The second love I have is my Hawg. Now for those who are not familiar with motorcycle lingo, a Hawg—in this case—is a 1948 Harley Davidson pan head chopper with a thirty-inch extended Springer front fork. It has a 74 cubic-inch engine, a hard tail, peanut tank and chrome out the ass. It's my baby. I bought it when I was seventeen years old as a basket case. Actually, if I am to be accurate, it was actually two baskets, three boxes, assorted shopping bags and stray parts. Three years later, I got it running and wrecked it for the very first time.

It was love at first bandage.

~ * ~

I was starting my third day of suspension when I got the call from Sam. He was at the police station and I was not feeling my best. The ringing of the phone was much louder than I could ever remember.

"I need your help," were the first words I heard. Maybe there was more said before that, but 7 a.m. came way too early for someone who had been up drinking 'til three o'clock in the morning.

"You and me both," was all I could muster in reply. My head felt like someone had used it for batting practice and my teeth felt like they were wearing sweaters.

"This is serious, Samson. You are the only person I could trust calling."

"Who is this?" I was trying my best to clear my head. Something was happening on the other end of the phone and I couldn't even remember my own name 'til the caller said it.

Speaking now in a very slow and deliberate manner, he said, "Samson, this is Sam Reynolds. I am at the police station and I need you to get down here and help me out. Someone was killed at the pool hall last night and the cops think I had something to do with it."

My head hung from sheer weight, and I had to admit, when someone says something like that, it totally takes away the buzz, if not the hangover, very quickly. "Who've you talked to?" I asked with an unwilling tongue.

"There's a Sergeant Ramos and someone named Bennett. They have been grilling me since four o'clock this morning. And the way their questions have been going the last hour, it seems like they think I had something to do with the murder."

"Who's your attorney?" I asked.

"The only attorney I know is Larry Burgess and he only does real estate. I've never needed an attorney for criminal action so I don't know who to call."

"Okay," I said. "I'll make a couple calls and see what I can find out. I know a couple guys that are real good at criminal law and we'll take it from there. In the meantime, keep your mouth shut and wait 'til someone shows up. I'll get there as soon as I can."

~ * ~

I know what you're thinking. This guy claims to be a cop and yet he tells a suspect not to cooperate. But you need to know something about me. I don't believe the customer is always right. And I don't believe every suspect is guilty until proven innocent. Besides, Sam is a friend of mine, and though I don't know Bennett very well, I can't stand that pompous prick Carl Ramos. As far as I can tell, he would have half the city of Monterey in jail just to make sure the prospects of crime would diminish by fifty percent. He doesn't need a reason to arrest. His perspective is to go for the most likely suspect, regardless of guilt, and then let them prove otherwise.

As far as attorneys were concerned, there really was only one I needed to call. Bill Wiseman was by far the best. And even though we had locked horns on so many cases I couldn't begin to count them all, I knew him to be a man of integrity, and, once he got a hold of a case, he was like a junkyard dog with a ham bone. Letting go was never an option for him.

I made the call to his home. He told me he would take care of all preliminary work and would get to the jail by eight o'clock. I hung up from Bill and called the precinct to find out as much information as I could before heading to town.

Deputy Tommy Billings—tall, skinny, with a honker you could set your drink on—answered the phone. "Damn, Samson" were the first words out of his mouth when he recognized my voice. "In all the years I've been here, you were never up at this hour."

"Don't give me any shit this morning," I said. "My head hurts and I'm too tired to try sparring with you right now."

"Enjoying your vacation, I see." I could hear the humor in his voice and it was pissing me off. I had known Tommy since he'd joined the force six years ago and he was a good kid as far as I knew. We didn't work the same areas so our contacts were only when certain cases came up that I needed to help him with. But everyone liked him and he seemed to have a good head for the job.

"Look, Junior."

I knew that would get his attention because he hated the name. His father, Thomas J. Billings, Senior, was a very successful real estate mogul and complete asshole. Tommy loathed the man for that and other reasons too numerous to mention. "I need to find out what's going on with the Sam Reynolds case. He's a friend of mine."

"You know I can't do that, Samson," he lowered his voice. "You're on suspension and the captain would have my shield if he found out."

We both knew the drill. He had to tell me what he couldn't do. I had to tell him he would be okay and nobody would ever find out. Then after several minutes of going back and forth, he would tell me what I wanted. He knew it. I knew it. But it's an unspoken rule that had to be followed for those of us who covered each other's backs.

~ * ~

Winning the Nobel Peace Prize wasn't necessary to figure out the frosty reception I received from the powers and politicos when I made it to the station. They were, after all, looking out for the people (not to mention the votes) of this fine California shoreline community. I was considered a disturbing element for those in charge. Hell, if it wasn't for the ice crystals hanging from a few noses, I'm not sure I would have noticed much difference from the normal pleasant environment I work in.

"What the fuck are you doing here?"

Ah, the words brought joy to my heart. Carl Ramos, by the tone of his words, was not happy to see me. He's arrogant, ambitious, and as far as I am concerned . . . dirty. I hadn't been able to prove it yet so it didn't matter what I thought about him. On the bright side, I never missed an opportunity to rattle his cage when I could.

"I stopped by to see how bad you were going to screw up this case you're working on," I said, issuing the first salvo.

"If the captain doesn't know you're here yet, he will in two shakes."

Yes, run to mommy.

There are two factions of the local police department. The first are the RCs. RC stands for real cops. These are the men and women that you can go into battle with and know, not just think, that your back is covered. The others are AKs. That stands for ass kissers. Those are the ones you want to lead you into battle, hoping they will get taken out. Frankly, I wouldn't care too much if it were from friendly fire. Ramos is a card-carrying member of the AKs. If they had an AK patch, he would wear it proudly on his sleeve.

I've thought about getting him drunk and having AK tattooed on his ass.

"Get your brown nose out of the captain's tunnel for a moment and tell me what's going on with the Reynolds case," I said.

I guess he was on a roll. "It's none of your gawd-damn business. You're a civilian now and you have no right to any aspect of the case. So get the hell out of here before I have you arrested."

"Come on, big boy," I taunted. "Don't cry for help. *You* arrest me. I tell you what, you get those cuffs on me and I'll buy you the best dinner in town, your choice. I'll even pay for your date, just the meal . . . not the hourly rate, if you can find someone hard-up enough to go out with you."

"You boys have *way* too much testosterone flying around for this time of day," Dakota Walker announced as she approached the gathering crowd. "I don't understand why you two just can't play with separate toys."

The smile on her face was infectious. We were friends and I considered her a smart, cool lady. Of course, it might have something to do with the fact that I knew she couldn't stand Ramos any more than I could.

"Now what would be the fun in that?" I replied. We smiled at each other, knowing the others' thoughts.

Dakota was the Assistant District Attorney of Monterey and one of the good guys in my opinion. She was someone you could depend on to do the right thing when it came to the law. That didn't mean she would always do what you wanted, which I knew from personal experience. However, if something had to be done to help us get to the bad guys, she would do everything possible and take the extra steps necessary to get us what we needed for support.

However, for the sake of full disclosure, for about eight months, twenty-six days and eleven hours, not that anyone is counting, Dakota and I used to be an item. That was ancient history, about ten years ago. I'd been a little too wild and she'd been a little too much of an attorney. No ending is ever good, but I think we made it through well enough.

"I think you and I need to talk in private, Samson," she said, not waiting as she turned and walked toward a private room.

~ * ~

"Are you trying to get yourself arrested?" she asked. I could see the flair of anger as her cheeks flushed.

"What?" I asked dubiously. "That prick is nothing but a blowhard and couldn't beat his way out of a paper bag."

Where was she coming from? I was just here to help a friend. What was the harm in that? (My shoulders probably hunched as I went through this imaginary, albeit very convincing, conversation.)

"I don't give a flying fuck about Ramos," Dakota said, "and *you* know it. But you, my friend, are suspended, and unless you have a really good reason for being here, your hanging around police matters could contaminate some very important cases I'm working on."

"Look, I'm just here to try and help a friend. Sam Reynolds and I have been friends for a long time, and it seems Ramos is trying to pin a murder on him." I hesitated for a moment. "You know how he is, Dakota. Shoot first; ask questions later. It's hard enough to sit back and watch him do it with strangers. There's no way in hell I'm going to let that asshole get his claws in Sam. This is one case he's going to have to prove before he destroys the man's life."

"Does he have any reason to think your friend is guilty?"

"Since when does he need a reason? You know how he operates. He takes the easy way out. He puts the squeeze on people and makes their lives a living hell. He gets people fired. He takes away their ability to run their businesses just to put pressure on 'em. And then . . . when he finally figures out they're innocent, he just moves on without concern for the carnage he's caused. I will *not* let that happen. *Not this time!*"

After my little speech, Dakota moved around the table, pulled out a chair and sat . The pause seemed pregnant and I could sense there was something more here than I'd originally thought.

"He's confessed, Samson. That's why I'm here. I didn't know you and Sam Reynolds were friends."

Now it was my turn to be quiet. This was something I did not expect. What drastic changes had happened since I'd spoken with him?

"When? How?—I don't understand. I just talked to him an hour ago and he told me he was innocent. Why did he change all of a sudden? This doesn't make any sense—"

Dakota stood up and came to me. She knew I was having a lot of difficulty with this one.

"I can't let you see him right now, Samson. Does he have an attorney?"

"Bill Wiseman... I got Billy to represent him."

"You couldn't have done anything more," she stated. "Your friend will need the best and Wiseman is the best. I'm sorry."

And then she was gone.

I was stunned by the news. I'd known Sam since before moving to Monterey. As a matter of fact, he was one of the main reasons I'd moved to Monterey to begin with. We'd known each other in the military. Saved each other's butts on more than one occasion. After the Army, we both went back to our own home areas, but had stayed in touch. He was from Baton Rouge and I was from a small town in Ohio that nobody'd ever heard of. He became a pool hall junkie and eventually became known as Mr. One Pocket for his prowess in that particular game.

I became a cop.

He moved to Monterey because while on the pro tour, he met Willie Davis (known around the pool hall circuit as Fast Willie, after having won the world speed-shot tournament three years running), and they'd become good friends. Fast Willie was a pool shark of which legends were made. When Fast Willie died, Sam inherited the business and in his honor, named the pool hall after his friend and mentor.

A few years later, after a long and bitter divorce, I left Ohio behind and moved to sunny California. We've been close ever since. Not only that, but now I can actually play a decent game of pool.

I was now in a situation I couldn't remember ever being in, sitting on the outside looking in. For me this was dark territory and I had to think of a way to help my friend.

Two

I left the police station, mind in a whirl. I climbed on Lu-Lu Belle, my motorcycle, my second love, and kicked to start her, failing to retard the distributor.

There was a peaceful feeling that went through my mind right before that sudden impact of landing flat on my ass as she backfired and sent me sailing through the air. For those not familiar with the workings of old motorcycles, if you aren't careful when kick-starting an old bike, sometimes they kick back. It's a clear reminder that keeping one's mind on the work is critical to getting where you want to go.

Lying on my back with a dozen people rushing up to me to see if I was okay was significantly more painful than the bruise I could feel turning purple by the minute. But being the consummate biker dude that I'd worked my whole life to become, I stood up and told everyone I was okay and they had no reason to be concerned. I brushed off the embarrassment, climbed on Lu-Lu Belle again—this time starting her correctly, with loving care and a retarded spark.

I rode a few blocks and turned onto Freemont. A few minutes later, I arrived at Fast Willie's to take a look around. The place was closed. Crime tape adorned the front and back doors as well as the parking lot in the back. A couple of black and whites were parked at the front of the building.

Without interrupting anyone, I decided to head over to see Manny Black.

Manny's a biker friend, an ex-cop, and a man of many talents. He, like myself, is not exactly fond of the way the rules of the legal system work in favor of the criminals. His current job *du jour* is that of a private investigator. He isn't listed in the yellow pages as such, but if anyone needs help finding anything or anyone, Manny is the guy to call.

"You have a lot of nerve riding that noisy piece of shit here this time of day," he said, standing at the front door, wearing a Guns N' Roses t-shirt and boxers. "You'll wake the dead, not to mention the neighbors."

"The only one in this neighborhood still asleep is your worthless ass," I replied. "I still don't see how you make ends meet looking like shit and sleeping all day long."

"What you don't seem to realize is that the people I work for don't care what I look like and the ones I track down don't keep bankers' hours. Besides," he continued, "I don't remember you being exactly an early riser yourself. What the hell are you doing here, Samson?" He stepped over to me, shook my hand, followed by the one-arm chest bump.

"My best to help a friend who seems hell-bent on screwing himself," I said. "I figured if there was anyone who could help me figure out why, it would be you."

"You talking about Sam?" It was more of a statement than a question.

"How the hell did you know?" I asked.

"Small town, big mouths," he smirked. "I figured you'd be around sooner or later. So I've already been doin' a little snooping...just to get the four-one-one on what really happened."

"And?"

"Doesn't make any sense so far," he stated flatly.

He turned and walked back into his house.

Manny didn't live in the ritzy part of town.

Monterey, like every city in the U.S., has both good and not-so-good areas. Of course, Monterey's bad sections are more expensive than most cities' good sections. It's not unusual for a small two-bedroom, one-bathroom house to cost over a half a million dollars. Manny was one of those who grew up here. He was one of the official natives of Monterey, and he'd inherited the house when his folks died several years ago. By looking around, it wasn't difficult to realize he hadn't spent much on renovations or upkeep.

"Want a beer?" he asked as he popped the top off one for himself. He must have seen the look of astonishment on my face. "What?"

"Humph. How the hell do you do that?" I asked. Just the thought of alcohol at ten in the morning was enough to make my stomach wretch a bit. Granted, I'm no choirboy when it comes to the brew, but morning beer just seems all kinda wrong.

"Hair of the dog," he said without a second thought. "If you want me to help you on this, I need a clear head. A beer is just the ticket." He swigged down a huge gulp and then a second one. "Ahhh," he dragged out the delight.

"Sam isn't a killer," I told him. "Sure, we had to do what we needed in the service, even killing. But, he isn't the kind of person to do something like that now."

"Are you sure?" Manny asked. I sensed he wasn't looking for an answer. He wanted me to look for the answer myself.

"I know anyone can do anything if the right—or wrong—reasons are presented," I offered in reflection. "But, I can't see any way he could be involved with this. He's a good man. And I'll continue believing that until it's proven otherwise."

"What about the confession?" he asked.

"You know about that, too?" I don't know why I was surprised. I guess I didn't think that information was out to anyone yet.

"I know about it. I have friends in small, dark places. There isn't much I can't find out in cop-land."

After pausing a moment, he asked again. "So?"

"Even with the confession," I said. "He would take the heat long before he would do the crime. I have no doubt."

"Then I guess we need to figure out what makes a good man confess to murder, before it kills him."

"How do we do that?" I asked. "This is the first time I've ever had to investigate without being a cop. I'm not even sure where to begin."

"We've already begun." He smiled. "We do what you've always done. We gather information, we follow leads, and then we gather more information. The difference is that we don't have to play by the rules cops do. Now, if you don't mind, I need a few hours to tidy up a couple of loose ends, and then you can meet me at my office at, say...two o'clock." He finished his beer and escorted me to the door.

"Don't worry," he whispered. "I love a good mystery."

~ * ~

I decided that the best use of my time at that moment was to go home, get cleaned up and start making plans on what to do next. Manny was a good friend and I knew he wouldn't let me down. But there was no way I was going to put my friend's life in anyone's hands but my own. Lu-Lu Belle was cooperative and as always, made the trip invigorating.

Jill was waiting for me at the door when I arrived, the bundle of vitality she always is. Lu-Lu Belle had announced my arrival, her loud pipes sounding off as I drove up the small hill to the front of the house.

"You are not going to believe the news I have to share!" she exclaimed. Jill was four years younger than me and had the energy of a teenager. She's never met a stranger, and you can believe me when I tell you that no one is stranger than her family. I can't brag too much about my relatives, but I find her family to be a soap opera waiting for a TV contract.

It didn't really matter how down I was or how agitated I might be from work, Jill always made my heart beat faster and somehow managed to put a smile on my face.

"So what's the news?" Inquiring minds wanted to know. However, somewhere deep down, I'm always afraid to ask. I could tell you stories that would curl your toes, but I'll leave those to another time.

"Tootie is coming to visit," she said with so much enthusiasm I didn't want her to suspect the "Oh shit!" that was going on in my mind.

"Really?" I said, as she jumped in my arms and hugged me around the neck. "Wha...? When did this wonderful piece of news arrive?"

What I really thought isn't something I should be expressing here.

Tootie Childress is Jill's father. His given name is Harlan, but everyone calls him Tootie, even his kids. He's more active than most people half his seventy-something years. He watches Animal Planet when he doesn't have anything better to do, and talks about sex like he's Dr. Ruth's bastard stepchild. Every problem with married couples, in his mind, could be fixed by adding a new sexual position into the mix. He's fun to be around in private or with the family, but he never ceases to embarrass me when we take him out in public. In the most simple of terms, he's a horn dog.

"So exactly when is this blessed event going to happen?" I asked, tongue in cheek. I was hoping beyond hope it wouldn't be anytime soon. Even cops, or in my case a suspended cop, can make wishes.

"I have to leave in an hour to pick him up at the airport," she replied joyfully.

I felt my stomach give a short heave. The hair stood on the back of my neck. I sat down.

"This is a little quick, isn't it?" I asked, clearing my throat.

"He wanted to surprise us," she said. I did not reciprocate her enthusiasm and she noticed. "Oh baby, it'll be a blast. He's so much fun and you'll have time now to spend with him."

"I can hardly wait." The smile was forced, but she was too much in her own world to notice.

"I love you, baby."

She hugged me and then—this is the best way I can describe it—she galloped into the bedroom to change.

Hey, what can I say? I'm in love with a woman who gallops.

~ * ~

After Jill took off, I was left with the reality of what was going on with Sam. It didn't make any sense to me. I've known the man for so many years and there has never been an indication of him being violent. He told me he was innocent. Now I find out he'd confessed to a murder. Every part of my being told me he couldn't be responsible.

But he'd confessed.

I needed to get ahold of the murder book. I needed to go over the scene, but didn't really think the department would give me access. I needed to get a list of his closest friends and any relatives in the area. What I really needed was to figure out how to do this while not being a cop.

The time was running close. I needed to leave to meet Manny when the phone rang. The caller ID said "restricted caller."

"Hello?"

"Is this the cop known as Samson?" The voice was muffled, but it was a woman's voice.

I thought about explaining my suspended status, but decided to play it out a little.

"Yes. Who's calling?"

That's an old cop trick. It doesn't happen often, but every once in a while when a person is nervous and thinking about something else, a simple question will induce an honest response. It didn't work.

"That isn't important, Mr. Samson," she said. "I just called to tell you that he's innocent."

"Who?"

What the hell? Nothing ventured, nothing gained.

There was a pause and a sigh. "Maybe you aren't as smart as I thought."

She hung up.

I never did like cryptic calls, but somehow this one seemed to have something real about it. Sam is the only case I'm working on, or sort of working on. The mysterious caller knew that somehow. Was it just my imagination that the information coming out of cop-land was as porous as a sieve?

~ * ~

I told Manny about the phone call when I arrived at his office. He studied my words for a moment and told me that for now, it simply reinforced my own thoughts. And because I had no idea who had called, we needed to focus on what we did know.

"Let me show you around the digs," he said. Manny was always saying things that were semi-cool in an out-of-date sort of way. "You might find some of my new toys interesting."

Well, maybe his vocabulary could use a little updating, but his "toys" certainly were state of the art. It had been almost two years since the last time I had visited his office and it seemed like his entire world came out of a Spies "R" Us catalog. He had listening devices that, as he put it, could "hear a fly fart at a thousand meters." He had infrared monitors that could see through cement walls and technology that NASA would have been proud to own. After the tour, we started back to his office when in walked an attractive lady of about thirty-something.

"Hey, Margie," Manny said. "Let me introduce you to a friend of mine."

"Detective Adam Shaw," she said, as if she knew me. She held out her hand and I shook it—her grip as strong as any man I'd ever met, "nice to meet you at last."

"Nice to meet you too," I replied.

Beyond that I wasn't sure what to say. I had no way of knowing how she knew me.

As if reading my mind, she said, "Three years ago you were the detective who took the Linda Samara case. She was raped and beaten."

She paused for a moment to see if I would recognize the name. I did.

"Yes, I remember. That was a brutal beating she received. It took time, but I nailed the bastard who did it."

"Linda is my baby sister. I moved here from Pennsylvania to take care of her. I'd heard so much about you that I did a little homework. You did my sister proud and I want to thank you."

"Thanks aren't necessary, but you're welcome. How is it that we've never met?"

"I've commuted between here and back east. I'd thought about contacting you and introducing myself, but decided to wait 'til the right moment. I guess now is that right moment."

"Well, now that introductions and accolades are done, how about we start working on the job at hand?" Manny suggested.

I looked at Manny and then at Margie. "She works for me," Manny smiled. Then his smile broadened. "She thought you weren't doing a very good job at finding her sister's attacker, at first, and hired me to make sure you didn't screw things up. She started helping with a few things here and there and...poof, we decided it could be worthwhile for her to stay. Been working for me ever since."

I looked at Margie and her faced turned scarlet.

"So?" she defended. "I wasn't going to take any chances and I didn't know you. I'm just glad you were better than the others I've met since then." She stood a bit taller. "I won't apologize for my actions."

"No need to apologize, as far as I'm concerned," I said. "I know those same people you're talking about. And I wouldn't have wanted them on her case either."

"Anyway," Manny continued, "I did a little checking before you got here. It seems one Bobbi Marshal was at the pool hall last evening before she was killed. According to a couple of the people there, she showed up around ten-thirty, alone and apparently already feeling no pain. She's thirty-two years old...or *was* thirty-two years old. No one interviewed so far seems to know her very well—just seen her in passing. However, and you know how it is at that place, it didn't take her long to make friends. If you know what I mean."

"Do you know if Sam knew her?" I asked. "Before last night," I followed.

"If he did," Margie jumped in, "he isn't saying so and nobody else interviewed so far has made any connection."

"Okay," I said, "so where do we go from here?"

"You tell us," Manny replied. "We're just the hired guns. You brought us into this, but you're on point."

My head was spinning. Don't get me wrong; I've worked many cases that were high profile. But this was the first time I've ever had to deal with saving a friend under these circumstances. Screwing this up wasn't an option.

I learned a long time ago that the first step to getting out of a hole was to stop digging. Sam had dug himself a crater and I had to make sure he didn't do anything more to make things worse.

"Can you get a message to Sam?" I asked them both.

They looked at me as if I had asked them if they could ride a tricycle.

"You write down what you want and we'll make sure he gets the message."

"Thanks," I said. "I need a list of everyone Ms. Marshal associated with. I need a background on her, including financials and the same with Sam. I need a list of Sam's employees and you can feel free to add anything else you may believe pertinent."

"Just so you know," Margie said, "I've spent a lot of time with Sam over the last year."

I guess the subtle aspect of my eyes turning to saucers with surprise gave her a hint that the information was somewhat shocking to me. I'm a regular at the pool hall and hadn't seen her before and Sam sure-as-hell never mentioned her to me.

"I'm a lesbian," she volunteered, anticipating the next question. "We didn't have sex...not that he didn't try," she added with a little smile. "He's been teaching me to play pool. I just thought you should know and maybe you could use some company interviewing the employees and several of the regulars. I know most of them and thought maybe I could grease the wheels when you talk to them. I know you know some of them too, but I think they might relate better with me."

It's at times like this when a true professional shows what he's made of. Opportunities of this magnitude will allow the cream to rise to the top. On the other hand, the "You're a lesbian?" question I squeaked out probably wasn't my best moment. I'm also sure the timing left a little to be desired. What can I say? I'm a guy and fantasies come into mind a lot more often than I can count. And, girl-on-girl action...Oh, stop it. Damn.

There was an awkward moment of silence. Hell, I couldn't believe what had come out of my mouth. Maybe my nerves were getting the best of me. Margie, however, merely smiled and asked, "So what do you think? Could you use some company?"

At least one of us was acting professional.

Three

Margie and I dismounted Lu-Lu Belle after a short ride and parked at Enrique's Mexican Restaurant—a family-owned eatery considered one of the best in the area for Mexican cuisine.

According to Margie, "Timmy Ramirez was the person working last night. All the employees at Fast Willie's work part-time and generally no more than three shifts a week. Timmy worked for Sam longer than any of the other employees and likes working the weekends because the tips are usually better than weekdays."

"Hey, Margie." Timmy was all smiles with a face full of teeth showing. "What are you doing here?"

"Hi, Timmy," Margie said as she gave the young man a hug and a peck on the cheek. "This is Adam Shaw," she stepped aside to make the introduction more formal.

"Hey, man, I know you," he said, with the smile never fading. "You're that cop friend of Sammy's, aren't you? We never met because you always stopped during the day shift and I work evenings. But, Sammy talks about you all the time. So I guess I know why you're here now. It's about Sammy, right, and what happened last night, isn't it? You want to know what I know about the girl's murder, don't you?"

I was waiting for the kid to pass out from a lack of oxygen.

"Well, actually, we came for the tacos," I said.

"Really?" Timmy's confusion was evident. Then, as if the magical light bulb turned on, he smiled. "Ah, man, you had me going there. I thought you were serious."

"I was serious. I've heard the tacos here are out of this world. But, now that you mention it, what do you know about it?" I asked.

"Nothing about the murder," he said. "But I worked last night and I can tell you from what I saw: that lady was an accident waiting to happen."

"What do you mean?" Margie asked.

"I mean she was on the hunt and she didn't seem to care who got devoured."

"Timmy," I said, "I've been a cop for a long time and I'm pretty good at trying to understand what people say. I'm pretty sure you're saying she was looking for something or someone, but I don't know what.

"I'm also sure she was aggressive in her looking. What I want to know is, do you know what or whom she was hunting for? Did she find it or him? And did she spend any time with anyone in particular?"

"I'm not sure what or who she was looking for," Timmy replied. "I know she was loud. She was drunk. I also know a few guys were doing their best to get in her pants."

"Was anyone successful?" I asked.

"As far as I could tell...yeah. I think a couple of them were."

"A couple of them?" Margie said.

Her mouth was open and she didn't hide her amazement well.

"Yeah," Timmy responded.

"And how did you come to that conclusion?" I asked.

"Well," he hung his head and shuffled his feet for a few moments. "When the first guy left with her, when they came back, her lipstick was smeared and her hair was messed up a little. Now that doesn't tell me that they went, you know, all the way. But, the smile on his face told me that they did a little more than hold hands.

"The funny thing, though, is that when they came back in, they went their own way. But, the second guy, now I know he got lucky."

"How do you know that?" I asked.

"He let me smell the perfume on her panties." Feet shuffled again. "Well, actually, that's what I thought I was going to smell. But I don't think she was wearing perfume, you know, down there."

There are times in life when holding back a smile is very difficult. This was certainly one of those times. After observing Timmy's scarlet face, I looked at Margie and I could tell she was having as much difficulty as I was. I just wasn't sure it was for the same reason.

If I had a knife handy, I could have cut the air. As it was, I thought changing the subject might be a good alternative.

"So you think she was looking for male attention?" I asked.

"Not really sure," Timmy said. "But she certainly found it...in spades."

"Is there anything else?" I asked.

"Nothing I can think of right now," he said, "'cept, were you really serious about those tacos?"

~ * ~

The tacos were even better than advertised. Looking across at Margie, I, at least in my mind, was being the male pig that men were always thought of being. She was one fine looking lady and I was a little distracted by the healthy lungs she displayed. There were, of course, two strong mitigating factors that prevented me from pursuing something beyond that of a business relationship.

First, I was married to a goddess I loved dearly. The second was that Margie was a lesbian. But then, being the arrogant chauvinistic male that I am, I was completely convinced that, given the chance, I could convert her back to heterosexual experiences. But alas, fate was against her having that opportunity.

Anyway, back to reality. The truth is, if not for the situation we were working on, she would never look at me twice.

"So what do you think?" Margie asked.

I hesitated a few moments and said, "I think the tacos are even better than advertised." I knew that wasn't what she was asking, but I felt compelled to act cool. "I also think you are a very attractive lady." Then I totally screwed the pooch by stammering, "For a lesbian, that is."

Now, that wasn't cool and I couldn't believe it had come out of my mouth, but there it was. I was caught with my lecherous thoughts and had no place to hide.

"Want to explain yourself?" she asked, "Or is your foot buried deep enough in your mouth that you might have trouble talking?"

The look Margie gave me indicated she was totally pissed off. I couldn't tell for sure because I was rattled.

She didn't let up.

"Your little visions getting in the way? Are you thinking about what it would be like? You know...your lady and me? Or is it your wife? Does she know you think about her being with another woman? And you, do you want to join in or just watch?"

By this time I was totally screwed. My mind was racing as I looked for a hole to crawl into or someplace to escape. Margie wasn't about to cut me any slack. She knew she had me by the balls and if I didn't do something soon, I was never going to get out alive. I could apologize. That would be appropriate, but I really didn't think it would do any good. I decided to take the offensive.

"You're having fun now, aren't you?" I said. It wasn't a major offensive move. More like a crawl forward. Unfortunately, it was all I could muster on short notice.

Her stern look stayed intact for several more seconds and then she broke into a smile.

"I'm having a blast," she said. "You look so pitiful. I wish I had a camera." She then laughed so hard I thought she would pee her pants.

"It's not funny to kick a guy when he's made a total idiot of himself. It's not kosher."

"If not then," she asked, "when?" She proceeded, still smiling, "Look, Detective Shaw, I know there are people who have a problem with gay relationships. Having already talked to Manny about you, I know you're not one of them. I am who I am and I make no apologies for that. Sometimes, like now for instance, I can actually catch someone off guard and have some fun with it, rather than always trying to pretend that my sexuality is something only others engage in. However, having said all of that, you need to know that being a lesbian doesn't mean I'm loose. I don't know your wife, but I don't go after married women, even if their husbands fantasize about it. I've gotten over that aspect of my life a long time ago. So, if you're a little reticent about my sexuality, then don't be surprised if you fall prey to my assault again.

"Any questions?"

I was stunned by her frankness, yet pleasantly surprised. "Maybe a couple things we need to get straight," I said, trying to keep a strong appearance. "First, I'm not a detective right now, so calling me one is a little too formal for my taste. Second, my friends call me Samson and my really close friends call me Adam. You have my permission to call me either. I haven't known you but for a short time. However, I'm a good judge of character and I think you can be trusted. Finally, I apologize for my awkwardness. However, I can assure you that you'll never get the better of me again. So enjoy it while you can."

There was a long pause. I expected her to take up the challenge.

"We have work to do, Adam. Let's go find some more answers."

~ * ~

We tried a couple more stops, with very little luck at reaching anyone, when I got a call from Bill Wiseman.

"You think you can stop by my office?" he asked.

"Sure," I said. "I'm about fifteen minutes away. I'll see you then." I dropped Margie off at her office and headed straight to Bill's. After a short greeting, he got right to the point.

"We've got a problem, my friend. Or to be more specific, my client and your friend is in a real pickle."

I was trying to act nonchalant about the comment, but felt nonplussed. I didn't respond, and he took it as a signal to continue.

"Ethically, I would normally not be speaking to you or anyone else about the conversation I just had with Sam. However, he insisted I tell you everything—verbatim. He said you would know what to do with what he had to say."

"Go on," I insisted.

"He said to me, 'I am responsible for the girl's death.' Those words are a direct quote and he insisted that I make sure you heard them exactly as he said them. He also said, and again I quote, 'I have no choice but to accept whatever punishment comes from my guilt.' I asked him if he could tell me the details of what happened and he refused. I asked him how he expected me to get him off if he continued in this manner.

"Want to know what he said about that?" And without waiting for a reply, Bill said, "He told me that I couldn't get him off. He said he would never change his plea of guilty. And that only the 'miracle man' could set him free. Doesn't that beat all? And frankly I didn't take the guy for being religious."

"He isn't," I said. "Did he ask or say anything else?"

"Only that he wanted me to drag my feet," the attorney said in disgust. "Look, Samson, I'm not a babysitter. I thought this friend of yours was someone I could fight for. But by the looks of it, he's just confessed himself into a slow boat to our max-security prison in Vacaville. I can't beat a confession, especially when there's so much compelling evidence building against him."

"You have to fight for him. He's innocent."

"What the hell're you talking about? He said he killed her."

"No…he didn't," I replied quickly. "He said he was responsible. He didn't say he killed her. He told you to tell me exactly what he said because he knew I would translate to you what he was really saying."

"Now I'm *really* confused."

"There's nothing to be confused about. When we were in the military, back in the day, an interrogation technique that was commonly used to accomplish a goal was to say what the enemy wanted you to say, only to say it in a manner that could be construed differently if someone looked at the words more carefully. In other words, when asked if he killed the girl, his response was that he was responsible for her death. Now, responsibility could be as ambiguous as he was the owner of the pool hall where she was killed. Or, it could also be that he owned a place that served alcohol and that because of his establishment, her defenses were lowered so she couldn't defend herself."

"That's stretching it a bit, isn't it?" Wiseman asked.

"Not really. If he's concerned that somehow his conversations are being monitored—-"

"They aren't," Bill jumped in. "Our conversations are privileged. There can be nobody listening other than the client's legal counsel. That's the law."

Ah…the sweet smell of naiveté. It's a blessing to know that the person you trust believes in playing by the rules. Unfortunately, it doesn't help when you knew the ones you were enemies with didn't play by those same rules.

"Since when do the criminals worry about your laws?" I asked.

"Even if they did hear the conversation," he responded, "they couldn't use any of it in court."

"Don't you get it?" I was almost yelling now. "They aren't worried about this going to court."

That caught the attorney off guard. He hadn't thought about it from that perspective.

"Look," I continued, "he said he would take whatever punishment he was guilty of. He didn't say he wanted to go to jail. And, if he isn't guilty, as I believe the first part meant, then the amount of punishment he's willing to accept is nothing. No guilt. No punishment."

"I guess that would make a lot of sense if what you said was accurate."

"I don't ask a lot from anyone, but I'm asking you to trust me on this one. He's innocent." I'm not much for begging, but if necessary I would make an exception for a friend.

"So what am I supposed to do now?" Wiseman asked, shaking his head and still looking confused.

"You do what he asked you to do. Buy him as much time as you can. We have to figure out what's going on and who's doing it to him."

"With him pleading guilty, I'm not sure if I can give you all that much time."

"Just do what you can. Delay, stall, lose paperwork or anything else you have to do. Just give him as much time as you can. I'll do the rest."

"I don't know what's happening here," Wiseman said, shrugging his shoulders, "but his miracle man needs to step up to the plate before your friend goes away for life."

"I will," I mumbled. "I will."

Four

I'm not much of a believer in drama. It's sort of a mantra of mine. Of course, that doesn't mean drama doesn't exist or that I keep it completely out of my life. I just prefer not to allow it into my daily routine. Then again, I'm married, and that alone can mess up anybody's personal mantra.

Let me demonstrate.

As I left Bill Wiseman's office, my phone rang. Jill, my beautiful, kind, wonderful wife, was on the other end and drama was now engulfing every fiber of her being. Like every good wife, she felt it absolutely necessary to share it with me.

"Baby," I said, trying to get through the hysterics, "what's wrong?"

"You have to come home...*now*," she blubbered.

"Are you all right?" I asked.

I know it's a stupid question, but what the hell? I'm a man.

"*Of course I'm not all right!*" she screamed in my ear. "*Do I sound like I'm all right?*"

Let me turn you on to a little clue about relationships. Over time, you get to know the person in your life. You get to know when some things are critical. What I mean by that is, there are times when you know when a situation you think is life and death is reality and you treat that situation as you should. Then there are times when it seems as if the roof will literally fall, only to realize that the roof is intact and life will go on. In time, you get to know the difference.

This call was of the latter variety, one that I just knew I could put off and deal with later. Yeah, right. When you're married, all situations are life and death and don't you forget it.

That is if you want to stay married.

"I'll be right home. It will take me about thirty minutes to get there."

"Turn on your siren," she squealed.

"Baby," I replied, in a calm and soothing manner, "I'm not a cop right now, but I'll get there as soon as I can. I promise. Now let me go so I can get on Lu-Lu Belle and head home."

She hung up without saying a word.

I called Manny and gave him a brief rundown on my conversation with Bill Wiseman. "Well, get over here," he said. "We need to get going on this right away."

"I have to run home first. The wife called and there's a personal matter I need to handle."

"Pussy," he said, and then hung up…just as the wife had. I hate friends who know the real me.

~ * ~

As always, Lu-Lu Belle announced my arrival. I didn't even have my kickstand dropped before Jill came rushing out to me. She didn't seem to be any calmer than when we spoke on the phone, and for an instant, I actually thought the situation might be serious. That feeling left as quickly as it came when I gathered that the problem was about Tootie.

It seemed, as best as I could understand through the fast-talking and hysterics, that her father had decided he was getting married...again, for the fifth time.

I said, "Baby, he's done it before."

"I know that," Jill said.

"Then why is this time such a big deal to you?"

She grabbed me by the hand.

"Come with me."

~ * ~

Living in the country is such a blessing. The air is fresh. Except for the birds and frogs, the noise is next to non-existent, and the neighbors are far enough away that, should you be inclined, getting an all-over tan is a reward all by itself.

All that goes away when relatives come to visit. Especially when that relative surprises you with an additional guest thirty-five years his junior and announces he's planning to marry her.

One look at the plastic-enhanced beauty before me, I couldn't decide if I felt sorry for her or jealous of him. The shock of the first view made me wonder if he had won the lottery; her being the grand prize. Of course one glance at Jill helped me decide that the jealous thoughts would have to be kept to myself.

"Hey, there. How's my favorite son-in-law?"

That, I'm afraid, is the greeting Tootie always gave me. It probably wouldn't be so bad if I wasn't his *only* son-in-law.

"I'm well, Tootie. How are you... or do I really need to ask?"

"Nope," he smirked. "Just seeing that trail of spit hanging from your chin and I knew the answer."

He laughed as I instinctively ran my hand across my face. Now don't go there. I wasn't slobbering. It was just a reflex and he caught me off guard.

"I understand you have good news," I said, and immediately felt a severe pain in my ribs—a subtle reminder that Jill was still close by. Have you ever noticed how sharp a small woman's elbows can be?

"Better than good," he said. "It's great. I've finally found the woman of my dreams. I want you to meet Bitsy, the love of my life."

Ever have one of those moments when someone gives you terrible news about a tragic accident or a close relative is stricken by a mortal disease? You know, the kind where all your senses go on overdrive and you mouth starts to water just a little as a precursor to a mad dash to the bathroom? That's what I was feeling at that moment.

Now don't get me wrong; she was a lovely young thing. This was purely a selfish reaction to everything I was going to have to deal with for a long time to come. Look at it this way: your wife is five years older than your new mother-in-law to be. That means your wife will be privately ranting about the disgrace of the relationship. She will be jealous that she doesn't stack up to the girl—and you can trust me when I say that this girl is stacked.

More important, sex will be out of the question. As long as the image of her father having sex with the little trollop is floating around in Jill's brain, there will be no hope for me ever getting laid. Ever! I had to think of something. I didn't know what, but I had to think of something...and soon.

"Bitsy is an unusual name," I said, as I shook her hand. "Where did you get it?"

With a southern drawl that poured like cold molasses, Bitsy said, "My mama use to read 'The Itsy Bitsy Spider' to my brother when he was just a baby. She thought the name was cute and decided that her first little girl would be a Bitsy, you know, like the spider."

"Yeah," Jill said, in a whisper, "an eight-legged hairy freak with her fangs in Tootie's ass."

"I'm sorry," Bitsy said, leaning closer to Jill. "I didn't hear what you said."

Jill started to repeat it louder when I interrupted, "She was just saying that Tootie seems very happy. So why don't you kids go to the living room and let me and Jill make you a drink. I'm sure I could use one after all the excitement."

Damn, this was going to be a *very* long visit.

~ * ~

There are times in every man's life when it becomes necessary to set the lady in his life down and demand that she listen to and agree with him. There are moments when that same man insists the woman set aside her petty wants and desires and look at the big picture. This was such a time.

Then again, I live in the real world. What I actually did was what every man does: I kissed ass. Of course, right after that I snuck out of the house when Jill was taking a bath. I simply told Tootie to tell her I had an emergency and would be back as soon as possible. I knew there would be hell to pay when I got home, but she was going to be pissed off anyway. Why listen to her yell about it before I leave and then again after I get home? Once is plenty for me.

Manny looked up at me when I walked through the door, "Snuck out again?" he grinned.

"Shut up," I said. "You don't know me as well as you think."

"Well?" he asked, with a smirk.

"Of course I did," I replied. "I'm not stupid, you know."

"That, my friend, is something I would never accuse you of being." The grin got wider. "But, pussy-whipped? That's something else altogether."

"Fuck you *and* the horse you rode in on."

Changing back to what we should have been discussing.

"Where are we?"

"I think you might want to talk to another one of the employees," Manny said. "You ever meet a lady by the name of Sophia Watson?"

I nodded. I knew her as Sophie, but knew exactly who he was talking about.

"It appears she's the go-to person at the pool hall. She seems to know everyone who comes in that place, and knows of or has seen just about everything the patrons have going on in their lives. If there's dirt to dig up on anyone, she holds the shovel."

"Okay," I said. "Is there anything in particular I should be asking her?"

I only asked him that because he seemed to be heading somewhere but was acting somewhat reserved.

"Nothing in particular, but I think you might want to lead her in the direction of the unusual visitors that evening."

"Why? She wasn't working there that evening. Jimmy was."

"It seems she has a tendency to visit the pool hall on evenings she doesn't work; especially Friday or Saturday nights. I have a feeling that if she was there, she would know who might stick out. She's also part-time, but her other job is just down the street."

Manny gave me the info on the job location and I headed out. Something about my conversation with Manny wasn't quite adding up. My thinking was that, if Sophie was so hooked up with the locals, why hadn't she come forward with anything that could help Sam? Also, if she was being so quiet about this, what else was she hiding?

I was about to turn around and talk to Manny again about these thoughts when my phone rang. "Hello," I said.

"So, have you figured it out yet, or are you still going to play dumb?" It was her again. It was the same voice that had called me before about Sam.

"I won't play dumb," I replied. "You sort of caught me off guard the last time. So if we can, let's start over."

"I'd like that," the mystery voice replied.

"Starting over?"

"No," she answered. "A man who knows when he's wrong and doesn't waste time try making excuses for his shortcomings."

I couldn't help myself, I laughed.

"Well if that's all it takes to impress you, according to my wife, I have enough shortcomings to make you sing my praises."

The phone was silent and I was slowly walking back into Manny's office when she said, "Don't do that, Mr. Shaw. Don't go inside and try tracing the call. First, you won't be able to, and second, it'll piss me off. I want to help Sam, but I need to know that you can be trusted. Can I trust you, Detective?"

"You can trust me to do the right thing," I replied. "But I don't know who you are and I don't know if you are trustworthy. I don't know if you are really trying to help Sam or sending me on a wild-goose chase. You can trust me not to lie to you, but you can also trust me to take your ass down if I find you're trying to screw me over. How's that for trust?"

"Acceptable," she replied.

"Oh, one more thing... where the hell *are* you?"

I was looking everywhere around me. If she could see me, I thought maybe I could see her too.

"Somewhere far away, Detective. Do you think the cops are the only ones capable of watching people?"

I knew that any straight answers were going to have to wait for now. She was talking more openly and I needed some answers.

"Well for the sake of honesty," I said, "I'm not a cop right now. I've been suspended from the force. I thought I should tell you that so you wouldn't get the impression I'm hiding anything from you."

"I know that, Detective," she responded. "I know a lot more about you than you might think. For the record, I do appreciate your willingness to set your pride aside and cooperate."

"Look, lady, as you probably know, I'm married. Pride went out the window a long time ago." I thought I heard something resembling a smile coming from the mysterious caller. "So if we can, let's set aside our little pleasantries for a moment. For the sake of honesty, tell me why you're calling so I can get on with what I need to do to help Sam."

"Well put," she said. "I'm soliciting you to help me free Sam. I thought you would have figured that out by now."

"You already know I am doing that, so why the cloak-and-dagger routine? Why not just tell me who you are and what you know, so I can get him out of jail? Maybe even put the bad guys away."

"I can't tell you who I am because lives are at stake. I will tell you what I can to help you, but some things you are just going to have to find out on your own. I can tell you this and I hope you believe me. Sam is innocent. People are threatening him with things that make him want to protect others, including you."

"Protect me from what?" I heard my voice rising. "What the hell are you talking about?"

"Find out what he's hiding and that will bring you closer to solving the case. In the meantime, there are not as many you can trust as you might want to believe. I will help you as much as I can. For now, go see Sophie. She does have more knowledge than even she realizes."

That last comment about floored me.

The only way she could have known about Sophie was having Manny's placed bugged. Whoever she was, she was good. Manny swept his place at least twice a day and yet she somehow managed to overhear our conversation. This woman was a pro. I don't know which agency she was with, but definitely a pro.

"Is there anything else you can tell me to help me out here?"

"People are watching you."

"No shit," I said. "Apparently you are watching me very closely."

"So are others," she stated flatly. "They know you have very little information right now, so they aren't too worried about you. When you start getting some answers, that concern will change. The ones you care about most will be in danger. I'll help you as best I can, but this is going to have to be done by you. Don't tell anyone we spoke," she added. "Not even Manny. I know he's your friend and will help you with his limited resources, but I still don't know if or how he might have an agenda other than the one you have. Just be cautious. I'll know more soon."

The abrupt click told me she had hung up and I felt like I was left hanging in the wind. Whoever she was, she knew way more than I thought possible. She had to be working for the feds or some agency I couldn't come up with. If she did, why the hell did she care about a local murder like this? Nothing was making sense and people were watching me. Is that stating the obvious? Of course people were watching me. How many, I didn't know.

~ * ~

Lu-Lu Belle has the answer to almost every problem I have. When I get confused or have problems of any nature, Lu-Lu Belle has the answer. I talk to her about everything, and she usually tells me exactly what I need to hear.

For the first time in as long as I can remember, she was silent. I know her pipes were loud, but under all that noise she would usually whisper truths to me. She has a way of seeing through all the messes and confusions to help me come up with the solutions I need. Only this time, her silence spoke volumes. Maybe, like me, she was getting a little scared. I'm not really as dumb as I sometimes come across.

Okay, maybe I am.

This time, I'm totally out of my league. I'm at least smart enough to know that much. What can I do? Sam is taking the rap for a murder he didn't commit. If there's one thing I believe in as much as anything in the world, it's not deserting a friend in need. Not now. Not ever.

Somewhere along the way, I found myself parked in front of Jessica's Hair Emporium, Sophie's other place of employment. I was just sitting there when I saw her leave, and I decided to see if I could find out what she might know. I wasn't even sure where to start, but knew I had to try.

"Mr. Shaw," she said, when she saw me approaching. "I was wondering when you would be getting around to talking to me."

Is it just me, or does everyone know what the hell I'm doing? When I was working as a cop, nobody seemed to know who I was. Now, it's as if my picture is being displayed on billboards all over town. I've met this woman maybe twice since I've lived in the area. How the hell could she remember me? I'm not exactly famous.

"Why's that?" I asked her.

"I don't know," she said, smiling. "I just figured you would want to talk to me about Sam. He's your friend, right?"

"Yes, he is, and I'm trying to figure out what happened that night. Do you know anything?"

Sophie is a hard person to describe. She's not very tall, maybe five-three, and looks like she could be of Hispanic descent. However, the few extra pounds she carries conceal her age and I couldn't tell if she was twenty-five or forty-five. Either way, she is attractive and seemed full of life. Her dark hair was in a ponytail, and her eyes penetrated to my core. That's what got my attention.

"I know lots of things," she smiled knowingly, "but I don't talk to cops. They don't seem too trustworthy where I come from."

"I'm starting to get the same feeling," I agreed. "Seems a lot of them have their own agendas and don't want to help as much as take care of themselves."

"That's exactly what I'm talking about," she offered. "You wouldn't believe the stories I could tell you about crap that goes down around here and nobody cares, especially the cops."

"Well this is my lucky day, then," I said. "Because, as of now, I'm not a cop. I was placed on suspension. I'm here as Sam's friend, not as a cop."

"So why are you on suspension?" she asked.

"Seems I have a way of pissing people off," I smiled. "This time I just pissed off the wrong person."

She smiled as well. "I like people who don't take crap from others. Too many people just suck up to what everyone else wants. They don't have any backbone. I don't talk to them. With them, I just listen. You'd be surprised how much you can learn by listening."

Something inside told me I was going to like Sophie. She knew something, but she wasn't just going to give it up right away. "Do you think Sam killed the girl?" I asked.

"Not in a million years." She stood straighter and gave off a vibration of someone ready to fight for her beliefs.

"Why not?"

"Because that's not his way."

I felt like I was pulling teeth with her. She wasn't exactly avoiding my questions. She just wasn't offering a lot of details with her responses.

"What do you mean, 'not his way'?" I asked.

She looked at me. I'm not sure if she was trying to cover a misspoken statement or if she was sizing me up for confidence.

"Sam is a player," she finally said. "He doesn't kill people. He gets his way, but not by force."

"I'm not following you. What do you mean, he's a player? And how does he get his way?"

"Look," she said. "I like Sam. He's been a good boss and I don't want anything happening to him. It's just... he has a way of getting what he wants. It seems he knows a lot of people and he knows a lot of things about a lot of people."

"What kind of people?" I asked.

"Important people," she volunteered. "He used to tell me, 'It's not who you know; it's what you know about them that matters.' I found out a while back that he needed a variance for some changes at the pool hall. The city wasn't going to give it to him and told him he was just out of luck. I overheard the inspector tell him that at work. A week later, he got the approval. When I asked about it, he just said that he and the zoning commissioner came to a mutual agreement. He said that it would be in the best interest of the community that he got permission. I took it that he knew something, but he never shared what it was with me."

"So, to get this clear," I said, "you think Sam blackmailed the zoning commissioner to get the variance he wanted?"

"I don't want to call it blackmail," she said. "I just think Sam knew something about the commissioner, or somebody the commissioner is afraid of, that the commissioner didn't want to be made public. So, rather than get into it with Sam, he just went and gave him what he wanted. Sam never took advantage of people with his knowledge. I mean, he never hurt anyone that I know of. He's pretty much into just living his own life. But, when Sam wanted something, he usually got it."

"Who else knows about this..." I paused for the right word, "arrangement?"

"As far as I know, nobody."

"Then let's keep it that way. I don't know what's going on with Sam and who killed that girl, but if he didn't do it, maybe somebody Sam was negotiating with did. Maybe they weren't as willing to cooperate as the commissioner."

"You think he was framed?" she asked. She seemed surprised.

"I think the whole truth hasn't yet been discovered. And, until I find out more, I would just as soon keep this part quiet."

"What about that other cop?"

"What cop?"

"Ramos," she said, losing some of the kindness in her eyes. "He was here this morning and asked a lot of questions about Sam."

"What did you tell him?"

"I didn't know anything," she replied. "I don't like him very much...seems to have a chip on his shoulder."

"Ramos is an asshole," I stated flatly. "He's got Sam convicted and ready for execution. He won't try to help Sam. I don't want to tell you what to do. And I certainly don't want you doing anything illegal, but I will say that Ramos isn't trying to help your boss and you need to take that for whatever it's worth."

"In other words," she hesitated and then smiled, "keep my mouth shut. Don't worry...my words, not yours."

I returned her smile and said goodbye. I would talk to her again soon, I was sure. Right now, I had a few things to clear up before knowing where to go next.

Five

I wasn't sure where the case was going, but I had to take a break and clear my head. I called the house and Tootie answered the phone. "Hey there, son-in-law," he said, with too much enthusiasm. "You sure got one pissed-off wife on your hands." I could hear the humor in his voice. Tootie was the kind of person who pretty much smiled all the time. However, he liked it even better when the heat was taken off him and placed squarely on the shoulders of some other sap.

"She's your daughter, you know?"

I was hoping beyond reason that he would at least offer to help calm her down.

"Not right now," he laughed. "Right now I'm her friend and listening to her tell me what a jerk you are for deserting her during her time of need." His laughter continued. "Seems to me like flowers would be a good peace offering, but that's just my opinion."

"She wouldn't be like this if you would date someone your own age."

"True, but if I dated someone my own age, I wouldn't have something as sweet as Bitsy, now would I?"

"She's too damn young for you. I'm surprised you can still cut it at your age."

"I can cut it just fine. Of course, there may be a time down the road when I can't cut the mustard, but I'll never be too old to lick the jar. If you know what I mean."

If anyone else had said that, I might have taken exception, but this was Tootie and somehow the old geezer seemed exempt from such things. Besides, I couldn't refute his argument. If I were his age and had someone like that to cuddle with every night... oh hell, I don't want to take a trip down that path.

"Can I talk to Jill?" I asked, hopeful.

"She told me that if it was you calling, I should tell you to go fornicate yourself...that wasn't a verbatim translation."

Tootie could no longer contain his mockery and laughed out loud. He loved it when he knew I was uncomfortable, and the fact that his own blood was the one causing the discomfort just made it all the better.

I said, "Right," and hung up the phone. I didn't need to deal with Jill right now and I certainly wasn't ready to go home and face off with her. I had to find someplace quiet and think. Lu-Lu Belle seemed to be calling and I took that as my only place of solitude.

Leaving Monterey, I got on the 1 and headed north toward Santa Cruz. I didn't really have a destination in mind. I just wanted to get some time alone. I wanted to close out everything in my mind and just let it all sink in. The open road seemed like just the ticket.

~ * ~

It's about a thirty-minute drive to Santa Cruz from Monterey and the traffic wasn't very heavy. For the first twenty minutes, I was able to clear my thoughts. The notion that Sam was blackmailing community leaders seemed to clarify in my mind.

Let's just say for the moment that it was true. Let's say that the person he was trying to get to was very public and had aspirations of getting beyond the local political arena, and what Sam knew could squash all those ambitions. What if this person had ties beyond the scope of the local arena? That would explain a lot. It would explain a motivation for someone framing Sam. It would explain how someone could get to him at the precinct. It certainly would explain the mysterious caller and her probable government connections.

All these thoughts were running through my head as I cruised up the highway.

What it didn't explain was who that person could be. It didn't explain what Sam had on him—or her, for that matter. It didn't explain how I could find the answers to any of the questions I had about this case, or even if the murdered girl was connected to all of this or if she was just a pawn in the wrong place at the wrong time.

The only thing it did was give me a direction.

Sometimes, direction is the only thing you need.

~ * ~

At times, Lu-Lu Belle seems to have a mind of her own and for some reason she took the exit for Aptos and headed for the beach. We stopped and for a minute I could've sworn that someone was *again* watching me.

I got off and decided to take a walk along a path that would hide me. If anyone was watching, they would have to expose themselves to find out where I was going.

A man in a suit and sunglasses started heading in my direction. I doubled back around a sea-retaining wall and bushes and got behind him. He seemed to have lost what he was looking for and turned around, surprised that a big man was standing in his face.

"Lose something?" I asked.

"Yeah," he replied. "I lost you."

"I'm not all that hard to find. Seems like I just might show up any old place."

"So it seems," he responded.

The man didn't appear concerned or frightened by either my size or my being in his face. If I were to describe his expression best, it would be one of relief.

"Well, now that you found me, what do you want?"

"Don't want anything. I was just making sure you were okay."

"Well now, that's just plain silly. You just happen to be hanging out around the beach and got concerned that I was in danger back here in the brush? Isn't that just neighborly of you? I assume that if I asked you anything about the real reason you are following me, you wouldn't tell me, would you?"

"Don't suppose I would."

"And if I were to knock you on your ass and just take off?"

"Wouldn't help," he replied with an air of confidence. "You seem to have a lot of people concerned about your safety these days. I'm just one of those a little closer than most."

"I think I'm getting a better idea of why you folks are called spooks," I said.

I wanted to get an idea if I was on the right track.

"Sorry," he said, squashing the idea, "you have us confused with some other organization. We just like making sure we protect our own."

"And...how exactly am I one of you guys?"

This whole thing was getting more confusing as the day went on and I really wanted some answers.

"You aren't one of us, Detective," he said. "You *are* considered a friend. We take care of our friends."

"And...who exactly are you protecting me from?" I asked.

He just smiled.

"Those we don't consider friends."

With that he turned around and headed back to the beach where Lu-Lu Belle was waiting. About twenty feet away, he turned again and said, "Watch your back, Detective. There are some people out there who aren't very nice. They don't want you finding the answers you're looking for and will do anything to make sure you don't."

"Who?" I yelled in frustration.

"Just watch your back."

He turned around and disappeared.

I hurried back to Lu-Lu Belle, trying to shake the willies crawling all over me. The stranger was nowhere to be seen. I couldn't help but wonder if I caught him off guard or if this was a planned meeting they just didn't bother telling me about?

I took off for Monterey, looking every few seconds for a tail that never appeared. This whole thing was starting to creep me out. I felt *way* out of my league, but didn't expect anyone to help me find the answers I needed. I was a pawn in some big game. It was as if the ancient gods were watching over me and taking bets on what I would do. I could only hope one of them was betting on me.

~ * ~

When I returned to Monterey, I had a message on my cell phone from Dakota Walker asking me to come see her. I was only a few blocks from the courthouse and hoped she would have some good news to share.

"What took you so long?" she asked with indignation. "I left you a message over two hours ago."

So much for the warm and charming reception.

At work, Dakota wore old lady glasses with large black frames. She could, at least under more pleasant circumstances, give a guy fantasies of the strict schoolteacher or maybe the over-covered librarian who would let her hair fall at just the right moment. Never mind. We'll save those thoughts for other times.

"I just picked up your message," I said. "I've been busy. What's the emergency?"

"Your friend seems to be on a suicide mission," Dakota said. "He's requesting a speedy hearing and my boss is pushing me to set it for early next week. I'm stuck here, Samson. I don't seem to have any options to help your friend."

"I see what you mean. Is there anything you *can* do, anything that will give me more time to find out what's going on?"

"The DA's called me four times in the last two hours to see when the hearing's been set. I've been putting him off. Do you really think he's innocent?"

"After what I've seen today, I know he is. I just need time to prove it and find out the truth about what's really going on."

The look on her face told me she was confused.

"Look, Dakota," I continued, "this whole thing is a sham. It goes a lot higher up the food chain than you think. Unfortunately, I don't yet know enough to give you details. Mostly, I don't want to compromise your position here. All I can ask is to just do the best you can to give me as much time as possible. I'll just have to do better at finding answers."

"I'm not sure I can do anything," she said, hanging her head. "But, I'll try. Samson, you need to tell me what's going on. I'm flying blind here."

"So am I, babe."

I turned to leave. She started to say something, but I didn't want to explain any more than I already had. I held up my hand and she knew to hold her thoughts. I left with a sense that I was betraying a friend. Under any other circumstances, I would have told her everything. If my life was in danger, I wasn't about to put hers in danger as well.

~ * ~

It was getting dark and I knew that sooner or later I would have to face Jill. She was standing in the doorway when I arrived with hands on her hips. I took Tootie's suggestion and bought flowers, but really didn't believe they would help much.

With an innocent smile on my face, I approached her and handed her the bouquet.

"Hey, Baby," I said and kissed her on the cheek. "How're you doing?"

"Are you just plain stupid?" she asked.

Okay. Maybe it wasn't the best approach, but let's face it, who the hell knows the best approach when it comes to women?

"Look, Baby..." I started.

"Don't you 'Baby' me," she yelled. "You had no right to leave me when I needed you here to help me deal with a major problem."

"What problem?" I asked, regretting the words as soon as they left my mouth.

"How dare you play dumb with me?" Now she was livid. "You know *exactly* what problem. My father shows up with some floozy he wants to marry and you treat it like all is fine in the world. How dare you do that to me?"

"So is everything okay now with your dad?" I was hoping to distract her with the real issue.

"Everything's fine," Tootie said from inside the kitchen.

Apparently he was eavesdropping. From what I've learned about the man over the years, he's a bigger gossip than the old women standing by a fence. The smile on his face let me know he thought he had the better of me and was trying to sink the hook in.

"Everything is *not* fine," she turned on him. "The idea of you just showing up with some young girl and thinking I would be okay with it...makes you as stupid as him." She turned and glared back at me. "You're both imbeciles. Neither one of you has a clue about relationships or how to take care of a woman."

"I can't vouch for your man there," Tootie grinned, "but you can ask any woman I've ever been with; they'll all tell you I know how to take care of a woman."

"Oh, yuck." Jill shivered at the thought. "Too much information."

Looking at me, Tootie finished, "Son, you and I need to have a talk about the birds and bees. My daughter deserves better."

"Oh, shut up, old man, and get your head out of the f'n gutter," Jill fumed.

"Maybe we should all just sit down and talk about this calmly," I said as I moved through the door.

"Calm?" Jill said. "You want calm? *I am calm!*"

"Baby," I said, "you aren't calm. You're upset and you have every right to be. I was insensitive because I placed my own issues ahead of yours and I'm sorry. What can I do to make it better for you?"

"First thing you can do," she said, her voice dropping an octave, "is tell my father that his choice of a future bride makes him look like a dirty old man. He's seventy years old, for God's sake. He needs a woman his age who is mature and understands his needs as a senior citizen."

"Well, Baby," I replied, "since he's standing right here, I don't think I need to repeat your words. However, let me ask you a question. How long have you known that your dad is a lecherous old man? And what makes you think for a moment he would change now?"

Jill looked dumbfounded by the question and didn't immediately respond. Maybe thirty seconds went by, a very long thirty seconds, I might add, when all of a sudden she burst out laughing. I looked at Tootie and he didn't seem to know what to do any better than I did, but the laugh was infectious and he too started laughing. I was smiling at them both when Bitsy stuck her head around the corner and asked what the joke was.

Jill walked over to her, hugged her and said, "You are, Bitsy. And if that makes Tootie happy, then good for you both."

Bitsy seemed both confused and happy at the same time. She wasn't the brightest star in the sky, but she seemed to light up Tootie's world and that was all that mattered.

Jill made spaghetti for supper and all seemed right for those few brief moments.

I was, for the first time in a long time, able to relax. Tootie told story after story about how they met and some of the adventures they both enjoyed. I actually thought about calling it a day and starting again in the morning. Somehow I had managed to let the magnitude of Sam's situation fall to the back burner.

When Tootie asked what I was working on, the whole day seemed to rush back into my mind.

"A friend of mine was arrested and I'm trying to help him out."

"What'd he do?" Tootie asked. "Rob a bank or something?"

"He was arrested for murder," I answered.

I really didn't want to get into this conversation at home. Jill and I have a loose understanding that my work pretty much stays out of the house. Tootie and I had no such understanding and the whole idea fascinated him.

"Damn," he said. "How can I help? I have been around the barn a time or two. Maybe I can help you figure out who done it."

"What makes you think he didn't do it?' I asked. "He was arrested for the crime."

"Because if he was guilty," Tootie explained, "you wouldn't be trying to help him."

The response was more logical than I expected. I guess even Tootie can surprise me every once in a while.

"I appreciate you wanting to help, but most of what I'm doing is just research, and that gets pretty boring."

"All the more reason for me to come along," he said. "I don't move as fast as I used to, so if there was any running and tackling bad guys, I probably wouldn't be of much help, but I can do research. Besides," he volunteered, "any more sex with Bitsy and I would be shut down for a week. I can't afford that."

He laughed at his own joke.

Bitsy's face turned red as I looked at Jill, who shook violently and said, "Ewww."

My stomach turned a full revolution.

Jill looked at me with a pleading in her eyes. She needed time with her and Bitsy alone. I could already tell that Jill was going to try talking some sense into the young woman so I reluctantly said, okay. "But, don't think for a moment this is a permanent arrangement."

I got up to leave and Jill came to me. She gave me a hug and whispered in my ear, "One good turn deserves another. When you come home, you'll have a treat waiting for you, too."

Now those were magic words if I ever heard them.

Six

Where Jill and I live is considered back country. The coast is only about fifteen miles from our home; however, the roads don't exactly travel in a straight line. By car, the distance is closer to twenty-five.

Carmel Valley Road is a winding two-lane—sorta—secondary road that will challenge the shocks and springs of any vehicle, domestic and foreign. Personally, I loved the trip, but I'm used to it.

Tootie, on the other hand, is more familiar with smooth and straight roads, and before we made it to the Village of Carmel Valley, I glanced over at him and thought we would be lucky to make our destination before he lost his last meal. After the Village, the road smooths out and so apparently, did Tootie's stomach.

From the Village, Monterey is about a twenty-minute drive with some very beautiful scenery.

Some of the best known horse ranches line the Carmel Valley Road, along with the Quail Lodge Golf Course and other stopping spots for the venturing tourist.

"Oh wow!" Tootie said, after we arrived in town and drove down Cannery Row. "So this is Monterey, California, nightlife."

I was thinking to myself, either he hasn't been out much or it didn't take much to impress the man.

"Yes, Tootie, this is Monterey nightlife. As you can see, it's exciting in a dull sort of way."

"You don't understand." Tootie looked at me. "I've been all over this country. I've seen and been to all sorts of places. From cowboy bars to the Vegas strip, with every kind of activity imaginable. But there's no place anywhere that tops this. The problem is... those of us who would love to live here can't afford it. But those of you who do live here don't appreciate it. The thing that really makes me proud is that you've brought my daughter to a place that most people can only dream of living. For that I want to thank you."

I didn't know what to say about that. Having known Tootie for a bunch of years, never in my wildest imagination could I think of a sentimental thought entering his mind, let alone saying it out loud. It caught me off guard.

Looking around, for the first time in a long time, I knew what he was talking about. The lights of the quaint stores, the smiling faces of the couples walking along, holding hands. It reminded me of when Jill and I first became a couple and I brought her here to show her the magic of the place. The memories brought a smile.

Maybe if Tootie hadn't said those mushy words, I would have seen the guy running up to the side of the car. Maybe I would have had more time to react.

Later, I thought about a lot of maybes.

When the Molotov cocktail came flying at the car, I only had an instant to react. The bottle hit the support between the windshield and the driver's window when it shattered and exploded. I saw the blast and the first thing I did was to look at Tootie to see if he was okay.

The car, Jill's 1969 candy red Chevelle SS, was on fire and I had to get Tootie and myself out before we became toast or marshmallows or whatever ingredient you prefer roasting over an open fire. Both sides of the car were ablaze but my side seemed to have more fire than his.

"Get out, Tootie! Roll on the grass. Now!"

I followed and was amazed by his agility. Moments later we were both staring in amazement at the fiery mass of steel burning away.

The thing I was most concerned about was how to tell Jill that her father and I were the victims of a car bombing and that the car being bombed was hers. That's when I heard Tootie. At first I thought he was sobbing. It would be an appropriate reaction to almost getting killed. Most people don't handle life-threatening situations very well. I turned to comfort him and was amazed that instead of sobbing, what I was hearing was him trying to keep from laughing his ass off.

He looked at me at the same time, and said, "Damn, son, you sure know how to show an old man a good time."

"Your daughter is going to kill me," I said. I wasn't really sure how else to react at the moment.

"Hell, boy," he said, "I won't tell her if you don't. I thought maybe you would take me down here for a hooker or maybe even get me drunk. But damn, I've done both of those before. This is a first for me. And trust me, there aren't too many firsts this old fart will get to enjoy anymore."

"Well, I'm certainly happy to be able to entertain you," I said.

"Me too," he applauded. "Maybe tomorrow you can show me a carjacking." Then he started laughing some more.

All I could think about was how in the hell I was going to tell Jill I almost got her daddy killed and ruined her car at the same time. She was going to kill me.

~ * ~

Tommy Billings was the first cop to arrive on the scene. The fire department showed up at the same time. Tommy came running over to us to check if we were okay.

"Yeah," I said, "we're both fine. Messed up some nice clothes, but we both seem to have all our fingers and toes. Nothing cooked, either."

"What happened?" he asked.

I told him what I saw and knew.

"You get a look at him?" he inquired.

"Not a very good one," I replied. "Young, maybe late teens or early twenties. He was wearing jeans and a black pullover top. He was Caucasian and wearing a forty-niners' cap under the hood. Not too many of those around these parts. Should be a piece of cake finding him."

Tommy noted my sarcasm and took it as my just not having a good moment.

~ * ~

Tommy was about finished when Carl Ramos drove up to the scene.

"What the hell are you doing here?" I asked.

"I was just in the neighborhood and heard the call," he said. "Wouldn't have come over 'til I heard you were involved. I just wanted to see what kind of public nuisance you were being. Looks to me like you made a hell of a mess down here. I'll be surprised if the department doesn't get sued for having one of our own causing the local businesses to have to shut down."

"Nice of you to be so concerned about our wellbeing," I said. "And to think that you *still* consider me one of your own. How nice. Makes my heart flutter."

I wasn't in the mood for his crap, but sometimes I just can't help myself.

"Of course you're one of our own, Shaw." His crooked smile did little to ease my contempt for the man. "At least you are until

I bust your ass and put you behind bars. That'll be a *real* feather in my cap."

"You make your best play, asshole."

I was getting some of my juices back and if he wanted some of me, he was more than welcome to try.

"Later," he said. "I still have a few pieces of a murder case to finish up. You know," he turned smug, "the Reynolds case?" He turned and walked away, leaving me smoldering as bad as Jill's no-longer-beautiful car.

"Not one of your friends, I take it." Tootie watched my fellow officer leave.

"Let's just leave it at that," I replied.

There wasn't any point going into detail about someone I cared so little about. Besides, I wasn't sure how we were going to get home yet. I figured one of my *real* cop buddies would give us a lift. When Manny showed up, I knew the ride home problem was solved.

"You sure know how to get attention, don't you?" Manny said.

He looked concerned when he first drove up, but when he saw us sitting on the curb, I could see the concern slip from his expression. Margie Samara was getting out from the passenger side.

"Why does everyone around here believe I had anything to do with this other than be a victim?" I asked.

"Maybe because we all know you."

"You don't know shit," I said. "Besides, if you're so damn smart, why the hell didn't you tell me someone out here doesn't like me?"

"I thought you knew that was a given."

Manny glanced at Tootie, who in turn was looking Margie up and down, so I gave introductions all around. Tootie practically pushed me out of the way to shake hands with Manny's employee.

"The pleasure's all mine," Tootie drooled.

Manny looked at me. I shook my head.

"You know," Tootie was talking to Margie, "sometimes, intense situations of life and death make a guy real horny." I just about choked and Manny burst out laughing.

Margie, ever the cool lady, said, "I know exactly how you feel. Every time it happens to me, I have to find a woman and just ravish her body. Is that what you mean?"

The look on Tootie's face would have been worthy of the cover of *Ripley's Believe It or Not!* I don't believe a woman had ever bested the man until this moment. Seeing it was worth a dozen car bombings.

The ride home was quiet until Manny asked the question of the night.

"Do you think it was random?"

I really didn't want to talk about it with Tootie around, but he couldn't leave my side.

I returned his question with one of my own. "Just how many random car bombings have you experienced?"

"Can't say I've ever seen one," Manny replied. "At least not a random one. That is if you take out the riots of L.A."

"I didn't see any riot tonight," I said. "Tootie, did you see any riot tonight?"

"Nope," he smiled. "But if you know where one is, I'm up for it." I figured he had regained his composure and everyone laughed.

I still wasn't ready to face Jill about the car. But I knew that as soon as we got home, Tootie would take care of making sure that she and Bitsy knew all about it.

Jill's a cop's wife. As much as anything, she would understand the gravity of what had happened. Bitsy, on the other hand, would assume it was just another adventure that Tootie would be able to talk about for years to come.

When we arrived home, I asked Manny and Margie if they wanted to come in for a while.

"You're just afraid of Jill," he said, "aren't you?"

I thought about taking the macho route, but figured what the hell?

"Damn right I am. You've never seen her when she gets on a rage."

"Well, as tempting as the idea is to me," Manny said, "we have work to do. Maybe you can tell me all about it in the morning. You *will* be by in the morning, right?"

It was put out there as a question, but came across more as a statement.

"If Jill doesn't kill me, I'll be there. I'll just have to charge out the battery on the Olds. I should be there around nine or so."

I am not, by any stretch, a wealthy man. I've been fortunate to get our home through someone else's misfortune. The cars I have are all old and I've worked them back into running condition. Jill's Chevelle was completely restored. So is Lu-Lu Belle. The Olds needed a fresh coat of paint, but was now a screamer, mechanically. Now that Jill's car was destroyed, I would have to fix up another one for her. Which one would be up to her.

"We'll see you then," Manny said. "Tootie, it's been a hoot meeting you. Hope to see you around again."

"Well, if I can survive being around this guy." Tootie smiled. "I'll see you soon."

He reached in and grabbed Margie's hand; kissing the back of it. "Give a guy like me one chance and I'll turn you for life."

Always classy, Margie replied, "Never before have I been so tempted. We'll just have to wait and see. Maybe I'll ask one of my girlfriends to join us."

"Damn, girl," he said, "I know you don't mean a word of it. But God as my witness, you made this old man's pecker jump."

They both were still laughing as Manny drove away.

"Well, Tootie," I said, "how do we do this?'

"We take the manly approach," he said. "We tell the truth."

We opened the door and saw the two ladies sitting on the couch.

"I was hoping you'd prefer the cowardly way instead."

~ * ~

Jill was stoic about her car and pissed about Tootie being so close to danger. She blamed me, as expected, but we got past it.

After some quality time and hugs, I left the next morning to see Manny. The promise Jill made the night before, to take care of me, was unfulfilled because of the fire bomb. Passing through the Village, I stopped to get a coffee and a couple of lottery tickets. I figured the 250 million it was offering would help me a lot toward retirement, should I be fortunate enough to win.

Jill once asked me what I would do if we ever won. I told her I would find a new wife because I could afford one then. No, she didn't think it was funny, either. Then she reminded me that if that were to happen, I would have to give up half the money. She asked if I would rather have some young thing who was spending my money or a wealthy broad who would spend her money on me. What can I say; I'm a greedy bastard.

The wife stays.

The Olds roared into the driveway as I arrived at Manny's office a few minutes before nine. I'd mentioned the coat of paint the thing needed, but a new muffler would also come in handy as well. I didn't bother knocking before entering. I was surprised to see none other than the "mystery man" I had run into the day before in Santa Cruz. He was still wearing the sunglasses, even though the fog had yet to lift along the coast. The suit was different, but still dark. He still looked like a Fed to me.

"Detective Shaw," the man started, "nice to see you again."

Manny was surprised and asked if we knew each other.

"Not really," I said. "We had a chance meeting yesterday up in Santa Cruz."

"Not so much chance as...fortuitous," the man interjected.

"Six of one," I came back. "So agent—," I was trying to draw out a name with no result. "What exactly is it we can do for you?"

Manny and Margie looked at each other. And though they apparently decided the conversation was between the man and myself, didn't offer to leave.

"Would you mind if we spoke in private?" the pseudo federal man asked me. "There are matters we need to discuss regarding your mishap last night."

Margie stood to leave, but I held out a hand. "What you have to say will get back to them anyway. You might as well just tell me here. They are, unlike those who profess to care, actually doing everything they can to help me get to the truth about Sam. Until I know better, they have more status with me and every right to know what dangers might lay ahead, assuming the dangers are what this discussion is about."

"I guess you're right," he said. The man took several moments—checking both of them, surveying the room—before continuing. "When we spoke yesterday, I told you to watch your back. At the time, we were of the impression that if you dug too deep, someone might try taking you out before you found the truth. On that front, we may have underestimated your role in all of this and how serious of a threat they considered you."

"No shit?" I replied.

"They who?" Manny countered.

"I'll get to that in a moment," he said, looking at Manny. "For now, just listen. There are two factions involved in this situation."

"Let me guess," I interrupted. "Good guys and bad guys. And you want *me* to believe you're one of the good guys." The man didn't appear to have a sense of humor. It was at that moment I *knew* he worked for the government.

"That's exactly what we want you to believe," he said flatly. "This is big time political, and somehow your friend, Sam, got caught up in the middle of it. He knows something about someone and when he tried using that information to his advantage, well, you know the outcome."

"This may come to you as a surprise," I said, "but I already came to that conclusion."

"When the hell were you going to tell me?" Manny blurted. "Damn, Samson, you're dangling my ass in the wind."

"*Our* asses," Margie added. "My ass counts too, you know?"

"And a fine ass it is, I might add. Look guys, I just sort of figured it out last night," I said, defending my lack of communication. "Besides, I was a little preoccupied, if you'll recall."

"Bullshit!" Manny continued. "People are trying to ice you and we're *way* too close not to know this shit."

"Girls," Margie said—softly, but loud enough to get our attention. "We now know. Let the man talk."

"Thank you," the quasi-federal man said. "As I was saying, the two factions are working at every level of government in order to control who may be placed in office now and for years to come. The, as you say, 'bad guys,' have invested millions of dollars in their future candidates all over the country. The loss of even one of them would set them back more than you could imagine. And that's where your friend, Reynolds, comes into the picture. It seems that, inadvertently, he has acquired something incriminating on one of the future candidates and the bad guys have no intentions of letting him or her go without a fight."

"Him or her?" I asked. "What the hell does that mean?"

"It means we don't know who the person is that Reynolds was trying to put the screws to," Mr. Dark Suit replied. "And now that they have a hold over your friend, we haven't been able to ascertain who the person is or what he knows. In other words, Detective, we're flying blind, just as you are."

"Oh, great," I said. "Sam fell in a shit-storm and you want me to fix it for you."

"Actually," the man stated, "your friend did indeed get himself into a shit-storm. And as we see it, there are two options available to us. The first is we could do nothing. If that's the course we choose, nothing changes for us and your friend goes away for life. The other option is we help each other, take one of their protégés out of the political arena, and your friend gets his life back. It's a no-lose situation for us. We did not come to you to be benevolent. That, I'm afraid, is not in our mandate. On the other hand," he continued, "you intend to pursue this matter as best you can, anyway. With a little guidance from us, you may actually succeed and . . . everyone wins."

I almost caught a smile when he said that.

"Except the bad guys," I corrected.

"Precisely."

"So exactly what is it you can offer?" Manny asked. "Surveillance? Equipment? Agents? What?"

"Intel," he replied. "As far as anything more, we can't do that, I'm afraid."

"Well, so far you haven't exactly been generous in that area," I countered. "As best as I can tell, you've managed to scare the shit out of me, watch my car get bombed and remain basically hands off in everything we've done so far. What sort of intel *exactly* are you offering?"

"The reason for our maintaining a low profile to this point is because we needed to know more about you," he started. "Frankly, at least from every indication we've managed to find out about you, Detective, you're a loose cannon, you have no sense of protocol *and* you go outside the scope of your jurisdiction in order to get what you want."

"I solve cases," I defended.

"We know that," he said. "However, we needed to see if you did your job for the right reasons, or if you were getting something in return. Maybe you don't know this, but there are some in your department who don't care much about doing what's right."

"Yeah, I do know. So what kind of information are you offering?" I asked.

"Right now, the best we can do is give you some leads to follow. We know some of the fronts being used and small players in the game. You need to work those to climb the ladder. We also know that everything Mr. Reynolds says and does is being monitored by our competitors, so he will be of little use to you.

"However, it's my understanding, based on your discussion with his attorney, that the two of you have some sort of secret code from when you were in the military. Maybe that'll come in handy in time."

"Jesus!" I said. "You heard that, too?"

"We know a lot of things, Detective," the man said. "You need to trust that we can be of use to you. We want your friend released as much as you do, albeit for different reasons. The desire is just as great."

"So who are these leads?" Manny inquired.

"I will send you a list within the hour," he said, and turned to leave.

"So what do we call you?" Margie asked. I had almost forgotten about her.

"Call me... Joe," he said.

"Joe," I said. "Let me guess. Not your real name?"

That one actually got a left-raised-lip Elvis smile as he turned and left.

The three of us just stared at the door for several minutes after it closed.

~ * ~

"Is this for real or what?" Margie asked.

Manny answered before I could. "It's for real, all right," he said. "The question is, can we trust them or not?"

"I don't trust anyone who can extract a pubic hair without me even knowing about it," I said. "What I do know is that they're good at their job and we have to find a way to get Sam out of jail. If they can help, I'll use them for that reason and that alone. In the meantime, let's go over what we already know. Maybe we can get a head start on the list."

Seven

At least on the surface, William Joshua Sheffield III is a twenty-four-year-old business major just a year away from graduating from Stanford. He's six feet in height and considered an attractive young man. His curly blond hair and blue eyes are the earmarks of someone who could get into places on looks alone. With the pedigree he offered to go with the good looks, anyone who met him would give him far more credit than he had earned.

I had never heard of the lad. I *had* heard of Sheffield Construction, which was the largest general contractor in Monterey County and maybe the third or fourth largest in California. I only mention him now because when our friendly neighborhood spook left Manny's office, I decided to go back and visit with Sophie at the pool hall to see if she had ever seen Bobbi Marshall before that evening. I thought it might be prudent to get a little more of the kid's background.

Fast Willy's pool hall would be considered a "throw-back" establishment from the fifties or sixties. The thick wood paneling on the walls was classic and the ceiling hadn't been painted since before smoking indoors was outlawed in California. The purple and gold-hewed carpet consisted of some kind of material with a 500-year half-life.

The winning ingredients, however, were the scattered portraits of various tastefully depicted nude models hung all around the place. Some people would consider them works of art. Personally, I thought they were tacky and an art form one step up from Elvis painted on velvet. But, that's just me.

"Actually, I've seen her four or five other times over the last couple months," Sophie said. "Always on a Friday or Saturday night and never during the week. She was always with some guy I didn't know, but eventually I heard his name was Bill Sheffield. I remember them because he always gave Timmy nice tips. To be honest, I was jealous and wanted to see if I could get them to come in during my hours."

"What was their relationship like?" I asked.

"'Hot' would be the best way to describe it, I guess."

"What do you mean?"

"He was always dressed to kill, and she was always showing more than an R-rated movie. They were always kissing and touching each other. Sam usually didn't approve of such activities at the pool hall, but when someone gives you a hundred dollar tip before he plays his first game, you let some things slide. They always played back on table thirteen. It's by itself so nobody seemed to mind."

"Was there anything unusual about the relationship that you saw?" I asked.

"Not really," she replied. "Except maybe the last time."

"What was different?"

"When they got here," she said. "they were just as frisky as always. Well, now that I think about it, it wasn't the same then, either."

"Tell me," I implored.

"Well, before, he was always the aggressor. He always took control and forced her to do what he wanted. You know... show a little extra... that kind of stuff. The last time I saw them, she was the one who was trying to get him to do things with her. She was really pushing the envelope, too. They were in the back, but when I walked by picking up empties, I overheard her asking him if he wanted her to have sex with someone else for the thrill of it. And if he did, to just pick out the guy and she would do him right there."

"What happened?" I asked.

"Nothing," she said. "He looked over at me and saw that I had heard what was said and told her to cool it. They stayed for another hour and when they left, I saw that she was crying. I don't know why, but you just knew it wasn't good."

"Was anything said when they left?"

"No. And it really sucked, too. Every other time he gave Timmy a hundred when he got there and then another hundred when they left. This time he just covered the tab and walked out. I haven't seen him since."

"When was that?" I asked.

"About two weeks before she was killed."

"What about her?" I asked.

"I saw her a couple times the previous weekend," she said, "but she only stopped in long enough to see if someone was there she knew. I figured something had happened between them and she was trying to catch him at one of his stomping grounds. She never said anything to me. But, you can tell when a girl's on the hunt."

"And you're sure the young man's name was Bill Sheffield?" I asked again to make sure.

"Positive," she replied. "You don't give someone hundred-dollar tips and keep your identity anonymous to me."

I smiled at the reply and thanked her for the help. She told me that anytime I wanted anything from her to just say so. Of course

I picked up on the not-so-subtle meaning of "anything." *I'm such a lady killer.* I then reminded myself that thoughts like that would get me killed at home.

~ * ~

I had just flicked the start switch on Lu-Lu Belle and was about to kick her over when Manny called to let me know the list had arrived and I should come back and go over it with them. The trip took all of five minutes, hardly enough time for my baby to get warm.

"There are six names on the list," Manny said. He's not real big on the hello and goodbye thing. "I think we should each take three and then get back together and share notes. It should only take a couple hours."

"Well, can I at least look at the list and see the names first? Or have you already picked the easy ones for yourself...or the cute girls?" I said.

"What about me?" Margie pouted. "I could take a couple and make the list go even quicker."

"I know you could," Manny said, "but you don't have enough experience yet to read faces and change things on the fly if necessary. Why don't you go with me and we'll use this as a field training exercise."

"Screw you," she said with a tongue-in-cheek expression. "If I want training, I'll get it from a professional. I'll go with Samson."

"I'm riding Lu-Lu Belle again today, dear," I said.

"So?"

"I noticed you're wearing a skirt. It may not be the best combination, if you know what I mean."

"Let me worry about my koochie," she said defiantly, head held high. "Maybe I'll use the opportunity to do a little advertising. After all, lesbians need loving too."

"How can you argue with logic like that?" I said, looking at Manny who started smiling.

I was trying to act tough and manly, but the PI laughed as he saw the panic in my eyes.

"She acts all prim and proper, but I tell you, man, she's a slut." Manny grinned, pushing the envelope with me. Looking back at Margie, Manny continued, "Of course, I mean that in the best and most professional way possible."

Everyone laughed and agreed to meet up when we were done. We also noted that cell phones were to stay available in case something interesting came up.

Manny made copies of the list for everyone and passed them out. It took me about two seconds to see the name William Joshua Sheffield III. I didn't know the kid, but was already growing a dislike for the little prick.

"I want Billy Boy," I said. "I've already heard the name once today and it seems more than a coincidence it should come up on this list."

I repeated the information Sophie had given me.

"Tread lightly there, my friend," Manny said to me. "The boy has a lot of clout behind him."

"He has money from Sheffield Construction," I said. "So what?"

"It's more than that," he continued. "Grandpa has a lot of clout in city hall. I did background on him a while back for another client. The man had me shut down at every turn and never batted an eye. He's got friends in low places, if you know what I mean."

"Junior's got the same friends?" I asked.

"If he needs them," Manny continued. "Grandpa will pull out any resource for him. Like I said, walk softly there."

I would think by now you'd know I would take anything like that as a personal challenge. We split the rest of the list, and Margie and I climbed onto Lu-Lu Belle and headed off to make our grand entrance.

I didn't know how to find the boy, but thought maybe the best approach was to go straight to the old man.

~ * ~

Pebble Beach is one of the few communities in America where, if you don't live there, you have to pay to enter. There is a guarded gate everywhere you can enter the town and if you don't have "called-in" permission to enter, doing so will cost you. If you do business in town, you can get a temporary entrance card to go in as if you belonged. I established a small checking account at the local bank and can enter whenever I want by just showing my card.

On the other hand, Pebble Beach is one of the most beautiful resort locations in the world. The golf courses cost a small fortune to play on. The single, small gas station will charge you more for a tank of gas than the price of a small car. The homes—what can I say but...damn! This is how the rich and famous live. Nothing is too expensive for those who can afford to live here.

I figured out the trick a long time ago how to enter without having to pay. It's always easy with a badge. However, since that wasn't an option, I had to take out my trusty back-up card, flash it to the guard and act like I somehow belonged.

There are two lines when entering at the main gate—residents and visitors. The visitors' line was heavy, so I went through the residents' line and passed right through.

The bigger problem was finding a way to get past Sheffield's individual property gate, which was something most of the huge mansions featured. For that, I decided to do something a little more sinister—I lied.

The Sheffield place was one of the older mansions of the area. It had been around and updated with all of the latest bells and whistles as technology had evolved and become available. The castle-like appearance emitted an old-world, renaissance-era feel and gave me the impression that jousting knights would be seen just around the next corner. I was somewhat surprised to see that the gate had security guards posted and by the bulges under their coats, I could tell their purpose was for more than collecting money.

"I'm here to see Mr. Sheffield," I said as if it were something I did every day. I had to assume the old man didn't have that many callers riding up on an old Harley with a motorcycle mama sitting on the back.

"May I ask who's calling?" the man asked in a very professional manner, seemingly unfazed by the bike or the mama.

"My name is Detective Adam Shaw," I said without hesitation. "It's about a situation where his name came up in a very heinous crime, and we just want to ask a couple questions to clear the matter."

"Let them enter," a man's voice said over the intercom.

"Yes, sir," the guard replied, moving out of the way to open the gate for us.

Lu-Lu Belle did not need or care for introductions, and with the driveway going uphill, she was loud enough to shake a golf ball off its tee on the course, which was right across the road from the estate manor.

I could only guess, but thought the mansion had to be over 4,000 square feet on each floor of the three-story building. It was certainly out of my league. I thought I had made a mistake trying to shake this old guy. I'm sure whatever I had to throw at him, he'd seen before.

Another guard was waiting for us as we parked in front—and the bulge he carried would have made the first guard jealous.

"Mr. Sheffield is waiting for you in the study," the guard said. "Please keep it brief, he isn't in good health."

"Thank you," Margie and I replied in unison. "We'll only be a few minutes," I said. "It's just a few questions and then we'll be on our way."

The man turned and opened the door without another word. His physique and mannerisms were definitely ex-military. I suspected the armory under the coat was as well.

The home was magnificent, as you would expect, and I told myself that I could never let Jill see a place like this. She would work me to the bone just to have a place as big as the man's foyer.

Mr. Sheffield was standing next to the fireplace when we entered and didn't turn around until the butler or bodyguard or whoever he was announced our arrival and closed the doors behind us.

"Detective Shaw," the elderly man addressed me, in what I suspected was an accent that didn't belong to the local area. He had apparently been around long enough to mask where it truly originated. "I understand you have some questions for me?"

"I do, sir," I said with as much consideration as I could muster for a man of his means. "But, first let me introduce you to my assistant, Margie Samara." The old man nodded his white hair but didn't express any other greeting. "I appreciate you taking a few moments with us," I continued without prompt. "We will be as quick as we can."

"I know you will, Detective...or should I say, *Mister* Shaw," he questioned with a slight smirk. "As a matter of fact, I've already made contact with your chief of police to determine why you were here. He seemed genuinely surprised by your presence."

"I'm sure he did, sir," I stated. "I'm also sure he told you that I am not on the force at this time as well."

"As a matter of fact," he said.

"Then I guess there's no sense trying to bullshit you about anything I might have tried," I continued. "So before the cavalry arrives and hauls my ass off to jail for impersonating an officer, I guess I'll just ask you one question."

"And that is?" he inquired.

"Was your grandson still dating Bobbi Marshall when she was killed? And before you give *me* a bullshit answer, please know for a fact that I will find out the truth about that and anything else you've tried hiding under the rug."

He looked in my eyes and knew I wasn't lying. Additionally, was that a glimmer of respect I saw coming from his withered face?

"He had broken up with her about two weeks before she died."

"Do you know why?"

"I don't make it a policy to involve myself with my grandson's personal matters," he said with an air of smugness. "I believe you've extended your welcome beyond your one question. Besides, someone has already confessed to that crime."

"I know," I said, "but what the hell. Sometimes what you see on the surface isn't what's really going on. We both know that, don't we? You might want to run interference against me. As a matter of fact, I suspect you already have. But, if you've done your homework, you already know your efforts won't stop me. If anything, they'll only piss me off. My friend, Sam Reynolds, is the man who confessed. I know he didn't kill that girl and I suspect you know it, too. What I don't know is *why* he confessed. I don't know yet who killed the girl or what your involvement is in all of this. What I will tell you is that I will get to the truth. You can help me or you can take whatever heat comes from hiding behind these walls. I don't mean you any harm or disrespect, Mr. Sheffield, but I want my friend out of jail. I will find a way to make that happen."

"You are a very loyal man," Sheffield said. "I wish I could help you, but I can't. I will, however, tell the chief that your visit was merely social so our discussion will remain between us."

"That's kind of you. I'm sure he'll believe you."

"It doesn't matter if he believes me or not," Sheffield stood taller. "Either way, he won't bother you."

"Thank you, sir," I said and started to leave.

As Margie and I were about to climb on Lu-Lu Belle, one of our finest in uniform drove up and stopped in front, blocking our exit. Then I saw him talking on the phone and before he exited the car, he backed up and left us just staring at his taillights.

"I guess he's a man of his word," Margie said, referring to the old man.

"So am I," I replied.

Margie got on the bike and placed the helmet on her head. I waited 'til she was settled and climbed on. Apparently she noticed my hesitation and asked me about my reluctance.

"Nothing," I said, trying to let sleeping dogs rest.

"Come on," she said. "Out with it."

"Okay," I said. "But remember, this one's your fault."

"I can take it," she replied.

I half turned my head toward her, unable to avoid the view and asked, "Do you really call that thing a...koochie?"

Eight

The next lead didn't pan out. Mr. Reinhardt wasn't home and wouldn't be back for a couple days, his wife told us. However, the next lady was at home.

Stephanie Shadows answered her door dressed in heels designed for a fancy evening out. As my eyes climbed for a more complete view, the black leather pants she wore looked as if they had been sprayed on. Her top, if that's what it was called, was filled exceptionally well. The material was silk, or something I was sure I could never afford for Jill, and left little to the imagination. I'm not complaining, mind you. I just wasn't expecting a view so breathtaking. I think you get the gist—she was lovely. The only thing I would consider a flaw was her platinum hair, only because it could not be natural. But what the hell—I didn't think God actually made a creature with looks like that anyway.

"May I help you?" she asked, standing there with a view of the ocean as her background.

"Hello. My name is Adam Shaw." I extended my hand and didn't get a response. "And we're here to ask you a couple questions about a mutual acquaintance. At least I'm of the impression that you know him. His name is William Sheffield the Third. Does that name mean anything to you?"

"Come in," she offered and gracefully stepped to the side.

As Margie entered before me, I couldn't help but notice Ms. Shadows' attention to her backside. I'm not a *total* idiot, but at the time I thought she was only interested in her skirt.

Once inside, Margie corrected an error on my part and introduced herself. As she held out her hand, Ms. Shadows extended hers as well, then took Margie's hand into both of hers.

"It's a pleasure to meet you," Ms. Shadows said, looking at Margie with a hunger in her eyes.

There was a long pause, so I began speaking again. "As I was saying, I was wonder—" She pushed a stop-sign hand in my face to stop me from speaking.

"I would prefer if Margie would speak to me." She looked again at Margie and asked, "Do you mind?"

Margie looked at me and I shrugged my shoulders.

"That would be fine," Margie said. "Do you know Mr. Sheffield?"

"As a matter of fact, I do," Ms. Shadows replied. "Or should I say, I did. We don't come into contact anymore, I'm afraid."

"Why's that?' I asked, but again there was the hand.

"Why's that?" Margie asked.

I could sense something transpiring here. I wasn't quite sure what it was, but the dynamics were getting all twisted around. At first I thought it might be that Ms. Shadows was also a lesbian and this was some sort of mating ritual, but there was more. I just couldn't put a finger on it.

"For now," she replied, "let's just say we came to a mutual agreement that seeing each other might be a conflict of interest."

I started to speak again when this time Margie gave me a quick look that told me to keep quiet.

Margie said, "Ms. Shadows, we are only here to help a friend who's in trouble and we mean you no harm. We just...need your help."

Margie looked at the floor as if embarrassed.

What the hell's going on? I wondered.

"Baby girl," Ms. Shadows said, "I have no fear of you." She then looked at me with a stare that seemed to expel disgust. "Or him, for that matter. You should know that by now. What does concern me is that the young man you are asking about comes with a lot of clout; clout that is bigger than the both of us. And since I don't know you, I will need to get to know you better before I'm willing to say too much." Then after a short pause, "You know so very little of me."

"Getting to know you would be a pleasure," Margie said. I could sense the lust oozing from her.

"I'm sure it would. You are a most intriguing specimen, one I would also like to get to know."

"Ladies," I interrupted. "I know you two find each other—" I paused to seek the right word—"special. But for now, could we stay on track?"

"We are on track," they both said in unison. Then Ms. Shadows continued after a smiling glance was given to Margie. "Your friend, what's his name?"

"Sam Reynolds," I said. "I don't know if you've kept up with the news, but he's been arrested for murder."

"My goodness," she said. "Sammy's got himself into a real pickle, hasn't he?"

I looked at Margie. She asked, "You know Mr. Reynolds?"

"Of course," she said. "We've had some business dealings in the past."

"Your business?" Margie hesitated.

"No, silly," Ms. Shadows replied. "He's not into that. I just needed some help for a friend and was told that Sammy could handle it or knew somebody that could. He was a dear."

"Well, I'm confused," I said, mostly to myself. They both laughed.

"Of course you are, dear," Ms. Shadows smirked. "You're either a part of the life or you aren't. You aren't."

"What business are you talking about?" I then looked at Margie and asked, "And how is it that you know about it? Whatever *it* is?"

"Would you be okay enlightening Mr. Shaw?" Ms. Shadows asked.

"It's only speculation," Margie started, "But, if I'm correct, Ms. Shadows is a dominatrix. *And,* if that assumption is correct, I was trying to find out if Sam was a client."

"Very good," Ms. Shadows cooed. "How did you know?"

Margie seemed a little embarrassed, but explained. "Obviously the outfit you're wearing screams 'dominant woman.' There aren't that many women, even those as attractive as you, who would have the guts to wear something like that. However, I didn't want to jump to conclusions. But when we came in, I noticed several pieces of furniture had been attached to the floor so they wouldn't move. That was my first real clue about what you were into. Then I noticed your ceiling hooks were reinforced and not located in the most practical locations for plants to thrive. Finally, and this was probably the most telling, I noticed the whips and paddles you left on your dining room table. I wasn't sure if that was for effect or an oversight. Either way, it was pretty much a dead giveaway."

"Damn," I said quietly. "I'm supposed to be the detective."

Apparently, I wasn't quiet enough.

Ms. Shadows said, "Like most men, you think with parts that don't see well. And when the blood rushes from your head, your vision diminishes greatly. You, like most men, Detective, become visually impaired when looking at beautiful women.”

Now it was my turn to be embarrassed.

“Don't worry about it,” Margie said. “I won't tell your wife.” She ended the comment with an unrestrained laugh.

“So now that we've gotten to know each other better,” Ms. Shadow started, “maybe there are a few things you should know about Mr. Sheffield. He was one of my clients. And let's just say he was very enthusiastic. I'm not going to go into any of the specifics, but it seemed to me that his appetite for pain and humiliation didn't have any limits.”

“Go on,” I encouraged.

“It started about a year and a half ago with me,” she continued. “But I could tell I wasn't the first to play with him. Let's put it this way, there were scars in places that wouldn't happen with a car accident. And if you do this kind of thing for as long as I have, you notice every inch of a person. When we started, he would visit about once every few weeks. Then it became every week. Toward the end, it was several times a week.”

“How did it end?” I asked.

Even though she showed a touch of annoyance, she replied. “About two weeks ago, maybe three, I was going to my car when a young woman approached me from the curb. She said she was William's girlfriend and I should stay away from him. She said she knew who I was and what I was doing and if I didn't stop, she would call the cops and have me arrested. At first I was simply annoyed with her, but when I mentioned it to William, he got very agitated and stopped our session. I haven't seen or talked to him since.”

“He just stopped and didn't give you any reason?” Margie asked.

“It's not like they're engaged,” I blurted out. “It's a business deal.”

After I said it, I realized I was expressing a touch of prejudice or maybe even disgust by the whole thing. I felt out of my element.

Ms. Shadow seemed irked by the outburst and then calmed herself. "You're right, Mr. Shaw. Even though my services are of an extremely personal nature, it was a business transaction. My services are more in demand than you could imagine and I didn't think much of his absence. I have more than enough business to keep me from worrying about the loss of one client. I work primarily with professional businessmen and women as well as politicians. I wouldn't say I'm insulated to the point of being able to get by with anything, but I didn't think the girl's threats were of any concern to me."

"Did you know the girl?" Margie asked.

"I never saw her before or since," she replied.

"Would you recognize her if we showed you a picture?" I asked.

"Of course."

"Then if you don't mind," I stated. "We'll leave you to do whatever it is you do. Also, would you object if we visited again soon?"

"Not at all," she replied, smiling and touching Margie's face, "as long as you bring this little thing with you."

Margie reddened at the comment, but I could tell she loved the attention.

We were just ready to leave when I turned back. "I do have one more question for you, if you don't mind."

"Not at all," she said.

"Have you ever heard of a koochie?"

The slap against the back of my head was indication enough that the answer could wait 'til later.

Nine

"You've got to get over this koochie thing!" Margie told me after we pulled back into Manny's parking area. "You're an embarrassment to men around the world."

"I suspect that most men in the world could care less about my fascination with the word koochie. Besides, if I can learn one small thing for mankind about women, I'll be enshrined with a monument next to the great Rocky Balboa."

"Who?"

"Never mind," I replied as my phone rang. "Shaw," I said without looking to see who was calling.

"Tootie's gone," Jill said over the other end.

"What do you mean gone?" I asked.

"What part don't you understand?" she responded, more harshly than I expected.

"The part where you need to give me a little more information," I said. "My crystal ball's a little foggy and my ability to read minds was never fully developed. What happened?"

"After you left this morning, Tootie and Bitsy were talking about your little adventure from last night. He said he thinks he would make a great detective and was going to talk to you about being a private investigator."

"Oh, great," I said, interrupting her flow. "That's all I need."

"Hush!" she exclaimed. "If he wants to be a private investigator, that's his prerogative."

"Yes, dear," I said.

I came to the conclusion a long time ago that you can both pacify and insult a woman with that phrase. This time it was meant to pacify.

"Anyway," she continued, "Bitsy told him he was too old to do such foolishness and he got real angry. He called her a few unkind words, jumped in the pick-up and took off. He said he would show her *and* me that he could do the job. He was real angry, Adam. I'm worried. He might do something stupid. Find him for me, will you?"

"Baby," I started, "I'm in the middle of something real important. Can't this wait? He'll cool off in a while and come back home. You'll see."

"There's one more thing," she said reluctantly. "I didn't know at first—"

"What is it?" I asked, getting a little frustrated.

"He took my Glock," she said.

"*What?*" I screamed.

I didn't realize how loud I was and Margie turned toward me, startled.

Living in the country, ten miles from the nearest community, has its advantages. It's peaceful and has so many wonderful attributes. However, there are dangers in the wilderness and it never hurts to have a little protection lying around. Since there were no kids, I never thought twice about keeping the weapons unlocked and accessible. Never in my dreams did I expect her father to be childish enough to do something this stupid.

It took me a few moments to realize that Jill was talking to me and apologizing over and over. I felt sorry for her.

"It's okay," I said. I could tell she was worried and felt real bad for his actions. "I'll find him. I still have a few friends who can also keep a lookout for him."

After a half dozen thank yous and several more apologies, she hung up and I made a call to Tommy Billings to see if he could have some of the guys keep an eye out for Tootie. I told him that if they saw him, not to do anything except give me a call. I didn't want any kind of a scene and I sure as hell didn't want him arrested for carrying without a license.

"Everything okay?" Margie asked, concerned.

"Nothing a long vacation and a stick of dynamite wouldn't cure," I replied.

"I get the vacation part. What's with the dynamite?"

"I'd stick it up Tootie's ass and send him on a new journey," I said, not wanting to keep the conversation going.

"That bad, huh?" she said.

"You have no idea."

~ * ~

Exasperated, I walked into the office with Margie. As we entered, Manny was sitting at his desk with his index finger plastered to his lip in the traditional keep-your-mouth-shut sign. I shrugged in the "what the hell's going on?" manner and he held up a piece of paper for us to read. "BUGS" was all the sign said, but it stated volumes.

"Talk normal, but don't say anything," the next note said. He then quickly scribbled, "In a minute we'll take a walk."

"Hey Manny," Margie said as if he were deaf. "What's going on?"

"Not much, Margie," he replied, "but you don't have to talk so loud. My hearing has come back to normal."

"Oh, I'm sorry," she said, realizing what she had done.

"Want to do me a favor?" I asked him. "Lu-Lu Belle is acting up. Would you mind taking a look at her?"

I figured that was as good an excuse as any for getting him out of the office, and that we should be able to talk outside without unwanted listeners.

"Sure," he said. "What's the problem?"

"Don't know for sure. She's just running a little rough. I thought maybe you could figure it out quicker than I could." I said this as we were walking out the door.

"What the hell is going on around here?" he asked. "I've swept this place every day for years and never found a bug. Hell, my friends have been giving me shit about being paranoid. I guess it isn't paranoia if someone is really out to get me."

"This is some crazy shit, my friend," I said. "Did you find out anything with your leads?"

"A big lot of nothing," he said. "None of them were home, so I figured I would try again after six. Maybe I can catch them at the supper table. What about you?"

He leaned down to give Lu-Lu Belle the once-over as if there were something actually wrong.

"She's fine," I said. "I used that as a ploy to get us outside."

"I know," he said, "but if they're listening inside, maybe they're also watching outside."

"Good point," I replied. "And yes, we did find out a few things. Like Grandpa Sheffield is not going to offer a lot of cooperation. And that if my gut is still working, he's up to his ass in whatever's going on."

I told him about William III's little extracurricular activities, which got his attention and then a big smile.

"Seems to me that we now have a motive for the girl's murder, don't we?" he said with a whistle.

"I would think so," I continued. "But it's not a lot at this time. If Junior is one of the bad guys, *and* if he has big political aspirations, it would make sense that his activities would put the kibosh on those plans, not to mention be a huge embarrassment to the family. I can't see Granddaddy sitting back letting that happen. He gives me the impression that he would be willing to do anything to keep his empire intact."

"May I ask a question?" Margie inquired. "If little William is really into this fetish, what do you think is the likelihood that he could actually quit? You know, go cold turkey?"

I looked at Manny and we both wondered why we hadn't thought of that.

"Where would a guy go to find a dominatrix around here?" I asked no one in particular. I looked at Manny again.

"Don't look at me," he said. "I'm not into that shit."

We all laughed, and Manny seemed to shiver. Then his expression turned dark.

I saw him reaching into Lu-Lu Belle's belly—above the undercarriage, between the motor and oil reservoir—and he was fiddling with something.

"I think I see what's wrong with your bike."

"There's nothing wrong with her," I replied. "She's running fine. Like I said before, I just wanted to get us outside."

"Well, I would put this under the category of not so fine," he said as he pulled out a small metallic container from its hiding place.

"What the hell's that?" I asked, taking a step backward.

"I believe it's something to get your attention," Manny said, slowly lifting the lid and flipping off the switch to a remote detonator. The explosive device was elegant in its simplicity. The container carried a cellphone, a switch and a one inch cube of what looked like C-4. It wasn't designed for doing damage to anyone but the rider. I just didn't like the idea that the rider would have been me.

Margie finally realized what it was. She gasped, her face turned the color of chalk, and she looked as if her legs were going to give out. I grabbed her and moved her away from Manny.

There was a note taped to the small device. It said, "Let it go. This is your last warning."

"I get the feeling that someone intends to keep this mess quiet," I said. "And they certainly got my attention."

"How? When? Why?" Margie tried talking.

"All very good questions," I replied. "But, the bigger question is, who? I don't see Grandpa Sheffield handling explosives at his age. That means he's either hired someone or there are other players to be concerned about. Hell, maybe both."

"We're running blind here," Manny said. "We're totally outgunned." He looked at Margie, who was visibly shaken, considering it had been her *and* my ass sitting right above the bomb just a few minutes ago. "It's safe now, sweetie."

"Maybe our good-guy friends know more than they've been telling us," I said. "These guys are big league. Maybe I should pay Sam a visit. Maybe he could shed some light on the situation."

"How're you going to do that?" Margie asked. The color was returning to her face. "You know they, whoever they are, are listening to every word he says. He'll never risk telling you anything that could cause him or you problems."

"I know," I replied. "But, maybe I can check to see if we're on the right track. He and I used a system a long time ago when we were in the military. I just hope it still works."

"It better, dude," Manny said. "Otherwise, we'll all end up splattered on somebody's wall. And frankly, that idea doesn't much appeal to me."

"Or me," Margie echoed.

"I'll be back in a while," I said. "You two just keep looking through what we have. And don't go anywhere. I should be back in an hour or so."

"What about the cockroaches?" he asked.

"Find them and destroy them," I said. "They already know we know they're around. So as I see it, they'll expect us to do that. I don't think it will send any bad signals. Just make sure that you remember to check for more as frequently as you can." I looked at the device he was still holding. "What are you planning to do with that?"

"Keep it," he said. "You know how difficult it is to get your hands on military-grade C-4 these days? Beside, you never know when it'll come in handy." He smiled.

I got on Lu-Lu Belle and thought *nobody fucks with my bike.*

~ * ~

"They aren't going to let you see him," the guard said. "He's on suicide watch."

"Suicide-watch, my ass," I replied. "I got permission from Dakota Walker. Call her, she'll confirm."

"The chief told me nobody sees him," he countered. "Not without medical authorization."

"Call her," I insisted. "She'll give you whatever authorization you need."

Reluctantly he picked up the phone and called somebody. After about five minutes, he hung up and said, "Follow me."

Sam was lying on his cot and didn't move when the door opened. He didn't move when it closed either, 'til he heard my voice asking if he was okay.

"Goddamn," he said. "How the hell did you get in here? They told me there wasn't a chance in hell you'd get in here."

"I wasn't sure they'd let me in, either," I said, giving him a hug. "But I still have a few people who don't hate me."

"Wish I could say that," he said, dropping his head.

"You have a lot of friends," I said, sitting down next to him. "You doing okay?"

"About as good as anyone in my position," he stated solemnly. "I guess I really fucked up this time."

"As best I can tell," I said, "you had help in that area."

"This is all on me," he came back. "I can't let anybody else take the blame for this."

"I understand what you mean," I replied. "Do you remember when we were on duty and the lights went out? There were snakes and all kinds of creatures coming out of the woodwork. We managed to get out of it then."

"This is different," he said. "Well, I guess in some ways it's the same, but I don't see how to get the lights back on this time."

"That's what friends are for," I said, trying to make the conversation as normal as possible. I think he knew where I was going, but didn't think he had any way out of his situation.

"Sometimes friends just need to walk away and cut their losses," Sam countered.

"Not *real* friends," I said. "Besides, I heard from a friend that there's a guy in Sacramento who just might be the ticket to getting the lights to come back on."

"I think I know that guy," he said. "From what I hear, he's a pretty good electrician. The only problem is, he works with a prick of a partner here locally. And that guy is running his schedule and making it difficult to get any work done."

"Do you know him?" I asked. "Maybe if I talked to him, he'd let the guy help me out."

"I'm pretty sure the guy is local, but I don't know his name."

"Damn," I said frustrated. "I was hoping to get some help."

"Well, there is one thing," he said, hesitating.

"What's that?"

"Okay...I don't know if it's true or not," he continued, "and I certainly don't want to send you on a wild goose chase."

"Right now, I'll take whatever you can give me. I need this specialist and I have to find a way to get to him."

There was a hesitation while Sam looked around the tiny cell. "From what I understand, he used to be a farmer, a pig farmer, but I think he's moved up in the world since then. I don't know what he's doing now."

"All right, that gives me something to work with," I said. "I can at least look into that."

"Is there anything I can do for you?" I added.

"Find the guy and take care of yourself," he said. "There's a shit storm coming, so you better keep your umbrella handy."

I smiled and said, "I already got a whiff of it. I'll come back as soon as I can. You just keep your head down. We'll be okay."

Sam did something I never expected. He stood up with me and gave me a big hug. There were tears in his eyes and then he moved back to his cot. He never said another word to me, but I knew he was scared.

~ * ~

Sometimes I'm not sure if Alexander Graham Bell was a saint or the devil incarnate. I hate phones – cell phones in particular. By the time I got out to Lu-Lu Belle, I had five messages; three from Jill wanting to know about Tootie, one from Ms. Shadows, and one from Tommy Billings. I had nothing to tell Jill, so she would have to wait. Ms. Shadows was certainly the most tempting, but Tommy got the first call.

"What's up, Tommy?" I asked the deputy.

"We've found your father-in-law," he said. "He's down on Freemont talking to the P.I. Ed Lafferty. What do you want me to do?"

"Nothing," I replied. "I'll go get him myself. Thanks, Tommy. I owe you one."

"Well, I'll see to it that you pay up," he laughed, "soon. You keep going the way you're going and debts from you aren't ever likely to get paid."

"I hear ya," I said and hung up.

~ * ~

Ed Lafferty was an old-time private investigator.

A long time ago, he'd made a name for himself having found the kidnapped daughter of one of Hollywood's local mega stars. He made a good living for a while, but then a few cases went sideways. He started drinking and now he mostly takes on divorce cases. He is okay as far as I'm concerned. I'd never heard of him doing anything under the table or illegal.

My old, battered pick-up truck was sitting in his parking lot, just as Tommy said it would be. I parked next to it and walked in.

"Hello, son-in-law," Tootie said with a big smile. "What brings you here? Got a big case for us to help you with?"

Ed stood and shook my hand.

"Tootie says you're letting him help you solve the Sam Reynolds murder case. I thought he confessed?" It was more of a question than a statement.

I was about to set the matter straight when Tootie jumped in. "Tell him about the fire bomb last night. It was one of the most intense things I've gone through."

Again, I was about to talk when Ed jumped in. "That car bomb last night was you? Damn," he said with a whistle. "Well...you certainly know how to bring a rookie up to speed real quick."

"Tootie!" I said above the excitement. "What are you doing?"

"My new job," he said. "Ed here doesn't think I'm too old to be a P.I. As a matter of fact, he thinks I could be a real asset to what he does."

"Do you even know what he does?" I asked. "No offense, Ed, but this is getting a little out of hand. Why, in God's name, would you need him in divorce cases?"

Tootie didn't wait for Ed to respond.

"Because," he puffed up, "sometimes a sexy senior can get into places a young buck like him can't reach."

"How much divorce work are you getting in nursing homes? Because those are the only places he would have the advantage."

"None," Ed replied, smiling, "but I'm branching out. I've got a couple cases involving elder care fraud. I think someone like Tootie could get into a facility and snoop around without anyone raising an eyebrow. He has the years to get in and the youth to be functional. He could really help me."

"You're both nuts," I said, raising my hands to clasp behind my head in frustration. "What about Bitsy?" I asked. "I thought you were going to marry the girl."

"I still want to marry her," he replied. "But, how long would it last if she thought I was too old to do anything productive? Besides, if she decides she won't stick with me, I can do some real undercover work at the homes. You know what I mean?" he asked with a wink.

"Jesus H. Christ," I said in frustration. "What about Jill? She's gonna have a conniption fit about this. She'll worry her ass off about you getting hurt. And just where do you plan on living while all of this is going on?" I really thought I had him there.

"Most of the time, I will be going from one home to another," he said without hesitation. "Look, I know there'll be some down time, so I figured you'd be okay with me living with the two of you."

I don't usually talk under my breath. However, Tootie brings out the worst in me.

"And what about Bitsy?" I asked. "Where's *she* gonna live while all of this is going on? Have you thought of that?"

"She ain't so big as to be a bother," he stated, as if it was a ridicules question. "Besides, she could help around the house. Then we could both have a kept woman." He laughed at his own joke.

I didn't think Jill would consider it as funny as Tootie seemed to.

"Give me the Glock," I said. "Now!" I caught my voice getting loud and didn't care.

"I need it for protection," Tootie insisted.

"You're *going* to need protection if you don't give it to me right now," I said and held out my hand.

Reluctantly he reached into his coat pocket and pulled it out. I grabbed it and said, "You should be glad I don't just shoot you myself. But I'll wait 'til you get home. Or maybe Jill will shoot you and save me the effort. I could probably get her off on justifiable homicide."

"You just need some time to get used to the idea," Tootie said, standing straight. "And don't worry, I won't try to take any of your cases away from you. That'll be our agreement right up front."

"Go home, Tootie, Jill's worried about you."

"Just where I was heading," he said. "I have to get ready to start next week. I got lots to prepare for."

I glared at Ed.

"Don't look at me that way," Ed said. "He came to me. I just happen to need someone like him to help with these cases. Besides," he continued, "Tootie will be a blast to work with. He's kept me laughing the whole time he's been here. We're gonna do great together."

"You tell that to my wife when she comes to visit," I said. "And when she brings the Glock back, it won't be to show you how pretty it is."

I looked at Tootie and repeated myself.

"Go home, Tootie."

I got on Lu-Lu Belle and was ready to take off, but decided that calling Jill was the right thing to do. I didn't want Tootie being the bearer of bad news and telling her how her father has officially fucked up our world.

Ten

Talking to Jill was about as pleasant as you can imagine. Normally she is a kind, beautiful, and happy person. With Tootie around, however, she was a different person. It was all my doing and, "By God, Adam Shaw, you *will* fix this," were the last words I heard before the line went dead.

Ain't love grand?

After that exchange of pleasantries, I called Ms. Shadows, but couldn't reach her. I then called and told Manny to have Margie ready to go with me over to the dungeon.

Look, the lady scares the hell out of me. She may be eye candy to an old fart like Tootie, but I'm not brave enough to tackle that broad alone. I needed a woman's help and she seemed to like Margie. In what ways I didn't want to know, but I thought Margie would be a good buffer.

~ * ~

The koochie girl was waiting for me. She climbed on board and we headed for the beach house. When we arrived, the door was opened a crack. It looked like trouble so I told Margie to wait while I went inside. Like every other woman in my life, she didn't listen *or* wait like she was told.

"What the hell are you doing?" I asked quietly.

"Staying with you," Margie said. "I don't want to be anywhere like this alone."

"There could be an intruder."

"And what, you want me to meet him alone? No thanks. I'm sticking with you."

"Okay. Just be quiet."

We stepped carefully into the entrance and noticed that some of the fixtures that weren't bolted down were knocked onto the floor. It looked like a struggle had taken place and I felt my adrenaline shifting into high gear.

Farther inside, lying on the floor, was Ms. Shadows. As we approached her, I heard a noise coming from downstairs. I told Margie to check if Ms. Shadows was still alive while I went through the rest of the house. The look on Margie's face told me she didn't want to do that, especially if the woman was dead. However, she knew she couldn't help me if there was trouble waiting down below—she would just get in my way.

I wasn't supposed to be carrying a weapon, but for once, Tootie's shenanigans were paying off. I checked the Glock to make sure everything was in order—bullets chambered and all that. Once everything checked out, I slowly made my way down the stairs into what could only be described as a real-live, honest-to-God dungeon. Hanging on the walls were a vast assortment of whips, chains and paraphernalia I had never seen and afraid to ask about. To my right was something that reminded me of a medieval rack and to my left something that was the shape of a man-size X that I could only guess about. Man, this lady was really freaking me out.

I heard a noise coming from the next room and knew that when I was a cop I would've been calling for back up at this point. For now, I figured I had to go it alone.

The noise was consistently inconsistent. It was something hitting something metal. I heard a muffled sound that could be human, but I not sure. I knelt down and got on my knees at the doorway. I've discovered that if a perpetrator was going to take a potshot at me, he would usually aim chest high. I happen to like my chest and preferred they miss me altogether.

I didn't know if the door would squeak. So I opened it slowly, figuring that if it did, I would push it open quickly to finish the process. If it didn't squeak, it could give a chance to catch the perpetrator in the act—giving me the edge.

The door opened about a foot and then squeaked. I shoved it the rest of the way open and rolled into the room, coming up to a shooting position. I was looking in every direction. When my eyes came to a stop, the gun was pointing at a man—who started screaming like a girl.

I say it was a man, but other than his bearded face, a girl was more what he looked like. He was dressed in a maid's uniform, including fishnet stockings and high heels. The little bonnet on his head looked ridiculous, but no more so than the ball gag in his mouth. He would have run like hell, if it weren't for the restraints holding him on his tiptoes.

"Is there anyone else down here?" I asked. I followed the question with, "Ma'am?"

He closed his eyes and shook his head to the negative. I took another look around and saw nothing out of the ordinary—I say that with tongue in cheek. The place was completely out of the ordinary. At that moment, however, I was referring to *anyone else* out of the ordinary, not any*thing* else.

I placed the Glock in my belt and went over to release his gag, hopefully to get an idea about what happened.

"Is Lady Shadows all right?" was the first thing he asked.

"She's fine," a voice spoke behind me. It was the *lady* herself entering the room with Margie. She was carrying a phone and told me, "Before we talk, the *maid* needs to make a call."

"To call off the troops," Margie interjected.

I had no idea what she was talking about until she dialed a number then placed the phone to his ear.

"This is Deputy Police Chief Howard Young," the fair maiden said. "You received a distress call from a Miss..." he looked at Margie and asked her name, "Margie Samara," he continued. "It's a false alarm, so release the cars to go to other duties. I will take care of this personally." That was followed by a list of numbers and letters I knew to be a security code for verification and then he said, "Thanks." He nodded his head to Lady Shadows.

This case was getting more and more bizarre as the day went on. I was standing in the dungeon of a dominatrix before the deputy police chief in drag, only an hour after finding a bomb on my motorcycle and a father-in-law dying to screw up my already screwed-up world. What the hell else could happen in one day?

I hadn't recognized the deputy chief before the call. I don't know why. Maybe it was the old "take a person out of his normal environment and put him in a dress" thing. In just a matter of a couple of days, everything I believed to be normal, in a community that gave the outward appearance of being above anything subverted, came to a crashing halt.

Again, I want to repeat, I'm not a prude. But at that moment, my sanity was taking a shot and the outcome was looking bleak.

"Can anybody tell me what the hell's going on here?" I asked.

There were no volunteers jumping at the chance to explain, so I took the direct approach. "I guess the correct name now is 'Lady' Shadows?" I queried, looking at the dominatrix. I could tell by the pack of ice she held to her head that she was not feeling her dominant best. She raised her head up and down slowly. Now that the emergency was over, the bad guys were gone and the cops were called off, she was just now able to let the reality of the pain and the situation sink in. She sat on a plush chair that looked more like a throne.

"Can you tell me what happened?" I asked.

"Not much of it, I'm afraid," she replied slowly. "After you left, I was thinking about what we'd discussed and I got to thinking about Billy. I had come to the conclusion that he would have to be getting his fix with someone else by now."

"Why's that?" I asked.

"I'm sure there's a lot about this lifestyle you aren't aware of, Detective. It can be addicting to some people. It's not something you can just quit once you become used to it. So that's why I called you and left a message. I wanted to give you the names of some of my sisters. I believe I can trust you to be discreet."

"That's my middle name," I offered sarcastically. Maybe I came across a little harsh, but frankly, at that moment, I didn't care if I hurt anyone's feelings.

"I've heard a few other names people call you," she said, "but that's another story."

"What happened here?" I asked leaving the name thing alone. "Are you going to tell me you tripped and fell and that's how you hurt your head?"

"No, Detective," she said, sounding insulted. "I'm a private person and I prefer it that way, but I will never lie to you. I may refuse to answer you or even tell you that something is none of your business, but I will never lie."

"I can live with that." I was beginning to admire the woman's frankness.

"Soon after my call to you," she continued, "Miss Young, or should I be more formal now, Deputy Chief Young, arrived—he was my next appointment."

Everyone looked at the deputy chief—tied and looking lovely.

"It's not necessary to be formal with me, Ms. Shadows. You can call him 'Miss' if you prefer." I looked at the deputy chief, who hung his head, and then to Margie, who tried, but failed, to keep from smiling.

"Thank you," she said, appreciating my sense of humor. "Anyway, Miss Young arrived as scheduled and we went about our normal preparation for the scene we were about to play. He was dressed and attached to the beam, as he is now, when I heard a noise upstairs. I wasn't scared, but rather curious as to what it could be. I have a very good security system and I didn't think it would be an intruder. I didn't see him at first, but then caught a glimpse of someone coming at me from behind. I took martial arts, Detective, and managed to fend off the first several blows. He was a much bigger person than me. I did the best I could, but as you can see—not good enough."

I could tell she was shaken up more than she would allow herself to show. I didn't know if she was keeping up the pretense for me or for the maid. He was, after all, the paying customer.

"If you aren't up for this," I said, "we can take a break and get the info later."

"I'm fine," she said. "Let's just get this over with." She paused for a moment and then continued. "I was knocked down, and I think he was about to do some real damage when he heard your motorcycle pull up. That's when he hit me and knocked me out."

"Did he say anything?" I asked.

"Just before he hit me he said, 'We aren't finished with you, bitch.' Then the lights went out."

"Did you recognize him or could you describe him?"

"His shape and size only," she replied. "He was wearing a ski mask and dark clothes. He was about six one or two, maybe two-ten in weight. Other than that, I don't think I can be of much help."

"What about distinguishing marks?"

"Nothing I can think of right now," she said, as if disappointed in her failure to be more helpful.

"Wait," she said. "There *was* something. Just before he hit me, I noticed a scar close to the Adam's apple. I don't know what it's called, but like someone who had a tube put in his throat."

"A tracheotomy," I filled in the blank.

She showed her appreciation with a slight smile. "I wish I could be more helpful."

"You've been a great help," I said. Then looking at the Little Princess, I asked, "What about you, Fluffy? Can you add anything to this, or were you too tied up to be of any help?"

The deputy chief was hanging and on his toes, wearing a pink chenille dress and heels, but decided he needed to take an aggressive approach to the situation. "You're going to have to keep this under wraps, Detective. Discretion is the best approach to handling this. And I want you to make sure no one ever hears about it."

With an aching head and pale skin, Lady Shadows practically jumped like a cat at the little man.

"What makes you think anybody here cares what you think or want? You are nothing but a little girl in a hell of a lot of trouble right now. If it wasn't for this headache I'm feeling, I would beat you to a pulp for even thinking for a moment that you mattered. These people are taking a huge risk trying to do the right thing for a friend. They're my friends and you dare to insult them by telling them how to handle this? I will plaster your prissy little ass all over the news if you think for a moment you're in control of anything. You *will* help them get to the truth. Do you understand me? There's no need to hide from these people. They already know what a fucking wimp you are"

Hell, I was in awe. I decided right then I would never introduce Lady Shadows to Jill. I wouldn't get through a week with someone like that.

The deputy chief hung his head and simply muttered, "Yes, Lady Shadows."

What more needed to be said?

I had already decided not tell anyone about the deputy chief's proclivities. But once she got finished humiliating him, I knew that doing so would do me no good. I would never do that to gain my job back or create influence. I'm sure he was okay. He, like most of us, just needed to handle an internal monster the best way he knew how.

"Do we need to take you to the doctor?" I asked Lady Shadows. I knew we needed to wind this down and get on our way.

"I'll be fine," she replied. "I have some unfinished work to do here." She was looking at the deputy chief.

"Ever the professional," Margie smiled.

"Would you like to stay and watch?" Lady Shadows asked her, with hope in her eyes.

"Oh my," Margie said. "Talk about an opportunity." She was giddy with the possibilities. Margie had read about such activities, but had never participated. "Unfortunately, I have work to do that's urgent."

"We'll keep it as a rain check," Lady Shadows said, disappointed. "I have a whole world for you to discover."

"I'll think about it," Margie said, trying to keep her enthusiasm in check.

"You want to leave, Deputy Chief?" I asked. "As much as I would like nothing better than leaving you here, I must give you the opportunity of freedom. I may be on suspension, but I still consider myself an officer of the law. How would it look if I left a fellow officer behind, restrained, and in the face of eminent danger?"

The deputy chief hesitated and then looked at Lady Shadows.

"I'll stay," he replied. "My therapy session isn't yet concluded. However, I do appreciate your offer."

"That's a good boy," I said with a smirk.

Oh, to be a mouse in the corner. His ass is grass.

~ * ~

It was well past noon and I was getting hungry. I asked Margie if she wanted to get a bite to eat. We stopped at a nearby Italian restaurant and sat outside on one of the hard plastic tables in order to have a little privacy.

"Well, this has been a rather interesting day," Margie started.

"Yeah," I sort of mumbled. I was deep in contemplation and wasn't feeling too chatty. No matter how much pressure I was feeling at the moment, I knew there wasn't time to feel sorry for myself. I looked up from my chicken Parmesan and asked, "So what's your take on everything so far, other than it being interesting?"

"I'm not sure." Margie fell silent for a bit, then said, "There are so many things going on at once, I can't seem to get my mind wrapped around it all."

"I know how you feel. Do you think everything we've seen today is relevant? Is any of it relevant?"

"I don't think it all is," she admitted. "But I certainly think some of it fits."

"Like what?" I asked.

Like her, I was feeling overwhelmed. I was hoping that by discussing it like this, a light would come on to the parts that mattered.

"Well, I don't think the deputy chief's little games matter all that much, but I do think the Sheffield boy's involvement does. I think that Granddaddy Sheffield knows more than he's telling and that he's involved somehow, but I don't think he's the one running around planting bombs. Of course, he's rich enough to hire someone who could do it for him if he wanted to."

"I agree. Anything else?"

"Not that I can think of. What about you?"

"When I met with Sam, he made it *very* clear that he was being monitored at all times. Our little code thing is rusty because we hadn't used it in over twenty years. As best I could tell, there is someone else involved besides the Sheffield kid. He said he had a partner of some sort."

"What kind of partner?" she asked.

"I'm not sure. He indicated that the other person was the one actually in control of whatever's going on and that the kid was somewhat lesser in the food chain."

"Do you think it's Granddaddy... or maybe some other faction?"

She seemed hopeful that her questions were helping. I could sense that she wasn't too familiar with the bantering process police officers did to loosen up the brain. The concept isn't difficult and not always beneficial. The idea is that if you do it long enough and often enough, a nugget will fall out and give you new direction.

"It could be Sheffield, Senior," I responded. "But, my gut's telling me it's someone else."

"Who?"

"Unfortunately, I don't know. What Sam said didn't make sense."

Margie leaned forward. "What did he say?"

"He said the guy was a farmer of some sort, but I don't see how that applies here."

"There's a lot of cattle ranches around here. Could it have something to do with one of them?"

"No," I said, somewhat dejected at not being able to decode the meaning of Sam's conversation. "He said the guy was a pig farmer. So that takes out the local ranchers."

"A pig farmer?" she queried, more to herself than to me. She seemed to be contemplating something, but hesitating to say what it was.

"What? We're just spitballing here. All thoughts are open for discussion, and none of them are wrong."

"Well," she said, "when you said the word 'pig,' my first thought was a cop. I'm sorry. I know that it's a term cops hate. But, that was what first came to mind."

"Oh. My. *God!*" I said loud enough for the people inside the restaurant to look out at us. "You're a friggin' genius. That's it! The other person is a cop. No wonder they've been able to keep a lid on Sam and the murder so tight. Someone on the inside is pulling all the strings so that everything can be manipulated to fit whatever they want."

I reached for my phone and called Manny. I told him we needed to meet at the location we both knew, to keep ears from hearing and eyes from seeing.

"Let's go," I said. All of a sudden, I wasn't hungry and I needed to move things along at a faster pace. The chicken was discarded and Margie barely had time to grab her purse. I needed to get ahead of the competition. I didn't have a name, but I knew the players. This was finally a game I could play. A game I was good at.

Eleven

It took about fifteen minutes to reach our destination, The Little Church by the Sea in Pacific Grove. It's located so close to the ocean that if you had a strong arm, you could pitch rocks in from the front door. We chose that spot after a friend's funeral because of sentimental reasons. The little stone edifice was isolated and no one could get to within fifty yards without being seen. It would make an ideal spot to meet, we agreed, if either of us was ever in trouble and needed a place out of the way to hook up. It was only used for extreme situations so that the other would know not only of a situation's importance, but also to take extreme caution when heading there. I could only hope the precautions taken would work. The people we were up against seemed to know and hear everything.

I parked Lu-Lu Belle about two blocks away and Margie and I walked the rest. Now that I had an idea of whom I was up against, I wasn't going to take any chances. Of course, I was thinking that all of this could be the ramblings of a paranoid freak. However, I decided it wasn't really being paranoid when people were planting bombs on Lu-Lu Belle.

Manny arrived about ten minutes after Margie and I. Fifteen minutes later, I had him caught up with everything we'd been through and the speculations we believed deserved merit.

"I'm just wondering something," Manny started. "How the hell did you get caught up in this shit? But more important, why the hell did you invite me?"

"I just knew how much you loved playing with danger," I offered with a smile. "Besides, who else would be better?"

"Well, nobody is better," he returned the smile. "I was just thinking that now would be a really good time to take a trip to Tahiti or maybe Fiji."

"What? And miss out on the glory and headlines you'll receive when we break all of this wide open?"

"Or the headlines we'll make for our funerals," he came back.

"So what do you think?" I asked.

"I *think*," Manny offered, "that you are out of your fucking mind for getting involved with this case. I *also* think that your observations could very well be right on the money. Unfortunately, you have very little beyond speculation and virtually no evidence. I *think* that if young Mr. Sheffield is knee deep in something and a cop or cops are involved, then you need to consider that whoever that cop might be is high in the chain of command. Nobody below detective or maybe even sergeant could pull off anything like this. Hell, it could be even higher up the ladder and we're not going to get any cooperation to help us get to the truth.

"You might also want to think about the possibility that these factions helping them are well funded. Much better than we are, I might add. And if that's the case, they may have other connections that could keep us even more out of the loop."

He stopped to get a reaction.

"Well, aren't you just a ray of sunshine?" I offered. "Here I thought we were onto something and you just managed to remind me that we don't have a shot in hell at beating them."

"That's not what I said at all," Manny shrugged. "What I'm saying is... you're probably right with everything you came up with. I'm merely suggesting we take this and add to it and think about the areas we might've overlooked."

"So you aren't leaving for Tahiti?" I asked.

"Oh, hell, no," he said with enthusiasm. "These people think they're better and smarter than we are, but they aren't. I *do* think, however, that this is the end of the road for Margie."

"Bullshit!" she objected "I'm staying and helping. Don't even *think* I'm walking away. I'm in this all the way."

"Margie, baby," Manny smiled, "This has gotten *way* too dangerous. You need to visit your folks back home or do something away from here. These people are playing for keeps and I would be very upset if you ended up dead."

Margie's head hung and Manny and I both thought she was defeated.

"I don't want to end up dead any more than you want me to," she replied, with her voice raised above normal, yet surprisingly calm. "But this isn't just about what you want. Hell, it's not even about what I want. It's about doing the right thing and helping an innocent man. I'm no hero, but I'll be damned if I'm leaving now. So take that and stick it up your ass."

"Damn girl, you turn me on when you talk like that," Manny smiled. "But it's really up to Samson. He's the one calling the shots here."

He looked at me to see if I was going to support his idea of getting her out of harm's way.

"I don't want you here, either," I said to her. "Manny's right. It's gotten very dangerous and you have no idea what we're up against. I think you should just leave."

I think Margie expected me to back her up and champion on her behalf. Her head dropped again and she looked as if the wind had been knocked out of her. She turned to leave, but after taking a couple steps, she turned back to me.

"No," she said. "I'm not leaving. You big-ass-macho guys are trying to protect me and I appreciate that. God knows I don't want to die any more than anyone else, but I don't run from problems. Most of my life was spent running or cowering from bullies and people who've wanted to control my life. Then my sister got in trouble and I realized that if I was *ever* going to do anything in this world that mattered, I had to stand up and fight for what I believed. I believe in what we're doing. I may not know as much as the two of you, but I can help. I know I can help. You're *not* going to send me away with my tail tucked between my legs. So fuck you both and tell me what I need to know to help you guys *and* not get killed."

The room got quiet and Manny and I just stood there staring at the determined woman. Her feet were parted—fists on her hips. She stood straight and tall and I had no doubts that she was determined to see this through. Unfortunately, what I also got was a warrior-princess image of a beautiful young woman out to save the world. I imagined Manny was picturing something similar, and we both busted up laughing.

"Okay, Wonder Woman," I said. "It's your ass. But if you get killed, my wife is going to be really pissed off. I don't do well when friends get killed. So keep your ass safe."

"I will, Boss," Margie smiled.

Time was running short and even though there was a lot of information to disseminate, we all decided we needed to take a break and let everything soak in. We'd meet again in a few hours.

~ * ~

In all the years of my existence, I believe there are very few things I can say are facts. One of them is that there isn't a man alive who truly understands women. It's a fact, and I'll be the first to admit I know less than most.

For example, I took the time while on break purely to do a good deed and go home to see if Jill was okay and if I could be there to support her. Many men would consider me a pussy for doing something like that. The rest would consider me stupid because it's a well-known fact that no good deed goes unpunished.

After a relaxing ride home, I didn't get the "Oh honey, it's so nice to see you" reward I admit I was hoping for. What I got was something considerably different.

Jill's greeting was, "Why would you let him do something like that?"

"I'm assuming you're talking about Tootie," I replied.

"Of course I'm talking about Tootie. And don't act so innocent with me. You let him take a dangerous job hunting down criminals and risking his life. You're allowing *my* father to risk his life... for what? Do you want him to get killed? Do you think I'll be more dependent on you if he's not around? Do you need to control me that bad? You're sick, Adam Shaw. You are sick and disgusting and I can't believe you would do this to me."

The thing about women that has always baffled me is their ability to change their minds on a dime and expect a man to understand. It's true they keep us guessing and sometimes it's even sorta cute...but damn—

"Well, hello to you. Nice to see you, too." I exaggerated my motions. "Oh, I'm having a great day, thank you very much for asking. And by the way, my friend is in jail for murder and someone planted a bomb on Lu-Lu Belle."

Crap...I knew I had taken it too far.

"A bomb?" she exploded. "What do you mean, 'a bomb'?"

"Nothing to worry about," I said, trying to calm her. I was hoping to defuse the situation. "It was a small thing that some amateur did for a practical joke."

"Somebody puts a bomb on your motorcycle as a joke? What the hell kinda joke is that? That's not funny in the least."

Tootie walked into the kitchen and asked, "Did I miss another bomb? Damn, you have all the good stuff happen to you."

"It wasn't a big deal," I said. "Just drop it."

"Do you think they'll use bombs at the old folks' home?" Tootie seemed to be getting excited. "Probably not," he mumbled to himself. "Nobody wants to blow up geezers."

"There won't be any bombs," I said. "There won't be any guns or arrows, for that matter."

"Who said anything about arrows?" Tootie asked. "I just want to catch some bad guys and stuff." He walked out for a second and returned with a suitcase.

"Where are you going?" I asked.

"Saint Michael's Nursing Home," he replied, as if I should have known. "I decided to start working today and see if I can catch someone ripping things off."

"Now do you see why I'm upset?" Jill asked. "He's leaving now and leaving *her* with me."

"Can I have your gun again?" Tootie asked me. "Since you don't seem to use it much? I thought maybe I could use it to scare someone into a confession. That would save a lot of time, don't you think?"

"Mother of God," Jill put her hands over her face in disbelief. "I don't believe this. My father is a lunatic and my husband is giving him a gun."

"I'm not giving him a gun! Tootie...no guns. You can't threaten people with a gun in order to get a confession."

"Why not? I've seen it lots on TV and nobody gets in trouble. What's the big deal?"

"For starters, it's illegal," I said. "And you would get in a *lot* of trouble. Maybe not so much in Texas. I don't know. But in California, you'd go to jail doing that."

"It's them damn liberal movie stars," he complained. "Isn't it? They think just because people are famous they can do anything or dictate whatever they want. Just look at 'em. They point guns all the time in movies. But you let a normal citizen do it and they'll haul your ass off to jail. I think they're all Commies, if you ask me."

"Look," I said, trying not to rip the hair from my head. "I don't know their politics, but I sincerely doubt they're all Commies. As for them pointing guns, it's only pretend. It isn't real and they wouldn't shoot anyone."

"Well, son-in law," Tootie said. He smiled like he just found a winning lottery ticket. "I wasn't gonna shoot anyone either. I was only going to pretend. So that should be okay, right?"

"If you keep talking about this," I said in frustration, "the only person who's going to be shot today is you. For the last time...*no guns!*"

I started to leave the room for some peace and quiet. I mistakenly believed the conversation was over.

"Just where do you think you're going?" Jill asked. "We aren't done talking about that bomb thing."

"There was no bomb," I said. "I was just making it up, as a joke."

"Well, it ain't funny this way either," she said. "And, why would you say that?"

"I guess I was just looking for attention," I replied. "How stupid could I be?"

"Well, I think if you want attention, son-in-law, I think you should do something nice for your wife. It goes over a lot better than these little tricks you're trying to play."

Okay, so let me rephrase an earlier statement. I will never understand women *or* old men. They're all a cup and saucer shy of a full place setting.

I'm sure I said it before, but I'm going to repeat myself—I love my wife. But at times like these, I get the feeling that Jill and hemorrhoids have a lot in common. They're both a pain in the ass.

~ * ~

Tootie left to join the circus. Jill was pouting in the living room. I had no idea where Bitsy was and didn't care. I was actually thinking it was a blessing that Sam was in jail and I had something to get me away from the chaos at home. I figured another day in this paradise and a bomb would sure look good for getting rid of my pain.

I just hadn't decided yet if it would be used on them or me.

~ * ~

There was a weather front heading toward Monterey that evening, so I decided I would take the old pickup, the same one Tootie had borrowed earlier. It's a '79 Chevy six-cylinder piece of crap that I used to take other crap to the dump. For those of you not familiar with the weather patterns of Monterey, the definition of a weather front during the summer is that the evening temperatures may drop down into the low fifties rather than the usually comfortable high fifties. Heck, we might even get some fog, to really mess with our heads.

In any case, I thought Lu-Lu Belle could use the rest. And if I had to take Margie with me, lord knows I wouldn't want to risk having a frozen koochie to deal with.

I drove back to Manny's office and parked the old pickup. Manny wasn't back so I decided to use the time to figure out the game plan.

We had players with motivation and opportunity, but there were still many aspects of this case that didn't make sense. I could use some help figuring out the police connection, but that might be a major problem considering my current state of affairs with the department.

The phone rang. I thought it was Manny calling to tell me when he would arrive.

Twelve

"Detective," the mystery woman said. "I'm glad I could catch you."

"Ah, my favorite spook-lady," I replied. "Of course you caught me. You're probably watching me as we speak. I'm sure you have your little death rays pointing at me so that you can hear my thoughts and all that shit."

The woman caller laughed in a manner of what I could best describe as sincere.

"You're an interesting man, Mr. Shaw," she said. "I like you."

"That is so special of you to say that," I said, as sarcastically as I could muster. "Frankly, I don't like you much at all."

"That's so unkind of you," she said, feigning disappointment. "Maybe you would like me better if there was something I could give you?"

"Yeah," I said, "how about a winning lottery ticket? It probably won't get my friend out of jail, but then I've heard we have the best police department money can buy."

"I see you've been making progress," she said, impressed. "How did you come to that conclusion?"

I'll be damned. I know something she doesn't, I thought, *Or if she does, I've managed to catch up with her, at least in this area.*

"For now, I'll keep my sources to myself. By the way, in case you haven't figured it out by now, I think you need to know something."

"What's that, Detective?"

"Well, it's simple. I don't know you. I don't trust you. And when you put those things together, I have no reason to do anything you ask. It seems to me that you don't know a hell of a lot more than I've already found out in just a short period of time. I figure if you give me another day, you'll be calling me boss. Now what exactly is it that you want? Or are you just trying to pump me for information?"

"You already know my agenda, Detective." She wasn't so cordial this time around. "I want the same thing as you. However, I came bearing information. Now if you don't want this information, so be it. You can keep your pettiness to yourself. I'm not asking anything from you; now or ever. If we can accomplish the same goals by assisting each other, I see no harm in that. Do you, Mr. Detective?" Her voice was sharper and carried more strength.

"I have no problems with whatever you want as long as it doesn't interfere with or harm Sam's chances of getting out of jail. So what is this information you were talking about?"

"It might be beneficial for you to go and have a drink," the mystery lady replied. "There's a nice little bar in the lobby of the Embassy hotel. Order a Black and Tan at ten o'clock tonight. If I'm correct, you could easily get lucky."

"Sorry, sweet cheeks; I'm already married."

"Just do it, Mr. Shaw. Do with your idea of 'lucky' what you will."

"Jesus, you guys just love your little cloak-and-dagger shit, don't you? So why not just tell me who I'm supposed to meet and what I'm supposed to find out. It would make things go a lot faster if you did. Maybe Sam could actually get out of jail in this decade."

"What would be the fun in that? There are so few pleasures in my line of work. Why would you want to take away what little gratification I can enjoy?"

"I'm not all that interested in your gratification," I barked. "I'm interested in doing what I need to for Sam."

"Very well. If you can solve the mystery of who killed Bobbi Marshall and get your friend Sam out of jail before ten tonight, then you have no reason to go. However, if you don't have all your answers by then, maybe you'll reconsider."

She hung up and I felt like trying to smack her through the phone anyway. Hey, I'm not one of those guys. I've never harmed anyone outside the line of duty. It doesn't mean a guy can't have the occasional fantasy when it comes to crazy spook women.

"Boo!" Manny whispered, right next to my ear. Apparently he'd had a relaxing little break and was in a playful mood. I, on the other hand, jumped and hit my head on the roof of the truck; my heart skipped a beat, my knee hit the steering wheel.

"Goddamn it," I yelled. "What's wrong with you?"

I really don't think he heard me because he was laughing so hard he couldn't catch his breath. He was bent over and almost fell to the ground.

"That crap is for the birds," I bellowed. "You do that again, you son of a bitch, and I'll shoot your ass."

The thing is, if the shoe were on the other foot, I would probably have done the same thing to him. But since he did it to me, I had the right to bitch about it.

"A little jumpy, are we?"

"Yeah, I'm a little jumpy."

"What's the matter, buddy? You find another bomb you haven't told me about?"

"No. I just hung up with spook lady. She gives me the creeps...or have I told you that already?"

"Is it something serious?" He tilted his head quizzically. "Should I make plans to talk to Jill about your new love?"

"You're an ass, and not funny. And stay the hell away from Jill. She doesn't need any help with the pickle jar she holds my nuts in already."

"Ouch," was all the reply he needed to let me know he understood what I was talking about.

"So what does our spook lady want?" he asked.

I filled him in on the discussion.

~ * ~

"Here's what I think we need to do this evening. You still have your list to go through and I'll hook up with the mystery guest at ten. In the meantime, I think I'm going to have a visit with our local fetish cop. We're going to need some inside help and I think he just might be the way to get it."

"Don'tcha think it's possible he might be the one helping these guys get Sam?"

"I thought about that," I said, after a moment of reflection. "But frankly, I think he has enough on his platter to occupy his mind than to be involved in this. At least that's what I'm hoping. However, if he is a part of this, I'll have some leverage to get him to help anyway." My real feeling was that I had to have some inside help and the deputy chief was the only person high enough up the food chain to be of any real assistance. It was my risk and I was willing to take the chance. "By the way, where's Margie?"

"Wonder Woman's at home doing some research for me. With everything we've discovered so far, I thought it might be prudent to get some background information and financial statements on all the parties concerned."

"Good idea. It also gets her away from us to minimize the danger she's in."

"You caught me," Manny smiled. "Stay in touch. I'll leave my phone on."

~ * ~

Deputy Police Chief Howard Young was not at all happy to hear from me. The man was small in stature and to a degree I felt bad for him. I was polite and didn't use any form of bribery or blackmail to entice a meeting with him. I did, however, compliment the outfit he'd been wearing earlier. But that shouldn't have had anything to do with his agreeing to meet, right?

"So how long am I going to have to pay for this?" he asked as he walked in.

I had decided we should meet at a little restaurant just outside town, where I knew the likelihood of extra ears was slim.

"Pay for what?" I asked with what innocence I could muster.

"You know damn well what I'm talking about," he said in a huff. "What I do on my own time is my business. Not yours."

"Deputy Chief," I said, looking him directly into his no-longer-made-up eyes. "If I were a police officer of good standing, I would have had no choice but to report certain things I had observed earlier—you know, the break-in...the injury? That could have been a cumbersome situation for everybody involved, don't you think? However, we both know that's not the case. So don't get your panties in a bunch 'til you hear what I have to say. Oh, sorry about the panty thing. It was just a figure of speech."

"So what, you're asking me to help you get your job back?"

"Not at all. Look, we both know I can be a smart-ass sometimes. And if the brass wants me to take some time off, so be it. I'm here for something else."

"What then?"

"I'm here about Sam Reynolds."

"Uh-uh. That's strictly a hands-off case, and that comes straight from the DA himself. I don't want any part of whatever it is you're scheming on that one. Besides, he's confessed. Why would you want to get bloody over a loser like that?"

His eyes grew wide when he noticed my not-so-subtle glare regarding his comment.

"Because it's a setup," I said. "He confessed because he had no choice. Someone has placed his life on the line to save his family or someone else close to him."

"And how the hell would you know that?"

"I talked to him. I know the man. I know he didn't do it."

"What proof do you have?" he asked, doubtfully.

"Nothing solid yet, unfortunately. But I have a lot of information that leads me to believe he's innocent. I also know that somebody doesn't want me to find the truth."

"What do you mean?" he asked.

I told him about the events of the day, including the bomb on Lu-Lu Belle.

"It could mean that someone just doesn't like you," he said defiantly. "That shouldn't come as a surprise."

"It could also mean I'm right," I countered, not totally discounting his smug yet viable alternative.

The deputy chief thought about it for a moment and asked, "So what does all of this have to do with me?"

"I need information. I need someone to help me prove Sam's innocence. I need someone high enough in the department who can ask questions without having to step over so many hurdles. What I *need* is you."

"You're asking a lot," he stated. "What's in it for me?"

"What? Are you looking for a bribe or something? I don't have squat. I'm asking you to be a cop, for God's sake. Has it been so long since you were one that you've forgotten what that means?"

"I know what it means," he said, looking a little hurt. "I'm talking about the other thing, this morning's thing. What about that?"

"Look," I said, recognizing his *real* concern. "I don't want this to come out wrong, so try to take it as best you can. I don't give a shit about what you do. If you want to play sissy games and get your ass beat with a belt, more power to you. I don't care. If you're asking me to forget it, trust me, I'll have nightmares for months because of it and probably need counseling as a result.

"However, I don't plan on using it against you if that's what you're concerned about. When this is all said and done, I may take a few liberties just for shits-and-giggles. I'm that kinda guy. However, what I need now more than anything else is for you to grow a pair, put on a jock strap and do the right thing. Is that something you can do?"

"Yes," he said, inflating his chest a bit. "I can do that."

"Good. Now here's what I need you to do."

I told him the things I needed and then said, "There's one more thing."

"What's that?"

"You'd look better without the beard," I said, trying to contain the laugh.

I caught him off guard. His face turned crimson as he lowered his head.

"Thanks. I'll keep that in mind."

~ * ~

It was getting close to the end of the business day so I decided to take a trip to the court house. I felt I had enough information now to give Dakota Walker an update and see how things were going from her perspective.

I saw her car in the parking garage and was glad to find that she was still around.

Then I saw that I wouldn't have to go all the way to her office. She was in the garage in a heated discussion with someone. I couldn't see who it was at first, but knew she could hold her own. I wasn't going to interrupt. That's what I told myself, but then I saw who she was talking to and changed my mind.

It seems that David Cromwell, our esteemed District Attorney, was not a very happy fellow and was taking out his anger on Dakota. As I saw it, she was a damsel in distress.

"Mr. Cromwell," I said, as I walked over, "so good to see you again." I acted as if we were old buddies when in fact we each had a very strong dislike for the other. Not only had we butted heads on numerous occasions, he was also the driving force behind my current suspension. The man just couldn't take a joke.

"Can't you see we are in a meeting?" the red-faced, angry DA replied.

"Well, it's not an official meeting, is it? I mean official meetings generally require a degree of respect and decorum, right? All I could gather from way over there was that someone was ranting at someone else. Now officially, if I can remember my rookie training correctly, that could be construed as a form of harassment. I just thought that whoever was being harassed might need a witness. Would that be the case, Miss Walker?"

Cromwell's face turned a more brilliant shade of red. Sweat started forming on his forehead, and if I wasn't mistaken, the veins in his neck had grown considerably larger than their normal size. But most interestingly, the DA maintained control by not saying another word.

Dakota kept her smile in check and replied, "Actually, Mr. Shaw, that won't be necessary. Mr. Cromwell is having a bad day and decided to share it with me." Then, looking at the DA, "Is there anything else, Mr. Cromwell? I have so much to do and so little time."

"No," he said to Dakota while scowling at me. "That'll be all." To me, he forced his lips into a smile and asked, "How are you enjoying your vacation, Mr. Shaw? I hope it's becoming an educational experience. I would hate losing one of our most successful detectives."

"You have no idea what I have been able to learn," I replied. "As a matter of fact, there's a very good possibility that I will be sharing what I've learned very soon. I think even *you* will find it illuminating."

"I can't wait to hear it," he said, not trying to hide his smug attitude. "Good day, Ms. Walker. I'll be seeing you soon, Detective."

"Sooner than you might think," I replied, as his backside was about to round the corner.

The DA turned again to look me in the eyes and I thought he wanted to say something else. After a moment, he twirled around and walked away without comment. I really don't like the guy. I can't stand bullies. That man is a bully.

"Damn you, Samson," Dakota said when the coast was clear. "Are you trying to get me fired?"

"I wouldn't think of it," I said, giving her my biggest, brightest, cheesiest smile. "That pompous ass needs his underwear let out a size or two."

"You just need to be careful around him," she said, with a look of concern. "He can make or break your career."

"If I let people like him dictate what I do," I replied, more casually than I felt, "I don't have much of a career."

I'm not stupid, for Christ's sake, I thought. *I just don't always do the sensible thing.*

"I understand," she said, with the look of someone who indeed understood, but couldn't do much about her own plight. "So tell me, what are you doing here? You know how things work around here. I can't discuss anything about the case with you."

"Then this is your lucky day." I kept the cheesy smile in place. "I came to give, not receive."

Okay, that was a little white lie. I wanted as much information as I could get from her. But, since she was being so tight-lipped up front, maybe a little info her way might grease the wheels.

"Samson," she said placing her hands on her hips. "How long have we known each other? Never mind, we both know it's been a long while. You never give anything to anyone. So why would you start now?"

Ah, hell, she caught me. Might as well 'fess up to the truth.

"I'm a changed man," I said. "I think you should know the fun I've had today and what it has to do with you. If you think it's of no value, I'll respect that. However, if you think it can help, I'll want something in return."

Okay, maybe it wasn't the complete truth, but what can I say?

"What do you want?" she asked, arms still on her hips and not believing for a second that I'd changed.

"What I've wanted all along," I replied. "I want you to help me get Sam out of jail. I want nothing more than everybody doing the right thing."

"We've been through this, Samson. My hands are tied. Why do you think Cromwell was crawling down my throat? I delayed things longer than I should have. He was really pissed off and I think he's going to replace me. I really screwed up here."

"He won't replace you." That came across a lot more confident than I felt. "You're the best and he needs to make sure he doesn't show any impropriety. The case with Sam is too high profile for him to be jumping ships now."

"Thanks for the vote of confidence," she said relaxing a bit. "So tell me, what is it that you wanted to share with me?"

I told her about my meeting with Sam and what he'd eluded to. I told her about the bomb on Lu-Lu Belle and my mysterious callers. I told her about Lady Shadows, leaving out the part about the deputy chief of police. I figured I would save that part for now. I also told her of my suspicions about the Sheffield family and how they may be involved.

"I'm telling you, Dakota, Sam did not do this. I need you to help me figure out who did and I need you to keep doing what you can to give me the time to prove it."

"Look," she said, stepping uncomfortably close. Her perfume circled my head. Her more than ample breasts were close enough to distract. *God, I hate being a man sometimes.* "I believe you. Things are not going as they should around here either. I'm concerned that Sam is getting railroaded and I'm a part of something I can't seem to put my fingers on."

"Let me ask you something," I said, as an idea hit me. "What did Cromwell do before he was the DA here?"

"He's been the DA for a very long time," she replied. "But before he was elected DA, he was a cop."

"I should have known that. I'm not sure why I didn't."

"Unless you asked about it specifically," she said, "you probably wouldn't have known. He wasn't a cop around here. He was a traffic cop in Santa Rosa and then broke a huge case there and eventually made chief. It's a small force and up there it's an elected position. He had so much notoriety, he was a shoe-in for the job."

"Then how did he get elected down here?" I asked, not really knowing where my questions were leading.

"He's actually from around here," she replied. "When the previous DA was about to retire, he threw his name in the ring and used his local connections to make it appear that he had been around all along. He had very little opposition and got elected again in a landslide. He's been the DA ever since. That's almost twenty years now."

"But doesn't a district attorney actually have to be...an attorney?"

"He *is* an attorney. He graduated from law school, passed the bar, but then decided on law enforcement instead of pursuing a law practice. When he decided to run down here, his background in law enforcement made him a standout against anyone interested in the job."

All of a sudden the concept of pig farming had a whole new meaning, or at least one that had more clarity. David Cromwell used to be a pig farmer. That's what Sam was talking about. He used to be a cop and he hired and fired other cops. Recruiting was part of the job. "Son of a bitch," I said out loud.

"What?" she asked.

"Nothing. I just had an idea I'll keep to myself until I know more. In the meantime, you need to keep doing what you do best."

I turned and started to leave.

"Samson," she said with a worried look. "You be careful out there. This is bigger than I ever imagined. People are going to try and stop you and I don't think they'll care how it happens."

"Of course they will," I said. I was pleased at the new revelation. "They'll try, but they won't succeed. I've got you on my side. How could I lose?"

I left there and thought I had to be really stupid to think I would get out of this unscathed.

Thirteen

As I was leaving the courthouse, Margie called and asked if we could meet. I still hadn't eaten and now realized how hungry I was. I asked if we could meet somewhere that had food. She suggested a little place close to the pool hall and we agreed to meet in fifteen minutes. That gave me enough time to place another call to our friendly, prissy little deputy police chief and add another name to his list. He wasn't happy with what I told him, but agreed to get what information he could.

When I arrived, Margie wasn't alone. She was sitting with another female type. After the way the day was going, I wasn't about to try guessing who the lady was or why Margie decided to bring her to our meeting.

"Samson, this is Annie Lee," Margie said as I approached them. "Annie, this is Samson."

"Good to meet you," I said, shaking the hand of the child-like, mocha-skinned girl. Looking at Margie, I asked, "What's this all about?"

"I know you and Manny are trying to keep me on the sidelines," Margie said. "You know it. I know it. So let's not pretend otherwise. Anyway, I had an idea I wanted to check out, and once you hear what Annie has to say, I think you'll agree it was a damn good one. Annie, why don't you tell Samson what you told me?"

"What about the money you promised?" Annie asked. "I don't know nuttin 'til I get my fifty bucks."

Looking at the girl, Margie tilted her head toward me.

"Samson is the money man. He decides who gets it." Then looking at me, she said, "I think it's worth the money."

I reached into my wallet and pulled out the money. Margie nodded her head.

"If you're wrong, this will come out of your hide," I said. Then I looked at Annie and said, "Okay, you've got the money. What did I pay for?"

"That night the girl was killed? Well I saw a guy hangin' around the back door...you know, of the pool hall. He looked around real nervous-like. I saw him hurt that girl, but when he saw me lookin' at him, he took off."

"Did you get a good look at him?" I asked.

"Sorta," she replied, looking toward the ceiling. "Actually, yeah, I got the look."

"Was it the owner, Sam Reynolds?"

I wanted to make sure she wouldn't be digging my friend's grave.

"I don't think so," she replied, and it seemed to me she was being evasive. "The guy I saw was younger than that guy. It was dark and everything, but Mr. Reynolds got a few pounds on the one I was lookin' at."

"So what were you doing there?"

"I was working," she replied, sitting straighter, sticking her chin out defiantly. "I was taking care of a guy in his car across the street. You know what I mean?"

"I'm pretty sure I can figure it out," I replied. "Did the guy you were with see the man leaving?"

"If he did I would'n' be doing my job very well, now would I?" she replied in a huff.

"I guess not," I said. "So could you describe the man?"

"Could do better than that," she replied. "I can show him to you. But—" she turned around looking to see if anyone was watching us, "that'll cost a whole lot more'n fifty bucks."

"What's the price for that piece of information?" I asked.

I didn't know where this was going, but I liked the idea that there was someone else who we could name as a suspect. Hell, anything was better than what we had. As far as hard evidence was concerned, we were running out of time and this could be the break we needed.

"I need ten large...and a place to hide," she said. She was getting considerably more agitated and seemed scared. "Otherwise, it's no deal."

"Ten thousand dollars?" I almost choked. "Who the hell is it, the Pope?"

"No money, no name," she said. "And don't forget the place to hide. Once I do this, I won't be able to do much work around here anymore."

"I tell you what," I said. "I don't carry that kind of money on me and the banks are closed. I can get you the place to hide and the money in the morning. However, you're going to at least have to tell me why the cost is so high. I'm not gonna buy a pig in a poke."

"What the hell does that mean?" she asked.

It's an old southern expression my friends from down there used to say, kinda like buying a bill of goods. I didn't want to get into all of that.

"It means your information needs to be worth that kind of money or it's no deal," I said.

"Well it *is* worth it," she assured me. "It was a cop. There's your pig inna pope."

That was good enough to make me realize this young lady should get whatever she wanted.

"What cop?" I asked, nearly jumping off my seat to go sit next to her. If she was going to tell me the name, I sure as hell didn't want her to say it loud enough for anyone else to hear.

"I don't know his name, but I can pick him out if I see him again." She waited for a second, then said, "One more thing... he wasn't alone. He had a friend. But that's enough for now. You need to get me some place safe. I'm already getting the heebie-jeebies about all of this."

"Why didn't you tell the police about this?" Margie asked.

Such innocence.

"I was going to," she said. "I was gonna call the cops, then thought they might need me to look at some pictures and stuff. Us girls gotta stick together, right?" she asked Margie. "I do my civic duties if they don't get me arrested. That's how I spotted him. I went to the police station and when I walked in to tell someone, I saw him. He looked right at me and I about freaked. I thought for sure he knew who I was."

"What did you do?" I asked.

"When he stopped looking at me, I lit outta there. I figured there's no way in hell I'm gonna say nuthin' to nobody. I figured I stay alive better that way."

"Then why tell us?" I asked.

"Your girl Friday here is why," Annie said. "I was just minding my own business when this lady here comes up to me and asks me if I was working that night. At first I told her no, but then it started botherin' me when she told me her friend was in jail because of what happened. She was just tryin' to find someone who could help her out. And then when I found out she wasn't a cop, I figured I would let her know what I saw. Look, I'm good people." Annie seemed determined to get me to believe her. "I don't much like what I have to do to make a livin'. I got a baby girl at home that needs food and stuff. That money will help me take care of my baby. You know what I mean?"

"Yeah, I do," I said. "We all have to do things we don't like at times. I'll make sure you get your money, and that you and your daughter are safe. Then I need you to start looking at some pictures so we can find out this guy's name as soon as possible. Can you trust me enough to do that?"

"Okay," she said. "I'll pick 'em for you."

"Margie, I'll kick your ass later for going behind our backs to do this. But for now, I need you to take Annie home to get her baby and whatever she needs. Then take her to your place. I'll get in touch with Manny and see you both in about an hour."

"Okay," she said.

The girls got up to leave and I picked up my phone to make a call.

I started to ask Annie one more question. "By the way, did you get a look at that other person, too?"

She never got the chance to respond.

~ * ~

None of us saw where the shots came from.

There were loud bangs, flying glass and then screams coming from everyone in the place. I looked at Margie first. She was lying on the ground holding her arm—blood dripping between her fingers.

"Are you all right?" I asked her. I could see the pain on her face. Her eyes were glued to Annie, but she shook her head up and down.

I then looked at Annie. She wasn't so good.

There was a lot of blood seeping out of her chest and head. I ran to her and did everything I could to keep her alive—pressure on the wounds, removing broken glass from her face—hoping it would be enough.

The shooting only lasted a few seconds, but seemed to go on forever.

The paramedics finally arrived. If the girl was still breathing, I couldn't tell. I thought I still felt a pulse, but wouldn't bet my life on it. They told me she'd lost a lot of blood. The floor around her told me that already. The only thing we could do was wait.

I was pissed off and ready to fight. I wanted to hit someone as hard as I could. I had no idea where to go to do that, but the thought wouldn't go away. When Carl Ramos appeared, I had what Oprah called an ah-ha moment. Right then I knew: Carl was as good as anyone.

"Shaw," he started, "what the hell are you doing here?"

Sometimes, words can't do a moment justice. I could tell you about the hatred welling inside. I could tell you how the noise of the sirens and the screaming of the people disappeared and there was nothing but silence in my head. I could even tell you that my vision narrowed and focused solely on one thing. I could tell you that, but I'm more about action and what I did was walk up to the son of a bitch and hit him square in the jaw as hard as I could. I wasn't going to take any crap from the asshole and I sure as hell wasn't about to give him a statement. Several of the officers came over and grabbed me. They held me so I wouldn't hit him again. When Ramos got up off the floor, I saw the blood oozing from his lips. It was enough to make me proud.

"That's all I need to arrest you, you son of a bitch," Ramos spat his words. Then looking at one of the officers holding me, he said, "Cuff the bastard. I'll show him what it's like to be on the other side of the law."

"Fuck you! You can't show anyone anything. If you could, it would only be because you know what it's like to be there. You're the damn crook—not me. You think you have so much going for you, you piece of shit, but you don't. I'll find your weakness one of these days and I'll take you down."

Okay. I know when I get pissed I'm not exactly the most eloquent orator you might expect. As a matter of fact, I had to look up those words—eloquent and orator—just to say something cool.

The truth is, I'm just a Joe cop who believes in right and wrong and very little gray in between. I didn't graduate from an Ivy League school, but I have excellent skills when it comes to human perceptions. Carl Ramos is scum. How do I know? Because my gut tells me and that's all the reason I need.

I felt the cuffs locking my hands behind my back. I knew I'd screwed up big time—again. But to be honest, hitting the bastard made the whole thing worthwhile.

"Take the cuffs off," a voice said from behind me. I recognized it as Deputy Chief Howard Young.

"The son of a bitch hit me," Ramos objected. "I'm going to bring charges against him."

"Not tonight you're not," the deputy chief stated with a confidence I hadn't seen before. "I'm sure that if he did hit you, Detective Ramos, it was because he's been under a great deal of stress. His friends were just shot. Of course, as an alternative, he could have done it because you said something outrageous or taunting to take advantage of the situation and he punched you because you deserved it. Now release him."

The cops holding me let me go and one took his key and released the cuffs.

"You haven't heard the last of this," Ramos turned and walked away.

"Thanks, Chief," I said.

"Deputy Chief, but I think you have bigger problems than Ramos right now," he replied in a whisper.

"Like?"

"Like living," he stated with a genuine air of concern in his voice. "Let's step outside and talk."

He didn't wait for me, but turned and stepped through the destroyed plate glass window and walked around the corner. I followed—hearing the crunching of glass beneath my feet. I heard the sirens of the ambulances taking off for the hospital.

Both women were hurt and I felt as if I were to blame. I would have to call Manny and let him know what happened and wasn't looking forward to the wrath that conversation would bring.

"Do you have a death wish?" Young said as soon as we were clear from everyone else.

"Not particularly," I replied. "We were just getting ready to leave when the shots came and I didn't see the shooter. I might as well tell you that before you ask."

"What were you doing here? Are you a magnet for trouble or what? And please, don't bullshit me."

"I wouldn't think of it, Deputy Chief," I said, almost sincere. "I was trying to do what I've been doing the last several days. I'm trying to figure out a way to get Sam out of jail. It just seems that it's getting bigger all the time."

"What do the girls have to do with it?"

"The one girl, Margie, works for Manny Black. I believe you know who he is. She's the one you met earlier," I said, as a reminder of our agreement.

The comment didn't faze him. He was totally in "cop mode" and wasn't about to be distracted from his objective. "And the other?"

"Her name is Annie Lee. I just met her tonight for the first time. She was about to tell me something that could help me clear Sam."

"What does she know?"

"I can't tell you."

Actually I could have told him. I was beginning to think I could trust the man to help. But I still wasn't going to take the chance.

"She got shot before she could tell me what she knew. Apparently, someone doesn't want me to know either. But, I'll need her guarded when, or should I say if, she recovers."

"I'll see to it. But you know, if she had told you, you're the one who would've been on his way to the hospital."

I waited for Young to continue.

"Did you know the Sheffields are connected to the mob?"

"What're you talking about?" I asked, truly surprised by the statement. "There aren't any mob ties around here. I know he's powerful in a lot of ways, but mob? I don't think so."

I was sure his information was bogus.

"It seems there are," he said. "It seems old-man Sheffield has ties with the Ramirez cartel out of Columbia. "He's pretty much retired at this point. From what I gather, people still owe him a few favors, and it seems you might be one of those favors, at least the part about making sure you don't get what you want."

"How did you find out about this?"

"Don't know for sure," he stated flatly. "I got a call about an hour ago telling me in detail about the old man. I did some checking after the call and it seems the caller was right."

I could tell he wasn't lying.

"Let me guess...a lady caller."

"How did you know that?" he questioned, surprised by my astute observation.

"Lucky guess," I said. "It seems we have a friend in high places after all."

"I don't know about the 'we' part, Shaw, but you sure as hell seem to. Mind letting me in on who these people are?"

"I'd be tempted to if I could. It seems Big Brother, or should I say, Big Sister, wants to stay anonymous for the time being, and I'm just flying by the seat of my pants."

We both stopped for a moment to ponder what we were discussing.

"By the way," I said, "what're you doing here? This ain't your beat. You live way across town. I actually expected the chief to show his ugly face...sorry, sometimes I can't help myself."

He dropped his head for a moment, face turned crimson, then smiled.

"I was on my way to visit a friend. Speaking of which, I'm late and there's going to be hell to pay. She hates when I'm tardy."

"Then you best get running." I returned the smile.

I wanted to say something smart-ass and totally degrading just for the hell of it. For some reason, I didn't.

It was at that moment we understood each other. He was who he was and that was all right with me. Neither of us was perfect. We both had baggage—something that challenges a conventional life. But we also both had a desire to do what was right when it mattered. The deputy chief was an R.C.—Real Cop—and it was good to know that someone had my back.

Fourteen

Manny already knew what was going on when I called him. As a matter of fact, he was already at the hospital with Margie. He told me the wound she'd sustained was more painful than debilitating. She would be released soon and they were waiting to see how things were going with Annie. According to him, it didn't look very promising. She was hit in the chest twice and one bullet had grazed her temple. He said she would be in surgery for the next several hours, if she made it that long.

"So what's your plan now?" Manny asked.

His concern for Margie was genuine but he'd been around long enough to know that the job was not done.

"I have a meeting in about an hour," I said. "It looks like our lady spook has made arrangements for me to meet someone. I just hope it's not some wild goose chase."

"She seems like she's trying to help," Manny observed. "Maybe whomever you're going to talk to has something that'll give us the break we need."

"Annie was the break we needed," I said, voicing my frustration. "Now she might not make it."

"Don't worry about that right now," he consoled. "That's out of your hands. Focus on what you can do. We'll keep an eye on Annie and make sure the baby's taken care of. You just find us something, or someone, useful."

"I'll do what I can," I assured him.

Of course I didn't feel very positive about anything at the moment. However, I couldn't let Sam down.

I decided to go to the hotel early to see if everything was in order. Who knows, maybe I could get something to eat, too. The shooting had interrupted my dinner and I was starving now. I know that seems callous of me, but what the hell. It's hard to ignore a loud stomach and a light head. I would've been happy eating just about anything.

I was about thirty minutes early when I got to the hotel and immediately ordered a burger and fries. I was hoping that whoever was going to show up would give me a chance to wolf it down.

As I waited for my happy meal, not the trademarked one but the one that would actually make me happy; I looked around to see if anything or anyone appeared out of place. There was nothing obvious and I was very happy that the order came out quickly.

Now don't get me wrong, a burger and fries is usually just a burger and fries. There are only so many things you can do with that combination. However, I was so hungry I would have sworn the chef had put his heart and soul into making it. It was five-star quality in my mind and I would have paid a king's ransom for a second. Unfortunately, time was short, and I was not going to be caught off guard by whoever was planning to show.

I ordered the Black and Tan as instructed, and then a second. The time passed. I realized that I could have had three burgers— and still nobody showed. I was about to leave when a young girl, appearing no older than eighteen, asked me if I was alone for the evening and would like some company.

"I am alone," I returned her infectious smile, "I'm expecting someone. It seems I've been stood up."

She lowered her head and lightly bit her lower lip. She genuinely looked shy.

"Well...maybe it isn't a total loss," she said, rocking back and forth like a teenager on her first date. "I could make things a lot better for you."

"I appreciate the offer," I replied, "but I'm married and, though you might be a tempting distraction, *that* isn't something I'm willing to consider. Thanks anyway."

The girl seemed dejected and turned to walk away.

I turned back to the bar, about to pay for my beer. I didn't notice the woman on the other side until she spoke.

"That was a noble gesture," the lady said. "Not many men would have walked away from someone so sweet and appealing to the eyes."

"I'm not most men," I replied, checking her out and wondering who she might be.

"I see that," she continued. "Why did you turn her down? Was it really the wife thing?"

"Actually, yes, it was," I replied. "When you have someone in your life you can trust, it seems to me it would be stupid to risk losing that for a few moments of pleasure you could never repeat."

"I'm sure for the right price she would make every effort to repeat it for you."

"Still not worth losing the trust. Besides," I continued, "I figure that if I go for something like that, I couldn't keep up with her. I sure as hell don't want to embarrass myself."

The lady smiled. I returned the smile and wanted to ask her if she was my mystery date. I decided, instead, to take care of the tab and leave. If she was the one, she'd let me know somehow.

"You know," she finally said, as I was ready to leave, "I think I've seen you before. You're that cop I've seen on TV."

"I used to be a cop. Right now I'm just your ordinary non-police guy."

"From what I hear, you're not ordinary at all."

"That's nice of you to say. It was nice meeting you."

I extended my hand to shake hers. She did likewise.

I turned to leave.

"You really should have taken the girl's offer," she stated to my back.

I turned back. "Why's that?"

"Because she would have taken you somewhere to help you with your problem," the nameless woman replied.

"Which problem is that?"

"The problem you have where you're looking for someone who can give you information about your friend Sam."

She spoke casually, as if life-and-death conversations happened all the time. I didn't know who she was, but now I was serious about finding some answers.

"What do you know about Sam?" I sat next to her again and leaned close.

"I know that if you want to get him out of jail, the only way for that to happen is to find the real killer," she replied as if she was totally at ease with the discussion. "I don't think talking to you in public would be in anyone's best interest. Annie tried. Look what happened to her."

"How do you know about Annie? She was hurt just a little while ago. I doubt it's even on the news yet."

"Probably not. I know Annie because she works for me. The young girl you turned down was outside the restaurant when the shooting took place. She told me what happened. She's pretty shaken up about it."

"Did she see who did it? Can she identify the shooter?"

"No," the stranger replied. "It happened too fast, and the guy was wearing a mask. I was hoping not to have to meet with you tonight. I figured that if Annie talked to you, told you what she knew, you wouldn't need to see me. That doesn't seem to be the case now, does it?"

"Who are you?" I finally asked out of frustration. "And what does any of this have to do with you?"

"My name is Faye White," she said extending her hand. "I am what you might call the person who introduces girls to men in order that everyone has a pleasant evening."

"In other words, you're a Madam," I said, more abrasively than intended.

"That would be right. Is that a problem?"

"With what I've seen today, you don't even rate top ten on my weird-o-meter. So, no, I don't have a problem at all."

"Good," she smiled, "Then, let's talk. Maybe we can help each other."

She got up and told me to follow her. We went to the elevators and took a ride to the fourteenth floor. The room was a suite, like every room in the joint, and offered a plush couch, plush carpet, plush everything. She sat on the couch and told me to have a seat next to her. I selected the chair next to the television instead.

"Are you shy, Mr. Shaw? I would never have thought you to be shy."

"I'm not shy, Ms. White. I'm cautious. Please don't fault me for that."

She laughed.

"I don't. I just thought maybe you'd want to look at these pictures."

She pulled open a drawer in the coffee table in front of her.

"It seems that some of your friends at work haven't been playing by the rules."

"I know that a few have taken some liberties," I replied, reluctantly, looking at the photos. "However, the use of your services, or your girls', is hardly newsworthy."

I didn't know what any of this had to do with Sam, but decided to let her get to the point on her own terms.

"Then maybe the bribes they're taking don't mean much either," she said with a shrug of her bare shoulders.

Looking more closely, I could see an ethnic blend. The ever-so-slight curves in her eyes that reflected the Far East and the smooth, copper skin featured in many of the Hispanic women of the region—not to mention Fort Ord—lead me to the assumption that she was probably the child of a military family. Whatever might be her history, what she had just said got my attention.

"Let me see that," I said. I took the photos from her and looked at them for several minutes. I saw four different cops accepting money from someone I didn't recognize. I did, however, recognize the cops.

"What are they taking bribes for?"

"To cover up a murder, I think, but it's hard to tell for sure. I have the movie version these pictures came from."

"You're shitting me, right? Please, excuse my French."

My heart was racing and I was hoping beyond hope she wasn't just trying to get one over on me.

"I don't shit people, Mr. Shaw. I run an illegal business and I need you as much as you need me. So I was wondering—would you be interested in making a deal?"

"What kind of deal?"

I was curious, but not liking where the conversation was going.

"The kind of deal where you scratch my back while I scratch yours—metaphorically, of course. I need you to make sure the cops leave me and my ladies alone."

"You said your name is Faye?"

"That's correct, Detective, Faye White. I'm just a local business girl looking for ways to keep my overhead down. I'm sure you can understand that."

"Of course, I understand. You somehow think that the best way of helping yourself is to rat out some cops on the take by making me a cop on the take."

"Well, I don't think that's exactly right," she pouted. "It's just a business deal to help each other."

"Lady," I said, not too pleasantly, "as much as I would like nothing better than to get those assholes for selling out the force, I can think of several reasons why your plan won't work. The first, and I think maybe the most important, is that for now at least, I'm not a cop. I'm on suspension for being a guy who doesn't crap on his beliefs. And if you think you can get me to do that for greed, you're just as nuts as the politicians who put me on suspension."

"So you aren't interested in helping me out?"

"Look," I said, "I don't give a rat's ass what you do for a living. You break the law, I'll put you away. I don't want my friend in jail and would do just about anything I could to get him out. But I'm not going to break the law to make that happen. I won't be put in a position to have you hold it over my head the rest of my life. I'll get Sam out without your tapes. Sorry to have wasted your time."

"It wasn't a waste at all," Faye smiled. "I placed this opportunity in front of you to see if you were as dirty as the rest. Because if you were, the tape I just made of you would be given to somebody else for the same reason as the others. The tapes are yours, Detective, without any strings."

She stood and walked over to me.

"Let me re-introduce myself. My name is Faye Wesley. I'm with IAD. This entire meeting was to see if you were willing to accept a bribe in order to help a friend."

"I can't believe this shit. I'm busting my ass to help Sam and you're out here trying to frame me? This is just great." I was upset, frustrated and then a thought occurred to me. "What about Annie Lee...and the young girl downstairs? Are they with you, too?"

"Annie is a working girl—a confidential informant, actually. The girl downstairs is an undercover detective who works primarily to help us get the drugs out of our schools. Her name is Debbie James and she's twenty-three. With her looks, she can transform down to a fourteen-year-old. She's invaluable and occasionally does side duty for me when I need her."

"Great," I said, feeling betrayed and upset.

"Don't be troubled, Detective. The department has some bad apples and we're just trying to find out who they are. We thought you were okay, but we needed to make sure."

"Well, did I pass?"

Faye laughed at the question.

"Of course, with flying colors. And Detective, just so you know, with what you have and what we have, maybe we can help each other."

"What do you have?" I was curious.

"I don't want to give out any names just yet. However, we believe there are at least three ranking officers in the department who're dirty. We haven't been able to nail them down as of yet; we think we're close, but not close enough for an arrest."

"And you think these men are somehow connected to the Sam Reynolds case?"

"We don't know."

"Then why are you talking to me? I'm not a cop and the only thing I'm interested in is getting Sam out of jail."

"The thing is," she said, hesitating, "we don't know what they're involved in. We know they sometimes look the other way for money. That'll get them a slap on the wrist. Sure, maybe they'll get suspended, but no jail time. We think that if they're willing to do that, they'll be willing to go a lot further if the price is right. That's why we are talking to you. If they are involved with the Reynolds case, you could help us put these guys away for a very long time."

"Do you really think for a minute that I'm interested in helping you do anything? IAD has been a proverbial pain in my ass for as long as I can remember."

"I don't expect you to do anything for us, Detective," Wesley/White stated.

"I'm not a detective, lady. You guys saw to that."

"Actually, we didn't. All of that was at the hands of your chief of police and the DA. They wanted you out of circulation. We want to know why. Just do your job. All we ask is that you let us know when you find a dirty cop. Can we count on you for that?"

"I'll tell you what you can count on. You can count on me to find a way for Sam to get released. You can count on me to find out who really killed Bobbi Marshall. *And*—you can count on me to make sure that whoever they are will be happy to come to you rather than deal with me. Is that fair enough for you?"

"Absolutely. I'll be in touch."

"Don't bother," I said, grabbing the tape as I left the room.

I decided to drive over to the hospital and check up on Margie and Annie. I needed a break and some rest. But I also needed to know that they were okay.

Fifteen

I know that everyone loves a hero, someone who can stand up to the world and keep going like that stupid pink bunny. When I left the hospital, I was exhausted and felt like the world was collapsing around me.

Margie was doing okay. She was still in the ER, but I didn't think they would keep her. The bullet that hit her was just a graze, like Manny told me earlier.

That's what they say on TV, isn't it? "It's nothing. It's just a graze." Well, until you've been "grazed" by a bullet and felt the searing metal rip the flesh from your body, you have no idea how painful a graze can be.

Annie Lee, on the other hand, wasn't doing so well. Apparently one of the bullets had nicked her heart and the other had done a lot of damage as well. Somehow she made it through the surgery, but the doctors said her chances were "iffy" at best. She was in the recovery room currently, then would go to intensive care. The doctor told us it would be several hours before she would regain consciousness. There wasn't any more I could do and I told

Manny and Margie to go home—that I was planning on doing the same. Even spending time with Tootie seemed like a break.

~ * ~

I was pleasantly surprised when I got home. The lights were out and the house seemed quiet. The way this day had unfolded, I half expected to see circus tents set up in the yard. There were no tents, clowns or elephants. There was nothing but the sounds of the frogs, the flow of the creek and the occasional hoot of an owl somewhere not too far away. I knew, or at least hoped, this day was finally over.

I took a shower, went to bed and spooned with Jill.

Do people still use that term—spoon? You know, the act where two people lie together and one person holds the other. Well, for those of you with dirty minds, it's usually a non-sexual act. It's just a pleasant way to tell the woman you are with that you love her and she's the most important person in the world. As far as sex is concerned, we haven't had any since Tootie and the teeny-bopper arrived. Frankly, I didn't see getting action anytime soon.

~ * ~

There seems to be a lot of fog hanging around tonight. That's unusual for these parts.

There's fog everywhere and somebody is after me. I can't see his face and I'm not sure if it is just one person. All I know for sure is that he/they are trying to kill me and I have to run to stay alive.

I can't see anything. The damn fog is keeping me from getting a bearing on my location. I hide behind a large boulder and I'm not sure if it's the same one I hid behind just a short time ago. I run some more and the next thing I know is that I am startled when I come face to face with Rocky Balboa.

What the hell? What's he doing here?

I think at first that he must be running too, but when the bell rings and I look down at my hands and see the gloves, I realize that somehow I am going to have to fight him for the right to leave where I am. I can't beat Rocky. Hell, he's the heavyweight champion of the world. Maybe if I just stay away for a little while, he won't beat the crap out of me. Then I feel the crushing blow of that huge left hand and feel myself falling and tumbling over the bar of the old saloon.

What Kevin Costner is doing playing Wyatt Earp and pointing a gun at me I can't imagine. This must be a dream, I think. Yes, that's what it is, it's a dream. It has to be. But when he points the gun at my feet and yells, "Dance!" I jump just like anyone else would.

"Baby! Adam! Are you all right?"

Jill was talking to me and shaking me.

Then the gun went off again and I thought I would piss my pants—if I were wearing any. I looked down at myself and I was hiding behind the bedpost, buck-naked, pointing a finger at a target I couldn't see. I guess I was going to shoot Rocky or Wyatt or somebody with my finger gun.

Bam!

Another gunshot. I finally realized that someone was indeed shooting a gun, but whatever danger I had perceived was imaginary.

"What the hell?" I said, as I realized Jill was looking at me with an all-consuming grin.

"Who the hell is shooting a gun at—," I looked at my watch, "seven-thirty in the morning?"

"Oh, that's Tootie," Jill replied, as if it were a stupid question. "He wanted to get in some target practice. I didn't think you would mind."

"At seven-thirty in the morning?" I asked again, like she was the biggest wack-a-doo I had ever known in my life. "And what's he doing here? I thought he was off to work at the nursing home?"

"Look," she said defiantly, "you're the one who got him a dangerous job. I think it's only right that you make sure he can protect himself. As for the nursing home job, he was told that his room wouldn't be ready for another day or two."

"I didn't get him that job," I defended.

I was so exhausted I wasn't sure about anything. I was pretty sure, though, that I didn't get him that damn job.

"Whatever. The sun is up and you should be out there making sure he's doing wherever he's doing it, right."

"You *do* know that you people are out of your friggin minds, don't you?"

"Just cover that thing up," she said looking down at the Mamba King—my now-erect soldier. "Remember curtains around here are not that big of a priority. We don't want certain people to get the wrong impression."

"What impression?" I said, standing a bit taller. I don't care if people think I have certain attributes.

"I don't want Tootie thinking we're having sex," she said seriously.

"Well, there isn't much of a chance of that, now is there?"

"Humph," she said, exasperated. "You men are all alike. You don't get any for a couple hours and you think the world is coming to an end."

"I'm not worried about the world right now. I just want a little peace and quiet."

She left the bedroom and I went to the bathroom to take care of some personal business of my own.

Walking by the mirror, I paused for a moment and thought I looked pretty good for a guy. Jill should be happy to have such a fine specimen like me. Of course, I was saluting the observation because I hadn't had my morning pee yet. I still couldn't figure out why women didn't understand the God-given right of men to give their best friend a name.

"You finally finished getting your morning nookie?" Tootie asked when I approached him cautiously. I figured that a crazy old man holding a loaded weapon was reason enough for me to think about another career.

"Good God! Jill and I weren't ...oh hell, never mind. It's none of your damn business anyway."

My favorite father-in-law laughed.

"She's a looker, even if she's my own kid. You best be taking care of that so as nobody else comes a knockin."

"Nobody else is gonna come knocking," I said with confidence. "I take care of business just fine...when there's business to take care of."

"I'm just saying...when a woman gets to looking like that, you best keep your eye on the prize. Otherwise, someone else will try taking it from you."

"I'll be sure to keep that in mind. But before we get off subject, what are you doing out here?"

"Target practicing," he said, confidently. "Not too shabby, either."

He turned, waving the gun at me and asked if I wanted to shoot some. I ducked as best I could, and grabbed the pistol from him.

"Damn! Anything to keep from getting shot."

He laughed, "Oh, you're such a baby. The safety is on. You don't have anything to worry about."

"Really?"

I pointed the gun at the target and fired off three rounds.

"I'll be damned. Good thing I didn't pull the trigger."

He then looked at the target where I shot, "Damn, son-in-law, you see that?"

I looked at the target and saw three holes that almost touched each other.

"You still think I need practice?"

"Nope," he said. "You just remember what I said about my daughter, though. Somewhere, there's an old horn-dog like me just a-waitin' for you to screw things up."

I didn't bother to respond. Instead, I removed the clip, ejected the last round and set the pistol on the bench.

"Now let me ask you again what you are doing out here. You don't need a gun with what you're doing. You're scaring the hell out of Jill talking about shooting people and stuff. And where's Bitsy? What's she got to say about all of this?"

"I know," he said, dropping his head. "I just don't want the girls thinking I'm a pussy. A man has a right to be looked at favorably. If they think I'm doing something lame, it just wouldn't be right."

I hated to admit it, but I understood what he meant. Women just don't understand a man's world. We were born to protect them and take care of them. Now it seems they don't need us and they trivialize what we do. It wasn't right, and I hated how it makes us do things that only get us in trouble.

"I tell you what. Let's make a deal. I'll make sure they think your job is dangerous and scary, if you promise not to do anything stupid. That way they look at you like they should and I get to keep my nuts from getting blown off. What do you say?"

"You'd do that for me?" Tootie asked with a big smile.

"Hey," I said, "Us guys have got to stick together, right?"

"Damn straight," he said. "And I'll do the same for you."

"That's okay," I replied. "Let's just stick to one plan at a time."

"Oh, by the way," Tootie said, smiling. "About what Bitsy thinks? I told her I was comin' out here to shoot and she got so excited it'll take a week for my pecker to cool off from that fire she's got."

"Oh hell," I said, to no one but myself.

"Just thought you should know."

Before that moment, I had never seen a seventy-something old man skip.

Damn, I hate that old coot.

~ * ~

I wasn't too fond of the way the day had started. Fighting with Rocky, a gun fight with Marshall Dillon, or whoever that was supposed to be, and then Tootie's all too graphic description just made everything go downhill. I was hoping to get a sign of better things to come. Maybe I'm as nuts as the rest of them. Who knows?

I talked to Manny before I left the house and he said Annie's condition hadn't changed overnight. He said he would keep checking on her throughout the day. We decided to meet at his office at 9:30, so I had time for a much-needed breakfast.

~ * ~

"So where do we go from here, boss man?" Manny said, as I entered a few minutes earlier than scheduled.

He was sitting at his desk and Margie was making noise in another room. It sounded like she was making coffee and I thought a cup would go real well with my lack of sleep. I started looking around and Manny understood what I was thinking about.

"Don't worry about the bugs. I got a new bug zapper and swept them all out. Seems our friends need to move up in the technology area. I found three I think they wanted to keep a secret."

"Good to know."

I'd thought about Manny's question, "Where do we go from here?" all morning before I arrived. I still didn't have a clue where to go next and told him as much. He suggested we have a meeting with our young socialite, Mister William Joshua Sheffield the third.

"Any ideas where to find him?"

"It just so happens I do," Manny said smiling. "Follow me."

Manny stood and I thought we were going to head out the door. Instead, he led me to another room and then to a locked door. When he unlocked the door, I heard the distinct sound of a muffled voice. When the light was turned on, I saw a young man bound to a bed wearing nothing but his boxers and a gag.

"What the hell are you doing? You do realize that this could be construed as kidnapping, don't you?"

"Shh," Manny responded with a smile. "We don't want to give the lad any ideas, right?"

"I suspect he's already thought that one up himself. What's he doing here?"

"I look at it this way: For the last forty-eight hours, you and everyone else connected to this case have been shot or shot at, bombed, fricasseed, arrested and just generally fucked over. I don't see that getting any better as we get closer to the truth. Somebody knows something, and it seems to me young Sheffield here may be the best source of information we have."

"It's still kidnapping," I said emphatically. "And the last time I checked, it's against the law."

"What about the car bomb, or the bomb we found on your bike?" Manny ranted. "Are those against the law? And what about the shootings of Margie and Annie Lee, are those against the law? Do you really think these assholes are playing by the rules? Do you think they'd give a flying fuck if any one of us died in order for them to protect their little secrets? *I don't think so.* And I'll be damned if I'm going to sit around and wait to get killed because you say it's the right thing to play by the rules." He took a deep breath and finished with, "If you have a problem with this, then maybe you should take off while I ask the gentleman some questions."

"I didn't say I had a problem with it, dickwad," I replied, hoping to knock him off his sanctimonious pedestal. "I just wanted to make sure you understand what you're doing before you go to jail for doing it."

"I'm not going to jail," Manny said. "As a matter of fact, I believe this little visitation will be forgotten before we're even through." Then he picked up a San Jose phone book and looked at the boy. "What do you think, Billy boy? Are you going to remember this as a horrible kidnapping or a visit with some new friends?"

William looked at Manny with very large eyes showing a fright that was easy to read. Manny removed the gag so our conversation could become a dialog instead of just one way.

"I think it's always best to make new friends," Sheffield replied in a whispered voice. "I don't think I have as much information as you would like. I'll tell you whatever I know, if that helps."

"Now, see there?" Manny looked at me. "He'll cooperate to the best of his ability. Don't you think that's commendable?"

I looked at the kid and then back at Manny. It caught me off guard and I'm sure it caught the kid off guard when Manny took the phone book and swung it backhand and hit Sheffield on the side of his head. The kid reeled sideways and if not for the restraints would probably have been knocked off the bed from the force of the blow.

I didn't need an explanation, but the lad was very confused at the strike.

"Why did you do that?" he asked with tears forming in his eyes.

"Because," Manny said, "I don't like you and I don't believe you. You're only going to tell us as little as you think you can get by with and that just isn't good enough for me." Manny hit him again and continued talking. "So what I propose to you is the whole truth and nothing but the truth or I will beat the shit out of you. Are you keeping up with me, college boy?"

"Yes, sir," William said. "I understand."

"This is a good thing," Manny continued. "So here are the rules. Well, actually, there's only one rule. We ask you a question and you answer it honestly *and* completely. If you do, you'll not feel any more pain. However, and this is the part where you really need to pay attention, son, if you lie to us or don't tell us the complete truth, I will take this phone book and beat you 'til it shreds into little pieces. Do you understand the rule now? Is there any part of the rule you don't understand?"

William Joshua Sheffield III was getting close to graduating from college and didn't have any misunderstandings about the rule or that it would be enforced.

"What do you know about the shooting last night?" I asked.

I didn't like any of this, but realized that Manny was right about one thing. If we didn't find out what was going on soon, one of us was going to get killed.

Hell, maybe all of us.

"I didn't know about the shooting 'til this guy said something about it last night," Sheffield said. "I don't even know the girls who were shot." Manny raised the phone book, "I'm telling the truth," he yelled at Manny. "I know some things. But I didn't know about that."

"Well then, let's talk about something you *do* know," Manny said lowering the book. "Tell us about your friend, Stephanie Shadows, or should I call her Lady Shadows for you?"

"Oh, God," he started to pale. "You know about her?"

"Yes, Billy boy," I grinned. "We know *all* about your little fetish. Now you tell us about why someone broke into her home yesterday."

"It was me," he volunteered. "I know that sometimes she tapes our sessions. It's her way of keeping control over her toys, as she calls us. I was trying to find the tapes so I could destroy them."

"Why didn't you just ask for them?" I asked.

"Because I knew she would never give them to me," he squeaked a response. "She's a violent bitch and would use them against me later."

"You think she's a violent bitch? Yet you kept going back to her several times a week. Why's that, Billy?"

"I went to her because it was something I thought I needed," he said, then sniffed. "I'm still not sure if it's right for me or not. I started going back more often because I found out about her taping the sessions. I volunteered to do housework and whatever I could to see if I could find out where she was hiding the tapes. I had it narrowed down to only a couple of places. I would never hurt her. She's mean as hell, but she only did what I asked her to do.

"I thought I could get in and out quickly and she would never know it was me. I didn't think she was home when I went in. When I heard her coming up the steps, I panicked. I tried to get her from behind, but somehow she saw me and just about beat the crap out of me. It took everything I had to finally get the upper hand. If you hadn't shown up when you did, I never would have hit her. I just had to get out and didn't want her to see who I was."

"You do realize that when we're done with you," Manny said, "there is a very strong possibility that we'll turn you over to her."

"Oh God, no!" Sheffield cried. "She'll kill me."

"I don't think she'll *kill* you," I said. "But you'll wish you were dead when she gets her claws into you."

"Please," Sheffield sniffed back tears. "I'm cooperating. I'll do whatever you ask. Just keep her away from me."

"I thought you liked that sorta thing, Billy," Manny said. "Why the change of heart?"

"Because—" There was a hesitation—real fear in the kids eyes. "Because she knows how to take me beyond my limits. Please, don't bring her here."

"Then tell us about Sam Reynolds," I said. "What do you have to do with his being in jail?"

"I don't know," he replied, then correcting himself, "I'm not sure."

"What does that mean?" Margie said from behind us.

None of us had heard her sneak into the room and we were all startled by her voice.

"Damn it, girl," Manny yelled. "You don't need to be in here."

Holding up her injured arm, Margie said, "I've earned the right to be here." Then, without any doubts about her position, she looked back at the lad and said, "I asked you a question, asshole. What do you mean when you say you're not sure?"

Manny and I looked at her then at each other—both surprised by the intensity in her voice. Neither of us argued with her. We took her cue and looked at the frightened young man for an answer.

Sheffield finally said, "I went to my grandfather and told him that I was being blackmailed by Sam. I told him Reynolds had information on me regarding what I was doing with Lady Shadows and that he was going to make it public if he didn't get what he wanted."

"What did he want?" I asked.

"At first, all he wanted was a zoning variance," Sheffield said. "I had enough contacts through my grandfather's business that I pushed it through without having to bringing Grandfather into it. Then it dawned on me that he would need something else sometime down the road and the whole mess would never go away. That's when I told Grandfather about him and what he was doing. Grandfather told me not to worry about it. He said he'd take care of everything. I just wanted to get the tapes back and make it all go away."

"So you could protect your precious name," Margie stated flatly. "You people are killing others just to keep your sick little perversions out of the news."

I'm not sure where he got the nerve, but he replied, "My sick little perversions, as you call them, are my problems and none of your damn business. If your so-called friend had left it that way, nobody would have gotten hurt. And what makes you think you're so much better than me? You have me tied up and you're beating on me. You think you're somehow better than me?"

"I think," I said, "that we should take a short break and talk for a minute."

The others looked at me and they looked pissed. I could tell they would have preferred to keep things going. However, I needed something from my partners in crime. They got the message and filed out of the room. I heard the lock click and then Manny turned to me.

Sixteen

"What the hell are you doing, Samson?" Manny asked. "The son of a bitch is talking and we need to get some more answers."

"I know that," I said. "But let me ask you this: Are you really buying what he's saying? I don't mean the part about Sam using him for his own gain. I know enough to know that's quite plausible. I'm talking about the part where he's laying everything off on dear old Granddaddy. Do you *really* think he's going to do that? Granddaddy has way too much clout for us to get to him. I don't know why, but I think he's leaving something out."

"Like what?" Margie asked. "Everything he's said makes sense to me."

"Of course it does," I reflected. "That's the beauty of a con. They use as much of the truth as they can in order to make the lie viable. I'm not saying he's lying about everything. As a matter of fact, I'm not saying he's lying about any of it."

"Then what?" Manny asked.

"I'm saying he's hiding something. Everything fits too well. There's something missing and I can't put my finger on it."

I thought about what I said and something clicked. I told them to follow me and we quietly went back to the room. As we entered, the boy was lying down with his fingers interlaced behind his head. Before he saw us he looked like he had won a fight or a big prize. When he realized we had entered, his mannerisms changed back to that of a shy and confused boy.

"Manny, "I said, looking directly at Sheffield, "may I borrow your book, please?"

Manny showed a flicker of confusion, but went along with me.

"Sure, want the shirt off my back, too?" he said, flashing what could not be mistaken as anything but an evil grin.

"Naw," I replied, "but you may want to keep a distance. I don't want to get any blood on the two of you."

"What's going on?" William asked. "I've told you everything you wanted to know. Everything I know." There was a genuine fear in his eyes.

"Have you now?" I asked. "I don't think so. And, Manny," I said, still looking directly at the boy, "did you not make it a part of your rule that total disclosure was necessary to save his worthless ass?"

"As a matter of fact, I did," Manny replied.

"Well then, it appears that our little boy here has broken your one and only rule," I said. "He needs to understand that you were serious, don't you think?"

"Absolutely," Manny said, as if he knew where I was going. "Do you want me to do it? Or...how about we call Lady Shadows and get her to finish? I'm sure he would confess the rest to her."

"What do you think, Billy?" I asked. "Do you want us to call your lady friend?"

"No, please!" he cried out and tears were forming in his eyes. "I don't know what you want. Just ask me something—anything— and I'll tell you everything. Just leave that bitch out of this. Please!"

"Then tell us about your daddy, William Sheffield the second," I stated. The room went quiet and for the first time I could tell that young William was at a loss for words.

"There is no William Sheffield the second," he finally responded.

"Then I'm confused. How exactly did you get to be the third if there isn't a second?" I asked. "Immaculate conception? I don't see you as the second coming of Christ, so your answer better be good."

There was a long pause before he answered. "My father is no longer a member of the family. He went to prison twenty years ago and my grandfather disowned him."

"William the second is in prison?" I asked for clarification. I wasn't going to let him make a general statement without looking deeper.

"First off," Billy said, "There is no William the second. Grandfather only had one child and that was my mother. She died when I was born. Her husband, my father, was already in prison for robbery and murder. He got out about three years ago."

"So if I'm getting this straight, your dead mother couldn't be called William the second. Your jailhouse daddy wasn't a William anything. So when you were born, your granddaddy decided he would skip a generation with the name thing and call you William the third. Does that about sum it up?"

"Yes."

"Why is that so important? What difference does it make what you are called?" Margie asked.

"Grandfather believes that with my name set as a generational thing, it would give me another piece of the political puzzle. As far as the world knows, my father and mother are both dead."

"I still don't get it," she pushed. "Something like that is easy enough to figure out. The court records would prove that William Junior doesn't exist."

The young man smiled. "Actually, the records would prove that he did exist…and died. Money can buy you whatever you want, if you plan ahead."

"So what you're saying," I jumped in, "is that you figured if you put us on the trail of your grandfather, he would be bulletproof enough not to get caught. On the other hand, if we went after your father, who theoretically is dead but in reality is an ex-con with a non-William name, he would go down for the murder of Bobbi Marshall? Damn, this is confusing."

"I didn't say my father did anything wrong!"

"But you believe he could have, don't you?" I pushed. "Did he know what Sam was doing? Did he know you were being blackmailed?"

The boy looked away. He didn't say anything, but finally nodded yes.

"What's his name, boy?" Manny asked with a bite in his voice.

"David Sheffield. He changed his last name to Mom's when they got married. My grandfather made it a requirement before he agreed to the marriage."

"Shit," Margie exclaimed, "did your grandfather take care of your momma on the honeymoon, too? He controls everything else."

Manny and I were both dumbfounded by the implication of the question. I hadn't seen that kind of fire coming out of Margie. Then again, she hadn't been shot before. We let it slide.

Sheffield didn't respond.

"I hope you don't plan on going anywhere soon," I concluded. "We'll make you as comfortable as we can. I'm sure it won't be up to your standards, but you'll get over that."

Manny and Margie both got the clue that I was done for the moment. We left the room and locked the door.

"We have some work to do," I said, and then walked out of the office. I needed time to think.

~ * ~

I thought I should have a word with Bill Wiseman, Sam's attorney. I hadn't really had a chance to get together with him since this whole mess started and figured it was time to bring him up to speed. I also wanted to get a pulse on the timing of the hearing and what else we could do to slow things down. I felt that I had a good idea what was going on, but I didn't have all the key players yet and needed time to finish putting everything together.

Bill invited me into his inner sanctum.

"I was just about to call you and get a progress report."

"I know, Bill," I replied. "I use that same line when I want people to think I am keeping them at the forefront of my thoughts when in reality, I can hardly see through to the next five minutes."

Bill smiled and asked, "So what's going on? Have you been able to get Sam to change his mind about the plea or find out anything else?" he said.

"No and yes. Actually, it's more of a definite maybe," I said. "I was hoping to find out more from you."

"You seem to be making a lot of waves, my friend," he said, keeping the smile. "I've heard some rumors that you're shaking things up downtown."

"I guess some people are getting a little nervous as I get closer to the truth."

"That's an understatement. I've got a preliminary hearing first thing tomorrow. If he doesn't change his plea by then, there won't be much I can do to stop this from happening."

"Tomorrow morning?" I was shocked at the news. "I thought we still had a few days before that happened. What the hell, Bill?"

"That's what I've been trying to tell you," the attorney continued. "You have people scared shitless and they want this thing to go away...as quickly as possible. Can you help me out a little?"

"What do you have in mind?"

"What I want is for him to change his plea to not guilty. I want him to say that his confession was coerced. *And,* I want you to get him to do that as soon as possible."

"Oh. Is that all?

I'm sure Bill caught the ever-so-slight bit of sarcasm.

"Yeah," he followed, not taking the bait. "If you can do that, I think we can pretty much make it all go away."

"Well, I'll just jump right on that." My sarcasm continued. "On the other hand, if I can't do that, what do you suggest?"

Bill stood up from behind his desk and walked over to the door and closed it.

"Barring that," he said, lowering his voice, "get him to do whatever he can to stop them from taking him to court. He could fake an illness. Attempted suicide would buy us more time yet. We would need to get a psychiatric evaluation and that could take a lot of time. They would have to have their psychiatrist review anything ours had to say. To me, that would be the best way to go. On the other hand, without his doing something, this whole thing could be over by noon tomorrow. Oh, one last thing, you never heard that from me."

"Heard what?" I asked, with a smile I didn't really feel.

"About the psychiatric—Oh, hell, get out of here. Buy me some time."

"Damn, I came here to get you to buy me some."

"Do this and you'll have succeeded for us both."

I left Bill's office no more confident than when I arrived.

~ * ~

I decided to go back to the office after making a pit stop. I figured I had to use everything in my arsenal. The passenger I picked up was my best bet to get me more answers.

"Oh, God, what's she doing here?" Sheffield yelled as I entered the locked room with Lady Shadows.

"Well, Little Miss Billy," I offered the young, bound man, "since you were so reluctant to give up your father, I figured you had a few more secrets you might be hiding from us as well. So here's the deal: you get one chance and only one chance to make amends. I have just finished a lengthy discussion with Ms. Shadows. I explained to her all about your visit yesterday. I can tell you right up front that she isn't very happy about this recent turn of events. As a matter of fact, she's asked me to leave the two of you alone for about thirty minutes. She also told me she would be able to extract whatever information I might desire. Now, I'm not exactly a sadist, Billy boy; however, her proposal has a certain appeal to me. You see we're running out of time for my friend Sam, and you seem to hold the key to some very important information I need.

"I'm fascinated with learning firsthand about your little fetish. Well, actually, I would be learning second hand, but that's about as close to first hand as I intend to get, if you know what I mean. So here's the deal. You start talking right now and tell me everything, *and I do mean everything.* The more you talk, the less likely I will leave this room. On the other hand, you stop talking and I leave you and Ms. Shadows alone to discuss your future. That is, if you actually have a future after she's done with you. So what do you say, Billy? Do we stay and talk? Or do Manny, Margie and I go for a walk and leave you alone with Ms. Shadows to discuss whatever's on *her* mind?"

"You can't do this!" He was shouting and crying at the same time. "I want a lawyer. You keep her the hell away from me!"

Lady Shadows walked over to Sheffield and lightly rubbed her finger over the scar on his throat.

"I can't believe I forgot about this scar," she said. "You told me all about it—how you were sick as an infant and almost died, and all the problems that were in your life back then. It was during your formative years, you said, and that's why you enjoy the look and feel of a powerful nurse. It was why having a strong woman control you and abuse you was so important that you were willing to give up everything your grandfather had planned for you."

Lady Shadows looked at me and said, "I'm sorry, Mr. Shaw. I should have remembered. I guess my head hurt more than I realized. You have every right to punish me for my mistake." The comment was followed by a sly smile that couldn't be mistaken for anything other than the offer she was making.

The room got brighter from the reflection of her brilliantly white teeth. I flushed just thinking about the image of her lying across my knees and decided it was best to leave the offer alone. Any reply on my part could leave me with a lot of explaining to do.

"I take it that you decided on a private chat," I told Sheffield. "That's okay. I need a break anyway. I have some calls to make, a few small errands to run...a cold shower. It shouldn't take me more than forty-five minutes, maybe an hour tops. And by the way, Billy, I'm not a cop, remember? I'm suspended because I have a really poor attitude with authority figures. So, we'll be back in a while. Good luck, you little prick."

I started to leave the room, but stopped short because of the lad's shouting and crying—actually more like pleading and screaming—for me not to leave. It seems Ms. Shadows created more fear in the young man than I could ever have mustered in such a short time.

"Okay!" he shouted. "I'll tell you what you want to know. I promise. Just don't let her near me."

"What I will promise you, Billy, is that if you don't give me what I want now, I'm going to invoke the promise she made me, the one where she said you *will* talk, very soon. Frankly, I trust her promises a lot more than I do yours. So talk to me. *Now!*"

~ * ~

While I'm thinking about it, let me tell you a little about Lady Shadows.

She wouldn't fall into the category of a classic beauty. She's so much more than that. She's tall, about five-ten, maybe five-eleven, taller with heels. So far, I hadn't seen her in any heels shorter than four inches. She was voluptuous in all the right places, if you like that sort of thing. Jill would simply say she's too perfect. Her platinum hair reminded me of Marilyn Monroe in the movie *Some Like It Hot*. She wore too much make-up for my taste, but I could easily overlook that with a little effort. I'm sure most of it is for the part she plays in her role as a dominatrix. Just looking at the way she was looking at Billy would scare the crap out of just about anyone. She had a look in her eyes that told me she would like nothing more than seeing blood—Billy's blood. Overall, she was one friggin scary, gorgeous chick.

"Okay," Billy started, "I'll tell you what I know. Just keep her the hell away from me."

"That'll be completely up to you."

I decided not to say anymore and waited for him to start. I figured he knew where to begin. My plan would be to just interject questions from time to time.

"Your friend Sam is a fucking idiot," Billy said. "If he would have just stayed the hell away from me, none of this would have happened. He's the one that got Bobbi killed. It's all his fault."

"Okay," I said. "I get that you don't like him, but did he garrote her?"

"What the hell does that mean?"

"You're going to college? *You're* the fucking idiot. Did Sam strangle her?"

"No," Billy replied. "I don't know who did that. I'm just saying that if he'd kept his mouth shut and stayed away from me, Bobbi would still be alive. Now she's dead and I'm never going to make anything of my life. All because the greedy bastard wanted something he didn't need to begin with."

"You're really starting to piss me off." I got in his face. "Do you want to stay on track or are we finished? I have important things to do. I'm sure Ms. Shadows here has a few words to discuss with you."

"Okay, okay," he relented. "After he came to me, I told you, I took care of the variance he wanted. At first I didn't think too much about it. He found out what I was doing; I got caught. It was a small thing, the variance. It was only after a while that I got concerned and talked to my grandfather. Grandfather said it would be taken care of. I didn't know what he was talking about at the time and still don't know for sure if he's the one who had her killed."

"But you think he did?"

"I think he could have very easily been the one to set it up."

"Go on. Who else could it be if it wasn't him?"

"That's the thing. It actually *could* be my father. I told him what was going on as well, and he also told me he could fix it for me. He was angry. I mean *real* angry. My grandfather didn't know I'd been in contact with my father while he was in prison. So when I told my father about it, it was like something was different. I don't know how to describe it. I thought he was going to blow up.

"In prison, my dad changed from a kind and gentle person to someone different. Yes," he explained as if reading our minds, "he was in there for killing someone. But, that was an accident. The robbery went bad and someone jumped him and the gun went off. He realized he did wrong and was going to take his punishment. When I first met him, I was fourteen. He really was kind with me. He was sorry for not being around for me. Then...something happened. I don't know what. He changed. He had an edge. He seemed harder somehow. He seemed mean. I regretted immediately telling him, but it was too late."

"Did either of them tell you what they had in mind as far as 'fixing' it?"

"No. I heard about Bobbi's death like everyone else, on the news. I knew it had to be one of them, but I wasn't going to say anything to anybody about it. I feel bad she got hurt."

"She didn't get *hurt*. She was murdered. She's dead. You feeling sorry about that isn't going to help her now."

I hate talking to rich people. They don't get that lives outside their own actually do have value.

"So, what else?"

The boy hesitated. He looked at Ms. Shadows then back at me.

"Grandfather has cops on the payroll." He said it as if purging himself of the knowledge. "They're keeping Mr. Reynolds on constant surveillance and listening to everything he says and what everyone else says to him."

"You aren't telling us anything we don't already know," Manny jumped in. "Who're the cops? How can we get past them? What can you tell us that will actually help?"

"I only know one of the cops, Carl Ramos. I've used him a couple times personally. But there're others. I just don't know how many."

"Carl Ramos is on your grandfather's payroll?" I bellowed.

"*Son-of-a-bitch!*"

Seventeen

It would have been very easy for me to go off half-cocked with the information I'd just learned. I'd like to think that I have control over my emotions. As a matter of fact, I did *not* leave to go shoot Ramos—though I very much wanted to. I had control. It helped that Manny tackled me as I was heading out the door, but let's just keep that between us, okay?

I was livid. I really wanted to hit somebody and I knew who that would be. However, Manny was right when he said that it was information we could use when the timing was right.

It also helped that the kid was able to tell us how to get the proof of Ramos's involvement. It was great information. Unfortunately, it didn't help get Sam out of jail. What it did give us was leverage to get other information we needed for that purpose.

I was just about to consider the morning a good one when the door opened and Tootie walked in.

"Tootie," I said, "how the heck did you know I was here?"

"I didn't. I came here because the boss sent me here to get some things I need for my new job. What're you doing here; you getting supplies, too? Are you still workin' that big case? Think your friend can get me a big gun? Hellooo, Mama! Damn!"

I saw Tootie's eyes looking at a point somewhere behind me and turned around to see Lady Shadows checking out the new visitor.

"Who's this handsome thing, Samson? Have you been holding out on me?"

"Like anyone could do that?" I replied. "Lady—er—Stephanie, this is my father-in-law Tootie. Tootie, this is Stephanie. She's—uh—helping with the case we're working on. And no, Manny isn't going to give you a big gun. You don't need a gun."

"Hey, man!" Manny said, "Don't speak for me. If the man wants a gun, that's one of the things I do for a living. I sell guns."

"I like a man with a big gun," Ms. Shadows said, smiling. "I think he deserves the biggest gun you have, Manny. Don't you?"

"Absolutely," Manny said. "For you, Tootie, nothing but the best."

"All right," I interjected, "enough with the horseshit. Tootie isn't getting a gun. You hear me? The last thing I need is bailing his ass out of jail, too. No guns...and that's final."

"Come here, Tootie," Manny said, waving him over to the side where I couldn't hear them.

"You should let him have a gun," Lady Shadows said. "I'll bet he really knows how to use one."

"What you need to do," I glared at the smiling woman, "is focus on a way to get more information out of our friend in the back room without making him scream. We wouldn't want to have to explain *that* to Tootie, would we?"

"I wouldn't mind explaining a thing or two to him," she replied, looking over my shoulder at my father-in-law. "As a matter of fact, I think it could be a lot of fun. Why don't we invite him in to help us with our interrogation? He could really liven things up for us."

"No!" I said, much louder than I should have.

Manny and Tootie looked over at me. I could tell they would both prefer talking to her than each other. However, when I gave them one of my patented "go to hell" looks, they both started talking to each other again.

"Look," I continued, "that man's an accident waiting to happen. If we get him involved, we'll probably all wind up in jail."

"If you insist," she purred. "Just don't be surprised if something happens. He may just be too much man for me to resist trying out for size."

"Jesus!" I blurted, "He's old enough to be your grandfather."

"All that means to me," she said, "is that he's experienced."

I don't get it. That old coot gets more ass than a toilet seat. I, on the other hand, have to beg for anything more than a peck on the cheek. I'm not complaining, mind you. I just don't think God's sense of humor is as funny as He seems to think. Here you have me, a loyal and devoted husband, who has to fight for a handshake. Oh please, read into that whatever you want. On the other side of the coin, you have Tootie. He's an old horndog who tells every woman he passes that he wants to sleep with her. To him it wouldn't matter if nine out of ten said no and slapped his face. His philosophy is that one of the ten says yes.

"I think we have everything taken care of here," Manny said.

Then, looking at Tootie, "I'll get everything together and have it ready by tomorrow morning if you want to stop by then and pick it up."

"No guns," I repeated myself.

"No guns," Manny replied. He looked at Tootie and winked.

"Works for me," Tootie replied. "See you tomorrow."

Turning to leave, he paused and looked at Ms. Shadows.

"I may be too old to cut the mustard, but I'll never be too old to lick the jar."

He burst into laughter at his own joke and walked out. It was the same joke he said before and like with everything else, he'll use the same line over and over again until he gets the reaction he wants.

I looked at Lady Shadows and couldn't believe my eyes. She was blushing.

"I'll be damned," I said, under my breath.

~ * ~

"Hello, Mr. Shaw."

Faye Wesley was sitting at her desk when I stepped into her office.

I decided that after Tootie left Manny's place, I needed to have a talk with someone on the inside. Someone I believed could help.

Manny said he had one more trick up his sleeve, but didn't want me around when he did it. His asking me to leave was not considered a request. He also asked me not to ask any questions. I'm not a brain surgeon, but could figure out pretty quick that I didn't need to know what he had in mind.

"Hello, Ms. White," I replied. "Do you have a couple minutes to spare?"

I suspected she would, since I knew she was already investigating me. However, not being one to assume anything, I thought it only right to be polite. The members of Internal Affairs were like vultures: they could smell blood a mile away. I could only hope that politeness would give me a leg up.

"Please, call me Faye when we're in private. The last name is Wesley, remember? I only use 'White' when undercover. Anyway, I believe there are times when we can skip formalities. And just so you know," she said with a smile, "I'll always have time for you."

"Thanks, Faye." I returned the smile. "Before I start—have you ever had this office scanned for bugs?"

"Why would I do that?" she asked. "There haven't been any bugs in this building since El Niño."

"I meant listening devices. You know, the little electronic gadgets that can hear what you're saying when you talk to someone? Not the multi-legged critters that multiply in wet weather."

"Good Lord, no," she said as if I kicked her dog. "Why would you ask such a thing?"

"Because I believe you may want to have your office checked out as quickly as possible. It's come to my attention that some things we've all been taking for granted, like privacy, aren't quite what they seem around here. Let's go for a short walk."

The woman didn't ask for an explanation. She just grabbed her jacket and we walked out the door.

Since her office was only one floor above street level, I thought a little stroll in the fresh air might be the best way to ensure the privacy I was hoping to achieve.

As soon as we left the building, she asked, "So what's going on, Mr. Shaw? Were you serious about the listening devices you mentioned upstairs or were you just trying to get my attention?"

"Dead serious. There are a couple things I need to discuss with you that you aren't going to like. However, I need your complete cooperation as well as your silence until I get a better handle on what to do. Can I depend on you to just listen for now? And to keep quiet?"

"I can already tell you I don't like the sound of this. But, if you're coming to *me*, with all the friends you have to go to, then I'm guessing it has something to do with the department. If that's the case, then you can be *absolutely* sure I can use proper discretion. So, what is it?"

It took me a few minutes to bring her up to speed regarding our little meeting with Junior, though I left out the part about kidnapping and smacking him around.

I then told her the most important piece of information—Carl Ramos. I also mentioned that there were others involved, but didn't know yet who they were. That was the reason for privacy.

Faye was silent for the better part of a minute. I thought she was reflecting on what I had just told her.

Instead, what she told me just about made my knees buckle.

"It's interesting you should bring this information to me." I could tell by her mannerisms that she was picking her words carefully. "You see, Mr. Shaw, those were almost verbatim the same words Detective Ramos said about you less than an hour ago. According to him, you are the dirty cop and he's even given us proof of that."

"Son of a bitch," was all I managed, then fell silent. I didn't know what to do. Usually I can get a sense about what to expect. This one gave me pause.

"What kind of proof. Can you tell me anything else he said?"

"You know the rules, Detective. I'm not at liberty to discuss anything involving an open investigation. Especially something as serious as the allegations he brought to me."

"You don't have to. You've already told me enough to know that you're taking him seriously."

"We have to. If what he told me—shown me—has *any* merit, you're in a lot of trouble, sir."

"I can't tell you what to do, Ms. White, er...Wesley. You're going to do whatever you want anyway. However, I *can* tell you this much. If Carl Ramos tells you anything about me, it's a lie."

"I would like to believe that. I don't like the man all that much. He gave me evidence that places you in a very bad light. What proof do you have that he's the one?"

"Right now? I don't have anything except the word of a stupid kid trying not to get in any deeper than he already is. But, if given time, I will find the proof you need. Can you do that? Can you give me some time?"

"I don't know. I'm scheduled to meet with the DA in a couple hours to go over with him what I have. If my thinking is correct, he'll want to put out a warrant for your arrest. Like I said, I can't discuss with you what was given to me, but there's enough to put you away for a long time."

I was about ready to leave, and then paused.

"I'm surprised you've told me what you have. Why did you?"

"The other night," she placed a hand on my shoulder, "when we first met, I totally expected to prove you were corrupt. I gave you every opportunity to take advantage of the situation I put you in. There was plenty of rope for you to hang yourself, but you didn't. You surprised me and I don't get surprised very often. I've read everything that's been written about you in the files. You're a tough son of a bitch who doesn't take shit from anyone. You're considered antisocial, a renegade, pious, and generally not liked very much by anyone of authority.

"What I couldn't find in the file was anything that told me you were disloyal to the force or any of the principles the department stands for. I have no desire to punish someone for carrying around a soapbox or having strong beliefs in what we do for a living. In other words, Adam, if I can still call you that, I want the bad seeds crushed. I don't believe you're one of them. However, you need to find me the proof that we're after the wrong guy. Otherwise, what happens next will be out of my hands."

"I understand," I said. "And yes, you can call me Adam. When we get through this, and we *will* get through this, I'll buy you a drink and we can celebrate together the cleansing of the force. All I can ask is that you do what you have to do. If you feel compelled to give me any slack, or extra time, it will be very much appreciated. If not, well then we'll both have to do what we have to do."

"Want to elaborate on that last comment?"

"Now that would be just plain silly of me. Wouldn't it? I don't want to say anything that could get me in deeper than I already am, now wouldn't I?"

"Never hurts to ask," she smiled. "I'm going out on a limb here, but I'll let you know what the DA has to say." There was a pause. "I used to be a cop...just like you, out on the streets. I learned early that a lot of what a good cop does is listen to his gut. Often times it's the only thing that keeps him alive. My gut tells me that Ramos is a bad apple, not you. It also tells me that you may be unorthodox, but you're okay. I want this to have a happy ending. So do whatever you can to get me the truth."

"I will. One more thing, get your office checked. I was serious about the bugs. The players in this game are very serious and have very long arms."

I walked away, discouraged and unhappy. I didn't like what I was told. I sure as hell didn't like the prospect of going to jail and spending time with my old pal, Sam Reynolds. I needed to find some answers—fast.

Eighteen

I needed some serious thinking time. The best way to do that was to get on Lu-Lu Belle and go for a ride. I knew time was of the essence. I knew my ass was shooting the moon for everyone to see. But, I also knew that running hard didn't make sense if you didn't have any real direction. I didn't want to be like the guy who, when the cop asked him why he was going so fast, replied, "I don't know, but I bet I get there in record time."

When I got home, Jill was surprised to see me, but immediately noticed the frown I was wearing. There's a yin and a yang to being married. The yin is that when two people are around each other as much as a married couple are, they get to know what each other thinks. The yang is that they get to know what each other thinks. I know the two statements are identical. However, the contradiction is in the similarity. It's nice to know what someone else is thinking—'til it's not.

"Do you want the full version?" I asked. "Or the condensed one?"

"Let's start with the condensed one." she reached for and held my hand. "If I need more, I'll ask."

So, for the first time since this entire mess got started, I confessed to Jill what was happening and how it was turning out. Okay, I didn't confess every detail, but I told her enough to let her know I could be in trouble.

I figured she would blow a gasket, get pissed off at me, or maybe something worse. What I got instead was silence. She didn't say anything right away. She just walked into the dining room and sat quietly. Finally, after a lot of thinking, she said, "So what do you plan to do about it?"

"I don't know," was as honest a reply as I could muster.

"Sure you do. You always know what to do. Sometimes the answers are muddied or hidden somewhere, but you know. So tell me what you need to do so we can fix this thing."

"I'm telling you, Babe, I don't have the answers this time."

I tried to get her to understand, but she wasn't buying it.

She paused.

"Do you remember the time when your old partner disappeared and you were stumped? You told me then that you couldn't figure it out. You said you were lost and out of answers. Do you remember that?"

"Of course I do. What's that got to do with this?"

"It's the same thing," she replied, as she straightened with a confidence only a purebred Texas woman can offer. "You thought *then* that you didn't have the answers you needed, when in reality you had 'em all along. They were just mixed up with a lot of information you didn't need. So, how did you figure that one out?"

I thought about that incident, that terrible time. I remembered what I did then to solve the case.

"I stopped everything I was doing and just got out a piece of paper and started writing everything down."

"Go on."

"When I had all the facts in front of me, I took out more paper and separated everything into three categories. The first category was what I considered to be vital information. I later discovered it wasn't *all* vital, but that was how I started.

"The second was important stuff, but not necessarily vital. It was information that was maybe vital, but I wasn't sure.

"The last category was what I considered unimportant details—information I didn't want to throw away, but didn't seem pertinent at the time. If you'll remember, the last page also helped me solve two other cases. So I was glad I didn't throw it away."

"Now you're thinking like the cop I remember." Jill smiled. "You already know everything you need to solve this. And what you don't know, you know how to get."

I didn't know what to say. Am I the luckiest guy in the world or what?

I was about to lean in and give her a kiss, but she held up her hand to stop me.

"Get out of here and fix this mess you got yourself into. And, just so we're clear, if you think I'm going to sit around here and pine for your ass while you're in prison, you're out of your friggin mind. I'll go out and find myself a new man in a heartbeat. He'll be clean cut and have a bigger dick than you. So if you want to snuggle up with this," she said, running her hands over her body, "then you better make sure you get busy and solve this thing."

She had the meanest look I've ever seen on her face.

"He may be cleaner than me, but be won't be bigger," I said.

It was too much for her and she started laughing. The laughter turned to hysterical laughter and then the tears started flowing. She ran to my arms and held me like never before.

After a long time she spoke, in almost a whisper. "You fix this, Adam Shaw. Don't you dare tell me again you can't fix this. I love you and believe in you. Don't come back until you can tell me it's done."

~ * ~

On more than one occasion Lu-Lu Belle was a lifesaver. She's a big old bike. She leaks oil like all the old bikes do, but gives me a fresh perspective on everything. Today was no different. I was taking my conversation with Jill to heart and started breaking everything down in my mind. I figured when I got to Manny's office I would do the same thing on paper. However, when Jill and Lu-Lu Belle work together on me, miracles happened.

I was less than a block from Manny's office when Lu-Lu Belle turned right instead of left. She sometimes has a mind of her own. I found myself heading towards the office of one Deputy Chief of Police, Howard Young. I knew he'd been doing some secret researching for me. Now was the time to see if anything had paid off.

"Hello, Samson," he said, as I entered. "I wasn't expecting to see you for a while. What's up?"

"If you mean besides my blood pressure, a lot's up. Seems I am now under investigation by IAD. You mind telling me why you didn't let me know about it?"

"I wasn't informed until about ten minutes ago myself. And even then I only found out by accident. I overheard the chief talking to someone. He wasn't going to say anything to me 'til I asked straight out what was going on. I still can't believe it. You taking money from the mob just don't seem like something I would expect of you."

"Because I didn't, dammit," I yelled. "I'm being set up."

"Thank God," he said, as if my telling him that made it all go away.

"What did he tell you?" He looked completely distracted to the question's meaning. "About the IAD investigation?"

"Oh," he said. "The chief said that some incriminating evidence was turned over to them that would prove you took money to kill the girl in the pool hall. I told him I didn't believe it, but he said the information seemed credible. What was I supposed to do?"

"So now they're saying that *I'm* the one who killed the girl instead of Sam Reynolds?"

"That seems to be the case. I'm still not sure what the information is, but the chief seemed pretty sure."

"I'm sure he does," I said, more to myself than the deputy chief.

"What I don't get," he continued, as if pondering out loud, "is how you could be in two places at once? I know you're good, but I didn't think even *you* could do that."

"What do you mean?" I asked, not sure where the conversation was going.

"I mean, how could you be home with your wife *and* in Monterey killing the girl at the same time? You don't happen to have special powers you haven't told me about, do you?"

"How could you know where I was at the time of the killing?"

The man hesitated and seemed ashamed to answer. Then he looked at me.

"Because I was having you followed. *I'm sorry.* I was being greedy. I thought if I could get something on you that proved you *were* seedy *and* get you kicked off the force, it would go a long way when it came time for my next promotion. Nobody knows about it except the two officers and myself. Not even the chief knows about it."

"So who have you told?"

My hopes were running high—that more people knew.

"I haven't told anyone. If the chief knew, he would have my ass. This was a sorta-off-the-books kinda thing. I'm sorry, Samson. I thought you were a bad guy when this all got started. I know better now, but maybe it's too late. Please don't be mad at me. You know things that could get me in a lot of trouble."

"First, I'm not mad at you, and I would never use what I know against you. That's not how I work. Second, I don't want you telling anyone about what you know. I want you to make sure that the officers you had following me don't say anything either. For now, let 'em think what they have on me is good information. We'll keep it as a surprise if we need it."

"I really don't want the chief to find out what I did."

"I'll try to figure out another way. But if we have to use it to keep me out of jail, then I'll have to call on you. Is that something you can agree to?"

"Of course," Young agreed. "I wouldn't try saving my own ass if it meant you going to jail. I would really appreciate you finding that other way, though. And for the record, I won't say anything to anyone until I hear from you."

~ * ~

After leaving the deputy chief's office, I called Manny for a progress report. It seemed Lady Shadows was better at her job than I expected. Billy boy was singing his heart out to her and anyone else who would listen. It was also good that Manny had the foresight to record everything the kid said. He gave us more information on his grandfather than we really wanted to know. However, I decided the information was a good thing when it came to some of the less scrupulous characters out there. I thanked him and asked if Margie was still hanging around. I needed her help and told him I was going to come by and pick her up. She was waiting for me when I arrived.

"Damn, I was hoping for another miniskirt."

She was wearing jeans and another conversation about her koochie seemed moot.

"You had your chance yesterday," Margie smiled. "Any more peeks into that territory will cost you."

"You sure know how to make a guy feel bad." I hung my head in mock embarrassment. "And if I—"

She cut me off.

"You're a nice guy, Samson. I like you a lot. You're funny and smart. I don't see that in guys very often. And if I weren't a lesbian, I would probably make a play for you. However, I *am* a lesbian and you're married. My koochie is only viewable under the most extreme circumstances. Maybe one of these days, you'll get lucky again. In the meantime, maybe I'll invite you to watch my lover and me. How does that sound?"

"Dear Lord," I said shaking my head, "You hate me. You want to kill me!"

At that we both laughed and she got on Lu-Lu Belle.

"Where're we going?" she asked, as she put on her helmet.

"We're going to visit old man Sheffield. It seems we have a lot in common. He's up to his neck in crap, but from what we've heard here, I think he may be getting played just like I am. I wonder just how much he realizes that?"

~ * ~

Pebble Beach is always a good ride on a motorcycle. It's scenic and everyone is required to drive slow and easy, ideal conditions for bike riding. However, this wasn't exactly a pleasure cruise and my visit would more than likely piss off the old man, AKA the mob guy. However, my friend was still in jail and, I suspected, not very long from being some guy named Brutus's new plaything. Barring that outcome, I'm sure Brutus would think me a suitable replacement. So with all due respect for the inmates of San Quentin or wherever Brutus resided, I liked my butt exactly the way it is, if you don't mind.

Old man Sheffield did not have a smile on his face when we entered. This time there were no kind remarks or gambits to saunter through. He came right to the point.

"Where's my son, you son of a bitch?" The veins were already sticking out from his neck.

"You need to take something to calm yourself, Mr. Sheffield," I grazed the attack with a thin smile. "At this pace, you'll have a stroke and neither of us will get what we want."

"Fuck you." His reply was quick. "I asked you a question and I expect an answer. Now!"

"You know, my superiors have the same problem with stress," I smirked. "The chief's solution was to get an aquarium. It seems the little fish swimming around have a calming effect. You should try it sometime."

The old guy seemed about to yell again, but apparently thought better of it. Instead, he walked back to his office. He didn't ask, but we followed anyway.

"What do you want?" he requested, calmly now. "I know you're holding my son hostage. What's it going to take to get him back?"

That was the second time the question was asked—both times about his son.

"You mean your son-in-law? Or your grandson? I get the family dynamics here mixed up sometimes."

"My son-in-law is family. He's my son now as far as I'm concerned and I want him back. So let me repeat, what do you want?"

"And here I thought you had disinherited the guy. Has that changed?"

"Things have changed, Mr. Shaw...family things that are none of your business. Now get to the point...if you don't mind."

"I want a couple things," I replied calmly, trying to get a better understanding. "The first is the answer to a simple question. Why do you think we are holding your son hostage?"

"Don't be coy with me, Mr. Shaw," the old man was getting agitated again. "You know damn well why."

"Actually, I don't. I'm holding your grandson under lock and key. I've never met your used-to-be son-in-law, now 'son.' So either you're really getting more senile than I originally thought, or you have a bigger problem than either of us knows. Which is it?"

"You don't have my son?" Reaching into the center drawer of the massive desk, he pulled out a large manila envelope. "Then what do you call this?"

I opened the package and pulled out the contents. They consisted of a ring, a piece of silk cloth and a note.

"If you want to save your son's life, you'll make sure Detective Adam Shaw's friend gets released from jail. You have 24 hours to get it done. After that, you'll start receiving body parts every six hours."

I read the note wondering who might have sent it. I was coming up blank.

"You think we sent you that note?" Margie asked, coming to my rescue and giving me time to think for a moment.

"Who else would have sent it?" he asked, incredulously. "It even mentions your name." He looked directly at me.

Margie was not to be deterred. "If Samson wanted the man released, he would have said to get Sam Reynolds out of jail, not Detective Shaw's friend."

I was proud of Margie for standing up to the old man.

"On the other hand," Sheffield countered, "it was the perfect way to get his point across and to let me know who I was dealing with, not to mention the sleight of hand to maybe throw me off."

Margie looked at me as if to ask for help. "He's got a point, you know?" She then shrugged her shoulders.

The old man could hardly contain the smile. As far as he was concerned, the battle was won.

"Give me my son," he said. "Do that and I'll let you both live. Otherwise, your deaths will not be quick and I can assure you that they will be painful."

The conversation was going downhill. The two gorillas who stepped inside the doorway just added to the feeling. It seemed that everyone was after my ass in one way or another.

And yes, I understood the implication about the deaths being plural. It wasn't just my ass on the line. I had to take a stand, and hoped the leverage I had was enough.

I looked and Margie and said, "Thanks. It's too bad the voice of reason fell on deaf ears."

She mouthed, "I'm sorry," in return.

I turned back to face the old man. "Before you go killing us off, maybe you would be interested in what your grandson had to say." I decided to go for broke.

"He wouldn't talk to you," Sheffield said, although he seemed a little uncertain. "Even if he did, it would only be hearsay."

"You seem sure of that," I replied. "Then the recordings he gave us about certain events will probably not mean anything, either." I knew it was a bluff. The kid had mentioned recordings and hopefully we'd get them, but for now, I had to do something.

"What recordings? I don't know anything about recordings."

"Well, it seems your grandson wasn't all that confident that you or others in your little organization were as trustworthy as he had hoped. So, unbeknownst to you or any of the goons you call your security men, little Billy recorded conversations about some of your—how should I say—less than legal activities. Seems he wanted to make sure he could grow up and get his Social Security benefits. Not that they'll mean a lot to him by then, but you have to give the kid kudos for the effort."

"I don't believe you," the old man grunted. "He wouldn't do that. He's family."

"Then I guess you need to work more on *your* retirement package," Margie said smiling. "Families just aren't what they used to be."

"Now *she* has a point," I followed up.

The room was silent as the old man thought about what we had laid before him. I guessed that he wasn't sure if we were telling the truth, but couldn't risk taking the chance. His son was still missing and now his grandson had apparently turned on him. I'm sure he didn't know what to do.

"Look," I said. "For now you'll have to take my word on this. You grandson is talking to me and a few friends, but I don't have your son."

"Then, Detective, what are you doing here? I thought you came to ask for ransom. I thought you were using him as leverage to get your friend out of jail. If you don't have him, then there's no reason for me to negotiate with you."

"Actually, there is, if you consider the information I have on you. But that's not why I'm here. It's true, I want to get my friend out of jail *and* will do whatever it takes to do that. That is, assuming he's innocent, which I believe he is. However, I have a theory as to what actually happened. I also think I know who has your son *and* who's actually responsible for killing Bobbi Marshal at the pool hall. If you're willing to work with me and help me prove what really happened, I'll find your son. We can both get what we want."

"What about the tapes?" he asked. "If I agree to what you're asking, you're still a cop and that puts me at a severe disadvantage."

"I tell you what, if we get through this and everything goes the way I hope, I'll give the tapes back to your grandson. It seems to me he's the one who has to explain that part to you. We'll both consider the information a rumor and I'll look elsewhere to catch you and put your ass in jail. That's the best I can do. You'll have thirty days to make whatever changes to your operation you need so I don't have any advantages. So, Mr. Sheffield, what do you say?"

The old man wasn't happy about the proposal. However, I got the sense that he liked me for the first time. Thinking about it later, I think I was the first person willing to stand up to the old guy in a very long time.

"You drive a hard bargain, Mr. Shaw. I've discovered over the years that there are times in every man's life when he has to trust someone. I've done some very deep checking on you, Detective, and if there's one thing that comes up as often as your being a hard ass, it's that you are a man of your word. I'll take a chance with you. If this works, we'll both owe nothing to the other. If it doesn't or if you go back on your word, then we'll have a problem your badge can't fix."

We left a half hour later with a good understanding of what needed to be done. It would take help, timing and a lot of luck to make it work, but for the first time in days, I felt good about keeping my ass virginal.

Nineteen

The phone call I'd been dreading came sooner than I had hoped.

"Samson."

It was Dakota Walker, my friend and the Assistant District Attorney.

"I need you to come down here. We need to talk about some things."

"Hello, Dakota." I was using my happy voice. "What is it I can do for you?"

"You can come down here so we can talk," she repeated. "Some things have come up on the Reynolds case that we need to clear up."

"Well, let's clear them up right now. I have about ten minutes before my battery runs out. Then it may be a while before I can get it charged again."

"Damn it, Samson, this is serious. You need to come down here right now. Whatever you're doing is just going to have to wait."

"Sorry, sweetheart, I can't do that. I'm out of the area," I lied, "and I don't know when I'll be back. Speak now or forever…"

"You're in trouble, Samson," she interrupted. "I need you to help me clear this up."

"What kind of trouble?"

There was a hesitation on the other end of the line.

"I can't say right now. I can only tell you that it's an order from the top."

"From the top? What the hell does that mean, Dakota? I thought we were friends."

"We are friends, Samson." Her voice softened. "I don't have many choices here."

She was upset and I knew she was torn. Unfortunately, I didn't have the luxury of being able to solve a crime, not to mention trying to keep my ass out of jail, by playing nice. She would always do what the law required. That was the great thing about Dakota. She was predictable.

"I know we're friends," I said, deciding to lighten up a bit. "I swear that when the time comes and I do come in to talk, I'll make sure your bosses know that you did your best to bring me in."

"I don't care about that." Her voice was getting louder. "I want you to come in so I can understand what's going on."

"Dakota," I said. "What's going on is way above your pay grade. I am being set up and I'm not going down without a fight."

"So you know?"

"Of course I know. Why do you think they had *you* make the call? They knew if for some reason I got wind of what was happening, their *only* chance of me cooperating would have to come from you. So let me bring you up to speed.

"I'm being framed. There are some pretty smart bad guys out there who have decided that the best way to make everything go away is to let Sam go and transfer the blame to me. They've gone so far as to create proof that I was involved in the killing of Bobbi

Marshall. Of course, I haven't actually seen the proof, so I can't even refute it yet. However, whatever they've concocted must be really good for you to buy into it as even a remote possibility."

I was waiting for her to say something, but she kept quiet.

"I need time, Dakota. I know you're bound by your ethics. I know you have to protect your career and whatever else you believe to be important. But right now, as far as I'm concerned, it's me against them. I'm not going to ask for your help. I won't put you in that position. But should you be inclined, I'll accept it gratefully. What I won't do is go down gracefully for something I didn't do and let some greedy asshole commit murder and get away with it.

"So here's the way it's going to go down. If you want to help, contact Manny and let him know what you know. In the meantime, I have things I've got to do. I'm going to get the proof I need to put the real culprit, or culprits, behind bars. Whatever you decide, I love you anyway."

I hung up the phone, shut it down and took out the battery. I couldn't afford taking the chance of getting traced. Even little burgs like Monterey have access to GPS capabilities.

After that, I found one of the few remaining payphones in the city. I called Manny to let him know our time was up. The warrant had been issued and I was now a wanted man. I had to go underground. We agreed to meet at a safe place and set our plan in motion. It was time this mess got back under our control.

I had one more phone call to make. I had to let Jill know what was going on and that I would be out of contact for a while.

Her response was simple. "That's okay. I'm just putting together an ad for the personals section in the paper. I figured I might as well keep my options open if things don't go so well."

Leave it to her to try saying things to cheer me up. I don't think she knew I heard her sobbing before she actually hung up the receiver.

~ * ~

I decided to drop Margie off a couple blocks away from Manny's office. I took Margie's cell phone because I didn't trust mine and hadn't yet had time to buy a burner. Margie could get a temporary one from Manny when she got to the office. There were plans to finish and things to do that would take a few hours. The more interruptions I had to deal with, the longer it would take.

Of course, Tootie was a major contributor to the perfection of Murphy's Law.

"Yes, Tootie." Was my response when I saw his name come up on Margie's caller ID.

"I thought I'd catch you with that cute lezzie. You didn't answer your phone so I thought I would take a chance with hers. You busy?" he said, as if the world revolved around his desires. The man had no boundaries. Nor did he have a sense of decorum. He was old, crazy and a little brash, but that was Tootie. He meant nothing bad about the lezzie comment. He had no prejudices, either. In his mind, he figured that if a person identified herself a certain way, then he would be rude to address her in any other way. I'm not sure if I agree, but you've got to give him his dues.

"A little. The battery on my phone died," I replied.

"Well, I need you to do something for me. It's pretty important."

"What's going on, Tootie?"

Someone else answered. "He's got a gun pointed at his head and won't make it through the night if you don't do what I tell you," the new voice explained. It wasn't one I recognized, but the caller certainly seemed serious enough.

"Let me get this straight," I said. "You want me to risk my life in order to save his?"

I started laughing at the absurdity of the request.

"That man has been nothing but a pain in my ass since I first met him. How much would I have to pay you to go ahead and shoot the SOB?"

"That's not a nice thing to say, Detective. Frankly, I'm surprised that you would care so little about your wife's father."

Damn it, I thought to myself. He would have to play the wife card.

"So what exactly do you want me to do for you?"

"You have something that belongs to me and I want it back," the voice said. "We'll make a trade. Your father-in-law for the item."

"Okaaay," I replied, more confused than ever. "What is the item I'm supposed to have?"

"You know damn well what item...the *list*," he said. "I want the list back. You have two hours to get it to me. Otherwise, the old man dies."

I had no idea what he was talking about. I could only imagine what the list was about. I didn't have any list, so I had to assume that dear old Tootie took something that didn't belong to him and now was *well* over his head. I had no idea what it was, where it was, or how to find it.

Thanks, Tootie. I can always count on you.

"I can't do that." I tried to get back a little control. "I don't have it on me and I'll need at least six hours to go get it and get back in the area. If you can't give me that much time, you might as well shoot him now and save me the trip.

"I have other things to do that are important, so I don't want to waste the time on a wild goose chase."

There was a long pause on the other end and then, finally, "Okay. You have six hours. After that, I'll blow the bastard's brains out."

"So where do you want to make the exchange?" This seemed like amateur hour. If I was going to kidnap someone, I would have at least disguised my voice.

"I'll call you back and we'll set it up then. Don't be late."

The phone went dead and I was left contemplating what the hell to do with this new item on my agenda.

But I figured that if the guy wanted to babysit my father-in-law for a few hours, at least Tootie couldn't get into any more trouble.

I know that's a little callous of me, but what the hell? I called Manny and told him what he needed to do to get some information for me. I followed with a code that told him we needed to meet again. It was time for us to get the ball rolling.

I couldn't afford any more distractions.

~ * ~

I gave myself an hour before meeting Manny. I needed some think time and my stomach felt like it was playing with my spine—I needed food. I still needed to make that assessment of what I had and knew as facts. I also needed to figure out who I could trust and who I might use for the cause. We didn't have much time left. I couldn't afford any mistakes.

I knew Carl Ramos was dirty, but I didn't know if Bennett knew the scum he was working with. I couldn't risk working with Bennett. Another issue of concern was who else in the department was dirty. Was Ramos the top dog of the police group or was he just another pawn—hired muscle? My gut told me he was arrogant enough to be one of the guns, but I didn't think he was the top cop of the bad guys.

As far as I was concerned, Manny was above reproach. If he wasn't, I was totally fucked. I also believed Margie was one of the good guys, but since I didn't know much about her, I first put her on the maybe list, then, after reconsidering, I concluded that she was trustworthy and moved her back to the "A" list. I was more concerned about how she would be under pressure and would she be able to do the dirty stuff if I needed her.

IAD officer Faye Wesley and Deputy Police Chief Howard Young were both okay, but I couldn't depend on them to go out of their way to help me. I believed they'd both do the right things when the time came, but as far as bending any rules to help, I couldn't count on them. The problem with bad guys is they don't play by the rules like cops do. That gives them a lot more latitude.

I had a few friends, cops and retired cops, whom I knew I could count on as back up. I'd have to take a chance on their support. What I didn't know was how well they could play together with old man Sheffield and his merry band of gangsters. It might not go very well, but I had to risk it.

There was something else, which had been bothering me from the beginning.

Why was the girl killed? Why that *particular* girl? Was there something special about her or could it have been anybody? I was beginning to believe she was the missing piece. Call it a hunch, but there was something special about Bobbi Marshall and I needed to find out what it was.

Margie's phone rang again and I thought seriously about not answering. However, the caller ID said "FBI Task Force." That got my attention.

"Detective Shaw." There was that anonymous female voice again. "Don't let the caller ID alarm you. It's just one of many I use to get someone's attention."

"It seems to work. It certainly got mine."

"Good," she replied. "I see you've made great strides in both solving the case and getting yourself caught in the crossfire. I would hope you don't plan on spending the rest of your life in jail. That would be a shame."

"Not to mention my dislike for jailhouse sex options." I felt the grin she must have been developing with that remark.

"That *would* be a shame. However, your sexual orientations are not much of a concern to me. So if you don't mind, let's focus on the problem at hand."

"Which problem are you most interested in?" I asked. "The one where my friend has been framed for murder? Or, the fact that some dirty cops are now doing their best to transfer the blame to me? Or...how about a mob boss who's decided he wants to be my good friend as long as I can find his son? Otherwise, he wants to fit me with cement boots. Oh, I know that sounds a little clichéd, but at the moment I don't really give a damn. Or finally, maybe your concern is about how my father-in-law has been kidnapped and I've been given a mere few hours to find some list I don't know about before they kill him. Tell me, Mystery Lady, which problem do *you* want to focus on? After all, it's all about what *you* want, right?"

"My, my," she said. "We are a little testy right now, aren't we?"

"Unless you have solutions to these little issues or the cure for cancer, this conversation is over."

I didn't have time for her right now and I sure as hell didn't want to play games.

"I see your point, Detective." There was a change in her voice that was slight, but gave me hope that something good might come next. "I do have a few bits of information that could be of assistance. I know you're going to meet Manny Black in a few minutes. You'll want to take a detour before you get together with him. Go to the Pebble Beach Post Office and ask the teller to give you a special delivery for Sammy Sosa—for the record, I like baseball. Inside the package you'll find some items that'll help you and Mr. Black get things rolling. Also, there's a cell phone in the package that will be your way to contact me over the next twenty-four hours. If you don't have things resolved by then, it'll be too late. So don't delay."

"Is that it?"

I wasn't sure if she could hear the sarcasm in my reply.

"Just one more thing, Detective. Be careful. Not everyone is who they seem. You have friends you don't know and enemies you consider friends. This is your battle and it's a fight to the death. I don't mean to appear melodramatic, but there's truth in my words."

She didn't wait for me to respond and that was a good thing. I didn't want her to hear the chills she was giving me. I knew I had to get rolling in order to get the secret package and hook up with Manny. I had a feeling that the next twenty-four hours were going to change my life forever.

Twenty

Manny seemed concerned that I was running late, but the package had information we needed. It seems our government friend was indeed a friend. She included detailed information about the Sheffield family for three generations. It also included information about Carl Ramos that included bank statements proving he'd been making deposits at regular intervals far in excess of his pay grade. I now had the information I needed to get rid of that dirt bag once and for all. It brought a smile to my face.

The problem I had was there wasn't anything included that helped me get Sam out of jail—or kept me from going.

If I freed myself from prosecution, everything would fall back on to Sam. And if I moved too fast with the information I'd just received, the only thing that would change would be getting Ramos put away. It wouldn't save Sam. The case was already in the DA's hands and they were moving too fast. Or maybe I was moving too slow.

"So what are we going to do with this?" I asked Manny. I was trying to get a different perspective because frankly, once again, I was running out of ideas.

"We take down the bastard," Manny replied, referring to Ramos.

You had to give it to Manny. He didn't necessarily see the big picture all the time, but he sure as hell liked getting things done.

"I like that idea myself," I said to my friend. "I want nothing more than putting that son of a bitch away for life. We just need to think bigger than that."

"Like what?"

"Like finding out who *really* killed Bobbi Marshall. I know that isn't all that important to you. You have an agenda of helping me get Sam out of jail and I know that's all you signed up for."

I saw Manny's look of frustration. I held up my hand to stop him from speaking.

"Hang on a sec. Let me ask you something. Do you really think Ramos is the brains behind all that's been going on?"

"That stupid ass couldn't connect a three-piece jigsaw puzzle. I have a dead spider collection with more brains than he has."

"Oh man, that's gross," I said, pretending disgust. "The point is, if he isn't the brains, who is? He has to be getting his lead from somewhere. And if you think about it, at least from our inner circle—cop land—the list is pretty small."

"Why stick to just the inner circle? Old man Sheffield could be the one pulling the strings. He certainly has the means, motive and, if I'm not mistaken, the opportunity."

"I thought the same thing. He wants his grandson to be a big wig politician. He owns half of Monterey County. And if he thought someone was trying to take away something he wanted, he could and would do something about it. But after talking to him, I don't think he's involved. At least I don't think he's behind what happened here. I wouldn't trust the man as far as I could throw him. However, he doesn't have any reason to lie about his son being kidnapped. I think he's being played just like we are. Someone else is pulling the strings and I think it's someone inside the house."

"I hear ya, man." Manny was shaking his head. "But with everything you've said, it still doesn't have to be controlled from inside. There could still be someone else."

I was getting pretty frustrated.

"We don't have time for it to be someone else," I shouted, more at myself than at him. "If the puppet master is outside the loop, it will be too late for us to find him in time to save Sam. And that's not an option."

"So that's the problem," Manny stated, as if just now understanding my predicament. "You could go in right now, save your ass and put away Ramos. You could go home to your wife and have great sex. You could probably get off suspension, after all is said and done. Your problem, if I'm getting it, is that you need to save Sam because he got mixed up in some shit of his own making.

"He's the one who pushed the envelope and tried bribing Junior Sheffield. Why do you need to risk getting blown up, shot at, and even imprisoned because of *his* greed?" Manny was more emotional at that moment than I could ever remember.

"What's really bothering you?" I asked.

I knew something was eating at him.

"What's bothering me? I'll tell you what's bothering me. You're bothering me. We've known each other for what...I don't know how many years. You've always been the smart one. I may be better looking, but you always got the girls. People love and respect you and frankly I know more than one person who'd be willing to take a bullet for you. And *that's* the problem."

I was totally confused and had no idea where this was coming from or where it was going.

"Have you been drinking? What the hell're you talking about?"

"What I'm talking about is you could stop anytime you wanted and no one would blame you if Sam went to prison. He fucked up somewhere along the way to put himself in this position. Maybe he didn't kill the girl. Maybe he was just at the wrong place at the wrong time. But bad shit happens to good people, and I'm not even going to put Sam on that list. What I'm trying to say is that you aren't responsible for saving the world. You figured out information that can take down a bad cop. That alone should be enough to get you through the day. But you have to risk your life fixing everyone else's problems. You have to risk dying."

Manny stopped. It was as if he had run out of steam. His head dropped and he turned his back to me.

"Look, Manny, I'm still not sure what you are trying to say. I'm a cop. I may be suspended for the moment, but I'm still a cop inside. It's my responsibility to right wrongs. It's my duty to help people who can't help themselves. You've never had a problem with that before. Why's it bothering you now?"

Manny turned around and looked directly into my eyes.

"Do you know how many people could be hurt if something bad happened to you? Or should I say killed?"

"Well, ya—me, for starters. As for the rest, they would just have to lean on their other friends."

"And that brings me to my problem with all of this," Manny said, as if I should already get it. I guess I'm not as smart as I think sometimes.

After a full minute of silence, I threw my hands in the air and yelled, "What? I still don't understand."

"*I don't have any other friends!*" he yelled back.

I guess that falls into the chronicles of the worst male bonding experience in history. Of course he has other friends, but I get where he's coming from. We have a history. We've seen the worst in each other and that is something that trust is built on. I got it.

This guy I've known for so many years was actually showing emotions and I was shocked by the outburst. Is this what male menopause was going to be like for me? Manny is a few years older than I am. Was I going to blubber with emotional outbursts when I reached his age?

Shoot me now, please.

I was about to touch his shoulder. I thought maybe the guy could use a hug or something. Maybe he should take some testosterone pills. I don't know.

"Get the fuck away from me," he said, before my hand touched his shoulder.

"Hey, I'm just tryin' to give you a hug."

"You touch me and I'll shoot you myself. You may be the only friend I have, but I'll shoot you as sure as I'm standing here if you ever tell anyone about this."

"Hell's bells." I grinned. "I can assure you I won't tell a soul. But just to be clear, I don't think I'll *ever* get those pitiful blue eyes out of my mind."

Manny thought about that last comment and swung his big fist right at my head. Thank God I was expecting it. I ducked just in the nick of time and almost fell over laughing my ass off as he stumbled then tried to catch himself.

I finally got control of the laughter and Manny calmed down.

"Call Ramos," I said to Manny. "I think it's time we had a personal visit with the slime ball. Set it up and make sure he knows that, for his own sake, our conversation should be discreet. He has a lot to lose if he tries something stupid."

~ * ~

"So where the hell is he?" I heard Ramos demand of Manny when he arrived at the designated meeting place.

I figured the best defense, under these circumstances, was to create a good offense. The location needed to be open enough to see if anyone else was around, yet with enough places to hide if I needed to make a hasty retreat. If Ramos was stupid enough to try something against everyone's best interest, I wanted to be prepared.

The eighth green at Pebble Beach was as good a place as any. It had plenty of cover nearby, but would take the invisible man to get to the tee without being seen. That's where we were to meet. However, Ramos met Manny at the clubhouse and together they would take a cart to the destination. I got to the clubhouse a few minutes before they did. For precautions, Manny would sweep Ramos for bugs and tracking devices.

Manny's phone rang and he answered in a professional voice, "Yes. He's alone. I understand."

I already had the information because I was less than twenty yards away, secluded behind a sign and pillar. We kept the conversation short so tracking would be impossible from cell tower triangulation and it was also a signal to Manny that I was leaving from my hiding place at the clubhouse and he would stop midway to the green to do the necessary electronic checking. That would be a more than adequate amount of time to get set up and hidden.

I enjoyed the sight of the two as they approached because Manny had instructed Ramos to place a pair of welder's goggles over his eyes. It made him look like Stevie Wonder's golfing instructor.

Ramos was swearing by the time they arrived. I made sure no one was following as they drove past me.

Everything was fine.

"You look dashing, Ramos," I said, before I let him remove the glasses. "I never realized how dapper of a guy you were. Maybe, if the warden lets you keep the glasses, you'll attract some really friendly inmates to keep you company."

Ramos snatched off the glasses and tried looking at me. The only thing that saved him was that it was a typical Pebble Beach day—the clouds were thick and the sun couldn't blind him as much as I would have liked.

"I don't know what you're up to, Shaw," Ramos barked, "but you're under arrest. You have the right..."

"Oh, shut up," I said with not nearly as much disgust as I felt. "Right now you're in no position to arrest me, or anyone else, for that matter. As a matter of fact, you're in a really bad situation and it's totally up to me just how bad I want to make it for you, you son of a bitch."

"I'm a police officer, at least," he tried, seeming confused about what I was referring to. The poor guy seemed to think that taking an aggressive approach was better than doing nothing. "You, on the other hand, have no authority to do anything but follow my orders."

Manny and I nearly lost it with that comment. However, I decided not to waste any more time and handed him an envelope with much of the information I had acquired from my mysterious friend.

Ramos took the envelope cautiously and looked at the contents. It came to me completely by surprise that a person of Hispanic ancestry could turn that shade of mottled gray in such a short period of time.

"As you can see," I began, "you have a lot to explain to people a lot more powerful than myself. So please don't worry about my lowly status. Now, by the looks of what you're holding, you are *definitely* going to jail. I would say that's a shame, but in your case, it's happening much later than it should have."

"So what do you want?" he asked. I was surprised he didn't try to deny the evidence. Instead he was looking for a way out. "You looking to get in on the action or what?"

The arrogant prick was trying to bribe me. I wanted to hit him and I guess Manny sensed it, too, because he grabbed my arm and squeezed it tightly.

"Oh, I want something," I said, looking him square in the eyes. "I want it all. I want all the money you took for the bribes and payoffs. I want the names, dates and places for everything you were involved in. I want to know who's pulling your strings and how your little group does things. I want old man Sheffield's son returned. But most of all, I want you to eat shit and die."

I wanted to wait for a response from the prick, but kept going.

"You tried to kill me, you son of a bitch. You almost killed my father-in-law. You planted a fuckin' bomb on my bike and then you had the nerve to try getting me put in jail for the shit you were doing."

"It wasn't personal," he said, as if that would somehow ease my agitation.

"Wasn't personal? How the fuck can you say it wasn't personal? You tried taking everything away from me that I cared about. That's not personal? Then what the fuck is it?"

"It was a job," he said, shrugging his shoulders. "Granted, I don't really like you very much. And to be honest, I did get a perverse sense of pleasure out of knowing you were going to go down. But if the target would have been someone else, it wouldn't have made any difference."

"So you admit the orders did come from someone else?"

"Of course," he said, as if he had just agreed to play tennis. "I don't decide who gets what. I have my orders and I follow 'em. It's as simple as that."

"So who do you get your orders from?" Manny asked.

Hell, I'd almost forgotten the big lug was still there.

"Can't tell ya," Ramos shrugged.

"Can't or won't?" I followed.

"Can't," he stated flatly. "I don't know who he is. That's not how it works."

"Then how does it work?"

I was really getting frustrated with the way the conversation was going. I was getting the distinct impression we were slowly coming to an impasse that would lead us nowhere.

"Look," he said. "I, more than anyone, can truly appreciate what you've managed to put together on me. On the surface it seems like I'm really fucked and somehow you're going to make all of this stick. However, I could confess everything to you that I've done and you could record it on DVD with graphic details.

The problem for you is that none of this will ever go to court. None of this will ever go anywhere."

"Why's that?" I asked.

"Because whoever's pulling the strings will never let it happen. The evidence will somehow disappear, just like you'll disappear. Your families will disappear. And after a few weeks or maybe a couple months, the memory of your existence will disappear. You're so far over your fucking heads you'll have to get on a stepladder just to see the bottom. Now gentlemen, if you'll excuse me, I have reports to file that a wanted fugitive resisted arrest. For the record, Mr. Black, shortly there will be an arrest warrant for you as well for aiding and abetting."

"What?" I said with a smirk of my own. "You think we're done with you? Puulllleeese. That's always been your downfall, Ramos. You never look at the big picture. I said I could decide how much trouble you'd be in if you didn't cooperate. Your assumption was that going to jail would be your worst-case scenario.

"I, on the other hand, can think of many things worse than that. As a matter of fact, I'll do you a favor by giving you one more chance to change your mind and fully cooperate. Otherwise, I'll have no other choice than see to it that your life will change dramatically for the worse."

"Fuck off," was the reply.

Ramos started to walk away. When he saw old man Sheffield standing directly behind him, he quickly turned back to me as if to ask for another chance. I shrugged my shoulders and Ramos' world went black. The stun gun is a very effective tool when it comes to garnishing the cooperation of ...just about anyone.

When Detective Carl Ramos woke up, he would be more than willing to cooperate. Unfortunately, I wouldn't be the one to question him. And I had a feeling I might not ever see the man again.

Everyone has choices in life.

Manny and I left the scenic Pebble Beach golf course. I told him we needed to have a meeting with a few of the "clan." I wanted to get together with him, Dakota Walker, Faye Wesley and Margie. He told me he would make the necessary arrangements and get back to me. I asked him to also invite Deputy Police Chief Howard Young. I wanted someone high up to know what was going on so my ass would be covered if anything went wrong.

The first call came from Manny telling me the meeting had been set up and we were going to meet at Lady Shadow's home. The thought of going back there sent a shiver up my spine. However, this was no time to get squeamish.

The second call came from old man Sheffield himself. He told me he had located his son and that "the boy" was okay. He also let me know the rest of what I had asked of Carl Ramos. The only part we didn't get clear information on was who the puppet master was; he was positive Ramos didn't know. The way he said it told me immediately that it wasn't necessary to ask how sure he was. If Ramos had known, he would have told the old man.

What I did get from the information were the names of Ramos' cohorts. Unfortunately, they were of a lesser stature than Ramos. They were young and just getting their hands dirty. Sheffield didn't have to give me the information, but I think he felt it was best if he cleaned up the old pipeline and start anew. That's the way he made it sound, anyway.

What I actually thought was that he gave me only enough to placate me for the time being and hoped I'd leave the other cronies he has on the payroll alone.

For the moment, I guessed I would.

Ramos, at first, confessed to killing Bobbi Marshall, but the confession wouldn't be enough to free Sam. Apparently, he thought it was better to confess that than to tell what really happened. Eventually, he changed his story and told the old man he didn't do it, but knew it was going to go down. He didn't know who the real killer was and didn't want to know. Either way, the evidence that had been planted was too strong and Ramos would never testify to that fact. He wouldn't be testifying to much of anything anymore.

Sheffield also told me that he would see to it that I had the numbers and passwords to all of Ramos's accounts. I could feel free to do with the funds as I chose.

He finished the conversation by saying, "Your last request of Mr. Ramos was also granted, but you'll have to figure that one out for yourself. Consider it a gift, unnecessary to repay."

I tried to get an explanation, but the phone went dead. Then I remembered what I'd said to Ramos . . . *eat shit and die.*

Twenty-one

Time was running out and I knew it. I wasn't worried any more about going to jail. That problem was pretty much resolved. I had the financial records of Carl Ramos, not to mention our conversation. However, there was still the matter of Sam being in prison. And even though Ramos had confessed, the likelihood of him telling the world, or anyone for that matter, was pretty much out of the question. His confession to me wasn't enough with me being on suspension. It would come across as sour grapes. I needed more.

Tootie was still being held prisoner, for some reason of which I was clueless. Finally, there was the matter of the puppet master. I had no idea who that person was and I was becoming less and less confident that I would find the answer. Without that name, I was afraid Sam would be staying in jail.

With Ramos out of the way, I headed to Lady Shadow's dungeon. This was going to be an interesting meeting.

"What's this all about?" Dakota wanted to know as I walked in the door. "You've got a lot of nerve having this big lummox practically forcing me to come here without any explanation."

The big lummox, I assumed, had to be Manny.

"I'm your friend Adam, and I thought we had a better relationship than this."

"Were you two married in another life?" asked Lady Shadow. "She hasn't stopped complaining since she got here."

I was pleased to see that the platinum beauty had the good sense to dress down for the occasion. I didn't want a lot of questions being asked about the lady and her occupation.

"I don't know who the hell you are," Dakota fumed, "but we've got a warrant out for this man's arrest and he's putting you and everyone else here at risk. So don't get all uppity with me. I still work for the courts and this is not looking very good for any of you."

"Dakota," I said, "shut up for a second, will you? A lot has changed since the last time we spoke. When everyone else arrives, you'll be brought up to speed. I can assure you, no one will have to be arrested tonight for being here." The look she projected was stabbing. "As for our friendship, don't get so high and mighty yourself. I believe it was you who tried to trick me into coming in and getting arrested. Where was the friendship then?"

Dakota looked hurt. Her head dropped and there was pink growing up her neck. She was about to respond when the last of the group arrived—Faye Wesley and Deputy Chief Young.

"Good," I said, "any trouble finding the place?"

I looked directly at the deputy chief and smiled.

With hardly a stutter, the deputy chief said, "No. The directions were good. Thanks."

I made introductions and left out anything that might cause problems down the road. I told them what had occurred during the last two hours, as much as I could, including the new information I'd received from Sheffield the first.

Lastly, I informed the group about Tootie, so they would also know about the time constraints there.

Lady Shadow seemed genuinely concerned for the old fart.

"Don't worry about him," I said. "I'll figure something out about that. Right now I'm hoping that by getting you all together, we can come up with some sort of plan to find the puppet master. Without that person's name, I'm afraid all of this will be for nothing."

"How certain are you of these facts?" Dakota spoke first. "It seems to me that everything you have is either circumstantial or, if not, there's nothing that will save Sam."

"We aren't in a court room," Margie jumped in. "We don't need everything to be in place and perfect to win this battle. We need a direction to go; something that may have been overlooked."

"That's right," I agreed. "We need to know who's pulling the strings at the police station and the courthouse. I know the place is bugged. I know that whoever the puppet master is has a lot of clout and is above reproach. That should narrow down the list, don't you think?"

"Well, the only one who could do anything like that would be the chief of police," the deputy chief stated with a degree of certainty. "He controls everything that goes on in the precinct. I just can't imagine him doing anything that would be illegal, however. He may be a jerk sometimes—you didn't hear that from me—but he sure seems honest. At least he has been in everything I've ever noticed."

"Who pulls his strings?" Manny asked. "Even a police chief has a boss."

"That would be the DA," Dakota said, without batting an eye. "The chief does whatever DA Cromwell says. And if you have these other guys following his lead, then there isn't anything he couldn't do."

I thought about what she'd said and had a light bulb moment. The DA had to be the puppet master. Cromwell had to be the one pulling the strings. He had all the clout necessary to make it work. He had the people in the right places to do whatever he needed done. And most importantly, I believed that if we looked closer at him, we'd find something that would implicate his involvement with the Sheffield organization. He had to be the one.

Now we needed to bring him down so we could get Sam out of jail. I would have to set a trap. I just didn't know how.

As if reading my mind, Manny said, "We could pull a Fast Willie on him."

"What's a Fast Willie?" Margie asked.

"It's a pool hall term used when you want to trick someone into believing one thing while all the time you are doing something else," I replied.

"Like what?" she said, looking for clarity.

"Imagine you and a bunch of guys standing around a pool table. There's a guy—a mark, if you will—that you feel is ripe for the taking. Lay a pool cue across the table and bet the man that you can roll the cueball the length of the table without touching that cue. He knows the stick is too low for the ball to travel under it and takes your bet. You pick up the cue ball, act like you are going to make something brilliant happen, then roll it *under* the table. You win. You take his money. And you piss him off. That's just one example of a Fast Willie. There are dozens of others."

"Isn't that cheating?" Margie asked.

"That's gamesmanship. It's a kind of hustle. It's not cheating."

I had never done a Fast Willie myself. I watched Sam do one a long time ago. It always worked and always really pissed off the mark. It was only used as a desperate measure and these seemed like desperate times.

"Will it work?" Dakota asked, not really understanding what it was we were contemplating.

"It can," I said, "but I'll tell you this right now. What we have in mind falls into the gray area and it won't be something you can be involved with. I can't risk you being a part of it."

"I want to help too, you know," Dakota came back. "I'm in this now."

"Not really," I said. "You're involvement has been on the edge at best. I'm going to need you to separate yourself from where we go now. That way, if we fail, maybe you can plead for a reduced sentence for me if I get caught."

"Or maybe insanity," Manny chimed in.

"What about the rest of us?" asked Faye. "Do we play a part or just sit back and watch from the sideline?"

"You'll have to sit this out, too, I'm afraid, as well as you, Deputy Chief. I can't let anyone involved with law enforcement be a part of this. It would compromise your career and I won't do that to you. When the time comes, you'll know what's happening. Whether I succeed or fail, you'll have your duties to perform. I want you to be there to do them right."

"Then I guess this is where we part company," Dakota stated, dejectedly. "Be careful, Adam. I don't want you getting yourself in any more trouble than you already are."

"You know Samson," Manny smiled. "He's never in trouble. He's a carrier."

~ * ~

Everyone had things to do and we all left Lady Shadows' place to go do our jobs. Taking one last look at the place before I pulled away, I couldn't help but smile when I realized the deputy chief's car was still there. I wondered if there could be something more going on than just business. When you are required to fix things, you have to determine what issues are most important, but you also have to figure out what is most urgent. To me, helping Sam was the most important, but the problem with Tootie was more urgent. And, as is the case with most things in life, the urgent issues get the most attention.

I knew that for me to pull off the Fast Willie, I couldn't have the Tootie debacle hanging over my head. I also needed time to put the pieces in place for the Fast Willie to work. Finally, I decided that the old fool just might be useful. He wouldn't necessarily be a big part, but he could do one thing that could pull plan together.

"You still with Manny?" I asked Margie. Since I wasn't as concerned about getting arrested at the moment, I decided I could give back her phone.

"No," she replied. "He just dropped me off at my place. What's up?"

"I need you to track down the PI Tootie is working with, Ed Lafferty, and meet me at that greasy spoon next to Costco's, the one with the pink and green cactus flashing in the window. Be there in thirty minutes if you can."

"Sure," she said and hung up the phone.

I figured I would go to the hospital to check up on Annie Lee before I met them. Sometimes it's easy to forget about others when you have so many problems of your own.

What I didn't expect was Detective Joseph Bennett dressed in a white lab coat standing next to Annie's bed. I sure as hell didn't expect to see him with a syringe in his hand.

On the other hand, I'm sure he didn't expect to feel of my 9mm pressed against the back of his head.

"I sorta knew you were up to no good, being a partner of Ramos," I said. "I didn't think you were stupid enough to try killing this poor girl."

"You got this all wrong," Bennett started. "This isn't what you think."

"Okay, let me guess. You've been going to Stanford Medical School on your days off? Or maybe they got some kind of new mail-order-doctor-on-duty study program I hadn't heard about? No? I got it. All the doctors here at the hospital were really busy and you volunteered to act as one till their workload eased up a bit. That must be it. Because I *know* that somehow, if I were to have what's in that syringe tested, it probably wouldn't come out as something all that helpful to our little patient here. Now would it?"

"You're not going to stop this, you know," he said, with more confidence than a man with a gun to his head should.

"Why's that? You got something special working for you? Maybe a certain DA we all know and love gonna help you get out of this?"

"Matter of fact, yes," he replied. "Whatever you think you have on me right now will be lost before daylight."

Where do they get these guys?

"You could be right about that. However, for now at least, I don't have anything to lose. If you're as well connected as you seem to believe, then the best I can offer at this time is the fact that I have the gun." I reached inside his white coat and pulled out his Glock.

Then I reached down and took his backup piece. "Now I have yours, too." I also took the syringe. "We need to go for a little ride."

Some people are good, others lucky. Though I believe her to be a good person, today... Annie Lee was lucky.

~ * ~

One of the problems with riding a motorcycle is that when you take down a bad guy, there aren't many places you can put him to keep him out of the way. That was never a problem when I wasn't suspended. I would just call for a black and white and let them take the perp to the station. On the other hand, there weren't many of us bike-riding fools out there and I was pretty sure Bennett wasn't one of them. So with a little smack on the back of his head, he gave me the keys to his car and off we went to the parking garage.

I called the deputy chief and told him what had happened and who I had with me.

"I need you to beef up the protection detail for Annie Lee...right now," I said. "If Bennett disappears from his friends, they may send others before long. We can't have that."

The little man with the funky fetish was really pissed. He told me he would be there in five minutes personally. He also knew a few men he could trust to make sure Annie would make it through the night. At least if she *did* die, it wouldn't be because of undesired extra help.

Detective Bennett was a pretty good-sized man. He was about six-foot one and maybe two-thirty. He was a little out of shape, but I didn't want to take any chances with him trying to run. I bring up his dimensions because a man of that size doesn't fit well in the trunk of an Audi TT—a little sports car designed more for ass in the seats than in the trunk.

I could tell by the way he complained when his head hit the trunk lid that he hadn't checked that part out when he bought the thing. Oh, well—at least it wasn't me.

~ * ~

Of course I was late when I got to the restaurant and knew Margie would bitch me out for it. Maybe down the road she'd figure out that I'm not the most punctual person in the world. On the other hand, if I live through this mess, she'll come to realize that when I am late, I usually have a pretty damn good reason.

"Don't yell at me," I said. I figured I would try a little preemptive strike. My old basketball coach used to tell me, "The best defense is a good offense."

"Why would we yell at you?" Ed Lafferty said. "We've been getting to know each other. I think maybe there's something special going on here."

The smile on his face told me volumes about the fact that he was seriously delusional.

The smile on Margie's face told me I was right.

"You really think so?" I had to ask. "What makes you think that?"

"She's perfect for me," he said, as if Margie wasn't sitting there listening. "She's beautiful. She's intelligent. She's got eyes like pools of deep water. I could go swimming in those eyes."

"She's a lesbian," I said, adding to the conversation.

"Nobody's perfect," he said, without blinking an eye.

"That's what I've been telling him for the last twenty minutes," Margie said. "He doesn't seem to get the idea of what that means."

"Of course I know what it means," Lafferty interjected. "I'm a lesbian, too. A *male* lesbian. It's just another thing we have in common. We both love women."

"Oh, good lord," I said. "You two love birds will have to deal with this later. We have a little problem that needs handling. Now I know why you hired Tootie. You both think alike, *and* you're both nuts."

Lafferty just looked at me as if he were clueless about what I meant.

"Speaking of Tootie," I casually continued. "Any idea why someone would kidnap him, or what list they'd be demanding to get back?"

I looked directly at Lafferty when I asked the questions.

"Can't say I do," he replied. When he lowered his head and looked away, I was pretty sure he was lying.

"You can't, huh? Let me tell you a little something about Tootie Childress. Tootie Childress is the father of one Jill Childress, who is married to one Adam Shaw. That would be me. Jill Childress Shaw, my wife, happens to care very much for Tootie Childress and would be totally pissed off if something bad happened to her old man. As a matter of fact, that little Texas gal happens to be one hell of a sharp shooter—and could slice a man's balls off a lot easier than the bulls she neutered years ago when she worked at the slaughterhouse back in East Texas.

"Now, my problem is this. If I go home and tell her that her daddy was hurt because of something he was working on, something she'll quickly point out she was against to begin with, she'll go ballistic and want to cut off my nuts. Now, Ed, I'm really fond of my balls. So I'll have to tell her that someone else could have prevented that from happening. *You*, Ed, could have prevented that from happening. She'll still be pissed at me, but she'll want to get revenge on the person that got her father hurt, and that would be you. Now you either tell me what's going on or soon you'll be speaking a couple octaves higher—and you'll never get your chance to convince Margie here of the benefits of male lesbianism. Do you understand what I'm saying, Ed?"

"Yeah, I get what you're saying."

His head was still hanging, but I got the sense he was about to come clean.

"I've been working on this fraud case the last couple months. It seems there's a lot of that going around these days and the Covenant Nursing Home was being bled dry. They asked me to look into it, and I discovered they weren't the only ones being ripped off. Matter of fact, there are at least three other places being skimmed and I figured out who was behind it. The problem is, I couldn't get my hands on the evidence myself. Seems men in their forties stand out in a place like that. Tootie however, fit the bill. I thought if he could get that information for me, I could bring down those guys."

"Go on," I said. "This is getting more interesting all the time."

"Well, he *did* get the information, just like I asked him. He placed it where I told him to and that's the last time I've seen him. Honestly. I don't know where he is."

"So where's this information he got for you?" Margie asked. Lafferty looked at her with puppy dog eyes.

"Oh, I still have it," he said. His back went straight and he seemed proud.

"In other words," I said. "You had no intention of going to the police with this information. You figured that with what you had, you could con the cons. You thought there would be a bigger payday if you sold the information back to the ones you stole it from in the first place. No harm, no foul. Only somehow Tootie was discovered, now he's about to be killed, and you forgot to mention to me that it was you they wanted all along."

"I couldn't tell them about me! They'd kill me."

"So you think it's better for them to kill Tootie instead?" Margie asked. "You sniveling little piece of shit."

Margie stood and walked over to Lafferty and smacked his nose with her fist. It wasn't a punch so much as an upper swing that caught him with the side of her fist.

"Tootie is a friend of mine. Jill won't get the chance to cut your nuts off because you won't have any when I get done with you."

She was leaning over and yelling in his ear.

I jumped up and grabbed Margie before she could do any real damage.

Lafferty was holding his nose and cowering from the assault. He was bleeding, but he seemed otherwise all right. The patrons in the restaurant looked at what was going on, but when Margie stopped yelling and the noise quieted down, they turned back to their respective burritos.

"Now you see what I was telling you?" I said to Lafferty, "You don't want to fuck around with women. You think this is bad? Wait till Jill gets ahold of your ass. You're total dog meat."

Though the situation was dire, I was enjoying the fact that someone besides me was getting the blunt of a woman's wrath.

"Okay, okay!" Lafferty yelled. Then he whispered, "Tell me what I can do to make this right. Just don't let her hit me again."

"What we're gonna do is get Tootie out of this mess and not let him get hurt. You got that?"

To say that Margie was upset would be an understatement. Instead of good cop, bad cop, she was playing bad cop and really, really pissed-off cop. I still don't get how Tootie has such an effect on women.

I brought Margie up to date on my cargo and why I was driving a new sports car.

She called Manny.

Twenty-two

There's a fine line between bravery and stupidity.

I've experienced my share of both.

Making a living as a cop, opportunity presents itself where we can make choices that will dictate which direction we'll go and what we'll be known for. I've been fortunate; I haven't been known for making too many bad choices when it comes to surviving a bad situation.

Tootie, on the other hand, is old in years and yet a novice in the ways of the world. It seems that even when confronted with the prospects of death, he believes that good will overcome evil. He believes that good people have some sort of *extra gift* that thwarts the bad and that death will happen when *it* chooses, not when someone dictates it.

For that I can only be thankful...and just a little envious.

The phone rang exactly at the end of the sixth hour. It was now or never, I thought. I could only hope that whoever held the old guy captive would have just the right blend of both intelligence and stupidity.

Smart enough to listen to me, and dumb enough to do the same.

"Do you have it?" the voice said. "Your time is up."

"I have it," I replied, as cool and collected as I could, given that my wife's father's life was on the line.

"Good. Then read me a few lines so I know you're not just bullshitting me."

It seems I got the first part of my request. The man proved to me with that small request he was nobody's fool. If I didn't know what I was talking about, he had no reason to meet with me and, of course, no reason to expose himself.

If I could accomplish what he wanted, then we both had what the other wanted and a legitimate negotiation could happen. Fortunately for Tootie, Ed Lafferty came through with the goods. It was a list of patients at several different nursing homes that, with just a cursory review, were those with substantial amounts of money. They weren't super millionaires, mind you, but their liquid holdings were in excess of half a million each.

There was also a list of people who worked at the homes helping the perpetrators, as well as a few insurance company executives, in the fray.

Finally, and I suspect most importantly, there were lists of numbers that, to me, were what these guys were really after. The names and assets they knew we could copy. Actually we did copy them. However, without knowing what the list numbers represented, just copying them wouldn't help us. The missing piece was the names of those running the show.

We would have to find that information some other way.

~ * ~

After dark, the wharf in Monterey is generally deserted. It's long and about forty feet wide—wide enough for cars and trucks to drive on. That made it difficult for either one of us to hide anyone. At the end of the pier, there were a couple of fishing shacks used by the local fishermen to offload their catch of the day. We were told to bring the papers to that location. They would meet us there. They gave me about fifteen minutes to get there. It was going down fast and all I could do was hope my plan would work.

That's the part where their stupidity would have to come in.

I got to the wharf and couldn't see anyone. It was close to midnight and the streetlights hanging overhead were old and did very little to illuminate the area. I could see all the way to the end, about fifty yards away, but there were too many shadows to know for sure if someone was lurking.

As I walked toward the other end, I couldn't help but think about Jill and how much I'd miss her if I screwed this up and got her father killed. Then it dawned on me... she might miss me too, if I screwed up and got myself killed. Jill is a tough bird, but I know she loves me.

"That's far enough, Mr. Shaw," someone said from the darkness.

I was about fifty feet from the first fishing shed and quite surprised by the metallic click of a cocking gun behind my left ear. I had stayed close to the pier's edge, trying to cut the possible lines of attack by half. I hadn't heard or seen anyone as I walked. Maybe I was in a little deeper than I thought. I figured the man must have been hidden in the shadows of the large pier logs wearing soft-soled deck shoes. The sounds were muffled by the ocean waves. It made me feel better knowing *how* I had been surprised, but considering the gun now pressing against my neck, I didn't feel *that* much better.

"So are you going to be an honorable crook," I asked the man at my ear, "or am I going to have to get really pissed off about this whole thing and take you down the hard way?"

I'm not always the cool composed dude you may think me to be. There are actually times when I would rather be doing something other than risking getting shot in the head or blown to bits. This particular night would long be remembered as one of them.

I was alone and the guy with the gun didn't seem all that concerned about what he would do with my remains after he pulled the trigger. I was still hoping for the bad guy to make that one critical mistake.

"You don't seem to have a lot of leverage, Mr. Shaw," the man said. "Besides, I would just as soon kill you and take the list. Unfortunately for me, I'm not the man who makes those decisions."

"Is that right? You mean there's more than one asshole here? I thought this was supposed to be a friendly exchange."

"It *will* be friendly," the voice at my back replied. "You give us what we want, then we kill you. We'll be very nice about it. How much more friendly do you want it?"

"I was hoping a *little* friendlier. It just doesn't seem right that you get what you want and I don't. What's fair about that? I tell you what, you give me Tootie, I give you the list and we just go our separate ways. Now that's pretty friendly. What do you think about that?"

"He thinks the idea sucks, Samson."

I turned around to see a face I recognized, but couldn't place. I figured he was another of Ramos's bad apples. Then I remembered. He had been associated with Ramos. He wasn't a cop, but I saw him visit Ramos a couple times over the last several years. I hadn't figured him to be in on this little scheme. On the other hand, the way this week was going, I figured anything could happen.

"I was wondering about the cloak-and-dagger stuff," I said. "It seemed a little over the top how you wanted to meet. Now that I know who you are, I can understand why."

"There's an old saying," the new man said. "'Know thy enemies.' I know you, Shaw. I know you're not stupid. I also know you wouldn't jeopardize your wife's father. That's your weakness—your loyalty to family and friends. I knew that would get you out here alone. I wasn't sure if you would remember me or not."

"It's Westbrook, isn't it?"

Lenny Westbrook had tried being a cop, but didn't pass the psych evaluation. I didn't know much about his past other than he and Ramos had been friends as kids. Somehow he managed to stay out of the system. If my guess was right, that had more to do with his friend than his intellect.

"Is that what Ramos taught you? How to be an asshole and fuck over anyone who got in your way?"

He paused for a moment and said, "Yep, that's pretty much it. Speaking of Ramos, where is he? He was supposed to meet us here. He wanted the pleasure of killing you. You wouldn't happen to know his whereabouts, would you?"

"Matter of fact, I heard he decided to do a little farming. I think he's up to his neck in shit."

Now, that would've been really cute, funny even, if Westbrook hadn't slapped me with the barrel of his gun.

"So hand me the list," Westbrook said. "We might as well finish this."

"Where's Tootie? He's the other part of this arrangement. We'll just make the trade and I'll be on my merry way."

"You really are stupid, aren't you?" Westbrook snickered. "Do you really think I'm going to just give you your father-in-law and let you walk away?"

"Wasn't that the deal?" I replied.

He hit me again.

"Give me the goddamn list!" Westbrook was getting agitated. "I don't have time to fuck with you anymore."

"Well, if you're gonna be that way about it, I'm not going to give you the list. You'll just have to get it some other way."

"Don't fuck with me, Shaw. I'll blow your fucking head off."

"I'm not sure I see that as a lot different from what you were planning anyway. Why should you be the only one who makes out here?"

"Because the old man doesn't necessarily have to die. That's why. Now give me the list."

"Damn, Westbrook, you're as much of a whiner as your buddy, Ramos. If you want the list, let me see Tootie. Then you let him go and I'll let you do with me what you want." I pulled an envelope from my jacket and wadded it up. "Otherwise, it goes in the ocean. I'm not sure if you just want the list out of circulation or if you need it for further use. And since I'm still alive, I suspect you need it."

My hand with the envelope was hanging over the rail. Even if he shot me, he would never see it again.

"Go get the old bastard," Westbrook told his counterpart. "I want to get this over with."

There was a pause in the conversation while Tootie was being retrieved. I stepped a little closer to the edge of the pier and looked down into the murky waters. I figured that if this didn't go well, I would soon be down there looking up. That is, if I wasn't dead before I hit the water.

I saw Tootie being led out of the fishing shack. His hands were tied behind his back and there was a rag tied into his mouth. I suspected it was put there in the very earliest part of the kidnapping. The man could be a total pain to listen to.

He didn't seem to be any worse for wear. I was thankful for that much. He came over to me and I removed the gag.

"Hey son-in-law, this has been real interesting. It was probably a couple hours longer than I would have liked. What took you so long? These guys aren't the nicest I ever met. But they aren't any worse than the guy down in Nacogdoches who ran the Skinny Dipper. That's a titty- bar, two blocks off Broadway. Let me tell you they had some fine looking women in that place. Anyway..."

"Tootie, shut up," I said. "These guys aren't playing games here and they sure as hell don't care about a titty-bar somewhere in Texas."

"Nacogdoches ain't just some place in Texas. What are they, homosexuals?"

Tootie acted as if nothing in the world should interrupt him after hours of being gagged. I knew I could count on Tootie getting them riled.

Both men pointed their guns at Tootie. I was close enough that I knocked Westbrook's gun from his hand and it fell harmlessly into the water. The other man saw what I did and moved to shoot me. All of a sudden he started dancing and floundering around like a fish out of water and shrieking like a girl. He hit the wooden pier and kept flopping.

That information was told to me later because I was still a little busy with Westbrook. Fortunately, for me, anyway, that didn't last long either. Sometimes it comes in handy being six inches taller and about fifty pounds heavier than the guy you're fighting with. Two blows to the gut and a couple to the head and the fight was pretty much over.

When I looked at the other man, he was still flopping around as 50,000 volts of electricity ran through his body.

"I was wondering if you were *ever* going to shut up," Manny said as he crawled over the edge of the pier holding the stun gun. "I've been hanging on to that slippery-assed pier-log so long I thought I wasn't going to be there for you when you finally decided to do something."

"Well, you could have gotten my attention somehow so I could see you were there. I thought for sure you were being fashionably late as always."

"You two fight like a coupla old women," Tootie said. "I'm hungry. There anyplace around here open so we can get some grub?"

Manny and I couldn't help but laugh. Tootie Childress was truly a piece of work.

~ * ~

I felt like I was living in the old west doing a round-up. Bad-guys were getting herded like cattle and I needed a place to store them until it was time to bring them all in. After a few calls, an old retired cop-buddy of mine, Benny Goldstein, took them off my hands and freed me to take care of my favorite father-in-law.

It was a pleasure feeding the old geezer. I called Jill and told her everything was fine. She was concerned about not having heard from Tootie so I told her that he was with me and we'd be home soon. She reminded me of what she had last told me: I wasn't to come home until everything was finished.

"I remember," I said. "I was just hoping to take a shower and get a little sleep. The person I need to talk to won't be available 'til tomorrow morning. I'll finish it then."

"Then get your sorry ass home. Maybe you can help me go through the list of replacement candidates I've narrowed down if you screw this up."

There was a pause on my end, and then I heard the laughing. It made me want to tear up—but don't tell anyone.

"You just won't cut me any slack, will you?"

"I'll cut you slack. Just as soon as I know you're okay. I mean *really* okay."

"I take that to mean that sex is out of the question."

"You give me what I want," she purred, "and I'll give you everything you've ever wanted and then some. I don't even care if my dad's around to hear the whole thing."

"Oh, good Lord, woman, you were doing great till you said that. Just the thought of him around made my pecker shrink."

I could hear the laughter on the other end of the phone. It sounded like heaven's choir at that moment.

"Just get home, mister. I need a hug."

~ * ~

I woke the next morning before the alarm was set. I usually don't do mornings very well, but this morning was different. I lay in bed for a while thinking about the previous several days and couldn't get my head around everything that had happened.

I knew Sam was in jail for a murder he didn't commit. I knew that someone framed him and that that someone was very powerful. I thought it might be the police chief, but that didn't really add up because of reasons given to me by Ramos—well, given to William Sheffield Sr., who then gave them to me.

I had originally thought Sheffield was at the bottom of all of this, but he seemed as clueless about the whole thing as I was. Now, I was convinced that the person at the top was none other than District Attorney David Cromwell.

All the pieces fit.

He had the political savvy to make it happen. He had the brains to pull it off. He was certainly motivated by the political gains. He also had the thugs on payroll to pull it off. That's motive, means and opportunity—the two Ms and one O I needed to make the case stick.

Of course, there was one little flaw with my plan.

It was a slight problem. One I hadn't mentioned to Jill last night before we took a shower together and did the nasty. Don't judge me. I'm a guy and omitting material information is what I do for a living. Besides, it serves her right for making me wait so long.

The problem was that, for then at least, I wasn't a cop. As a matter of fact, I was a cop who wasn't seen in very good standing with the force and was on suspension. That may not seem like a lot, but for something like this, it's huge.

You don't go into the district attorney's office and accuse him of murder, or at least conspiracy to commit murder, without everything completely lined up. They would give Sam a pass and make sure that I was the one spending the rest of my life in jail.

Everything had to work out.

I'm not one to pray all that much. But if there was ever a time to give it a whirl, this was it.

Twenty-three

I met Manny in front of the police station. He had the prisoners cuffed and wearing leggings as we walked them into the barracks.

Detective Bennett, one of the police department's finest, was the first pushed through the doors, followed by Westbrook and the other thug we met at the pier last night. A crap load of cops surrounded us. They must have thought we were off our rockers for pulling such a stunt. None of them, however, stopped me as I pushed the prisoners in front of the desk sergeant.

"What in the hell's going on here? What the hell are you trying to pull having Detective Bennett trussed up, Samson? You ain't a cop right now. You're not the law. There's a warrant out for your arrest."

I was about to respond when Deputy Chief Young spoke for me.

"He's brought them here for me. Billings, escort these criminals to holding. I'll take care of the warrant issue myself."

"What're the charges, Chief?" the sergeant asked.

"For this piece of shit," he replied, looking at Bennett, "murder and two counts of attempted murder. For these other two, we'll start with attempted murder. We'll fill in the rest later. You got 'em, son?"

"Yes, sir," Billings replied. The young officer looked around the room and then at two officers. "Give me a hand."

"Your timing may not be the best," Deputy Chief Young said to me. "I didn't know, but the chief is heading to Sacramento this morning. I would have told you, but I just found out ten minutes ago myself."

"No problem," I said looking down at the little man. "He's not the one we need to talk to anyway."

I gave him a smirk of a smile that, I believe, he took as me knowing what I was doing.

I was actually thinking about him dressed in panties and trussed up like a Thanksgiving turkey. I don't think I'll ever get that image out of my head. On the other hand, if he backs up a good cop and saves lives, like I was now watching him do, he could wear pink lipstick, a push-up bra, and heels for all I cared.

In my mind, the thing that makes a good cop has never been about what he wears on his chest. In my book, it's what he holds to be true inside that counts.

~ * ~

As I've said many times before, life is strange and you don't know everything it's going to throw at you. That would be the case with this story.

Yes, I'm telling a story. It's what happened just a short while ago. Yet, it seems like yesterday and a lifetime ago, all at the same time.

Sam Reynolds has been my friend for a very long time. Since this case began, and with everything I've since discovered, our friendship will no longer be as strong as before. I'm sure he knows I can't be a friend with someone who uses people to get his own way, or scares them into submission with threats. I'll always be grateful for the friendship we've had all these years, but I won't be playing pool so much anymore. Those days are gone for me.

As far as being a cop, that's something I'll have to think about for a while. It's in my blood to bring down the bad guys. I like doing that a lot. However, I've seen a lot of corruption recently and it's coming from a place I considered above reproach. These were friends who have betrayed the most sacred aspects of my being. And now I was going to have to take down the biggest betrayer of them all. It was time to take down the district attorney. He was the leader of this madness. He had destroyed the lives of many people, and I was sure I hadn't done anything more than touch the surface. It was time to end this.

I met with Deputy Chief Young, Dakota Walker and Fay Wesley in front of District Attorney David Cromwell's office at the courthouse. Manny was also with me, mostly for moral support, I suppose. Manny was the only person who actually knew what I was going to do. The rest were invited because I needed witnesses to the impending chaos.

"What are we doing here?" Dakota asked. "I have a very important matter to handle. We're going to arraign Sam in just a few minutes."

"In that case," I replied, "I don't want to keep you waiting. However, if you want to get the real killers of Bobbi Marshall, you might want to postpone that hearing for a few extra minutes."

"What're you talking about, Adam?" Dakota asked. "Sam's already confessed. We've talked about that. We've eliminated the evidence against you that Ramos provided, but so far, everything we've gotten against Reynolds is still there. Everything that's been discovered isn't going to just go away. There's nothing more we can do."

"Oh, I think there is. Follow me and watch." I didn't wait for any response.

I walked into the district attorney's office, right past his receptionist. She stood up in protest, but when she saw everyone following me, she didn't say a word.

"What the hell is going on here?" Cromwell asked. "I'm busy, so get out and set an appointment if you want to meet with me."

He then looked at the rest of the members of my little group and asked Dakota, "What the hell are you doing here? And it better be pretty damn important or I'll have you fired and everybody else locked up for a very long time."

"I invited them here," I said before Dakota could respond. "I told them I was going to make a citizen's arrest regarding the murder of Bobbi Marshall. And just so you don't get the idea that I'm playing here, I figured it would be appropriate that the Assistant DA and IAD were also present, so that everything would be on the up and up. If you'll just take a seat, Mr. District Attorney, this will only take a few minutes and then you'll be on your way to the rest of your life in Pelican Bay or San Quentin or wherever they want to send that scrawny ass of yours."

"You think I had something to do with the Marshall woman's death?" Cromwell asked. "That's very funny. I had nothing to do with it other than make sure the son of a bitch who killed her would go to jail. I'm doing that as we speak. Now get the fuck out of my office."

There was a glimmer in his eyes. For some reason he believed, or maybe knew, he wasn't going to go to jail. He was cocksure that he was in charge and wasn't about to let go of the reins. It was time to turn the screws and bring all of this to a close.

"You want me to believe you just because you say you're innocent," I said. "Well guess what? I don't care if you're the President of the United States. You do a crime, I'll bring your ass down. And I can prove it."

"All right." the DA was smiling now. "Prove it. And when he's done making a fool of himself, Deputy Chief, I want this S.O.B.

and his renegade buddy there arrested. I'll make up the charges later. Do you understand me?"

"I hope you know what the hell you're doing," Manny whispered to me, shuffling his feet. "He seems *really* pissed."

"Thanks for the vote of confidence, man. I thought you had my back."

"I do, but my complexion doesn't go well with prison orange."

"Don't worry," I replied. "He's the only one that's going to be doing any bending over."

"Just get it to hell over with," the DA growled. "I have a murderer to put behind bars."

"William Sheffield is a major contributor of yours and he had a problem. It seems his little boy—or grandson—was straying off the path that dear old Granddad had in mind for the tike. It seems he has an affinity for whips and chains. I know this because I've had a heart-to-heart conversation with his dominatrix. She told me that he'd gotten to the point where it had become somewhat of an obsession. And that's not all. It seems that his on-again, off- again, girlfriend, Bobbi Marshall, also knew about this situation and confided the information to Sam Reynolds.

"Now Sam may not be the most honorable man, but he wouldn't just blab this information to everyone in the world. No, sir, Sam is an entrepreneur and he thought he could use the information to better his situation and get some things he wanted. He made a phone call and got a zoning variance. However, apparently he got a little greedy and thought the information he possessed was the gift that would just keep on giving. He thought grandson Sheffield would keep paying for his sins. Then again, maybe Sam didn't ask for anything else, but the boy thought he might. Either way, the information train was running down the tracks and had to be derailed.

"Old Man Sheffield wasn't about to have his grandson, i.e., future governor of California, maybe president, held for ransom because of some no-good weasel like Sam Reynolds. No sir. He came to the one man who could get things done if it were really important, and in a way that his hands wouldn't be dirty.

"He didn't come to you for the little things, did he? He only used you for the most important situations. It basically came down to one issue: if you wanted to be elected again as district attorney, you would find a way to make this go away. Two people knew about his addiction, Bobbi Marshal and Sam Reynolds, and they had to be taken care of."

"This is all very interesting, *ex*-detective Shaw, but you have no proof of anything you've just stated. I'm beginning to believe you'll be spending a lot of time behind bars."

The DA said this with a degree of certainty that momentarily made me question myself. However, I was already up to my ass in alligators; I figured I might as well finish draining the swamp.

I plowed on.

"Carl Ramos has been working for you for a long time. It seems the two of you liked the finer things in life and didn't mind bending a few rules to get them. That's why, when you broached the subject of killing Ms. Marshall, he didn't hesitate. There were promises made and money to collect for a job like that. I would guess in the hundreds of thousands of dollars, considering what was at stake for the old man. Ramos didn't have any trouble killing. My guess, though it isn't something I can prove yet, was that he'd done it before.

"Of course, killing her wasn't the only issue at stake here. Sam also had to be shut up. So you pointed the finger at him. That way, his word would be totally discounted if he ever did say anything. Were you going to have him killed in prison, Mr. District Attorney? Was that the next step to your evil plan?"

"This is ridiculous," he scoffed. "Nothing you've said so far can be proved."

"That's not the same as saying 'I'm innocent' or 'I'm being framed' now, is it? Anyway, we'll get to the proof part real soon.

"Carl Ramos also had a couple of cohorts in crime: Detective Bennett, whom I assume you all know," I said, looking around the room, "and Lenny Westbrook, a local slime-ball I'm sure will be a pleasure for you all to meet. Carl, it seems, wasn't willing to completely roll over on you. It seems that Detective Bennett, on the other hand, doesn't have the same degree of loyalty to you as Ramos. He told me his friendly DA would see to his freedom. You see, last night he tried to kill Annie Lee and Westbrook tried to kill me to keep me from getting any closer. However, being the fine, upstanding and excellent cop that I am, I foiled his plan and we had a very long conversation last night about what happened. *And* . . . he's willing to testify, for a somewhat reduced sentence, to all the facts related to this case. It seems you've been a very bad boy, Mister District Attorney. And the only one who will be going to jail right now will be you."

"This is an outrage," the DA jumped from his seat. "I had nothing to do with any of the things you just discussed. I had nothing to do with killing that woman. This is all a lie."

His face was red with anger. If his blood pressure went any higher, I was sure he would have a stroke.

"Is everything you just said true?" Dakota asked, as if she couldn't believe what had just happened.

"It's all true and available to you for the mere price of a deal with ex-detective Bennett," I replied. "It seems he's more than willing to cooperate if you'll work with him."

There was a long pause and the room got very quiet. Dakota seemed as if she didn't know what to do. Then she looked at me, then at Deputy Chief Young, and said, "Arrest him, Deputy Chief, for conspiracy to commit the murder of Roberta, a.k.a. Bobbi, Marshall."

The district attorney was yelling louder than a rock concert at a pitch only dogs could translate. Many of the words were incoherent; the gist was that he was innocent. He didn't do it. He was being framed. This was wrong. He was going to see me in hell. Something like that.

I, on the other hand, was very proud of myself for doing a good deed. I knew it wouldn't be easy, but I also knew that somehow it had to work.

I looked at Dakota and asked, "Would you do me a favor?"

"Anything," she replied.

"Would you please get Sam out of jail? I think he's had enough of playing the martyr."

"It would be my pleasure," she said smiling at me. "You did some really good work here. I'm proud of you."

Dakota gave me a hug. It isn't protocol for a cop to be getting hugs from attorneys of any kind, especially the district attorney kind. But it was Dakota and I would take a hug from her anytime she wanted.

"Thanks," I replied. "I'm just doing what I used to get paid for." I smiled at her in return when I believed she got the implication.

"We'll take a hard look at that suspension," she said. "Maybe there'll be a way to shorten the time a bit."

"That reminds me," Faye Wesley interrupted. "Why was Sam so willing to take the fall for killing the girl?"

"I'm not positive yet," I replied. "Maybe we'll have to ask him when he gets out."

"You took a big leap there," Manny said, putting his hand on my shoulder. "You also know that this isn't a locked-down case. There's a lot of circumstantial shit going on here."

"I know. The guy is powerful and he has a lot of friends. My guess is he'll be out before sundown."

He wasn't out before sundown. Not that day or even the next day. It seems as if even someone as powerful as the district attorney gets shunned when he gets accused of murder. The morning of the third day I got a phone call.

It was good news. Annie Lee was no longer unconscious and she wanted to talk to me. This would be the last straw for David Cromwell, our ex-district attorney.

~ * ~

I really didn't know Annie beyond our brief conversation when we'd met at the restaurant. She had been unconscious for the better part of a week. The skinny little girl looked extremely frail when I went to her hospital room. My momma would have said that she was "no bigger than a hand full of minutes."

But when she saw me, her smile seemed to come from an old friend. It tugged at my heart. I guess, in a way, I believed I was somehow to blame for her almost getting killed and that was something I was going to have to live with.

I looked at the tiny person in front of me and said, "I'm so happy to see you're doing better."

"Don't know how much better I am. I just know that getting shot ain't a whole lot of fun."

"I can vouch for that...I've been there a time or two, myself."

"So what, you want to compare war wounds or something? Yours bigger than mine? You got more so yours are more impressive?"

I will never understand women. She looked serious and I was getting uncomfortable standing in front of her. I thought I had insulted her somehow.

She noticed my discomfort, and then a smile crept onto her lips.

"I'm just kidding! Damn, can't a girl play around a little bit after she's been shot? I'm just jerking your chain a little."

"Damn, girl," I said, my face getting flush. "I already feel bad enough for getting you into this mess. I thought you were being serious. I'm sorry for getting you hurt."

"You didn't get me hurt, dummy. I screwed up. I thought I had more time before that cop and DA person got to me. I guessed wrong."

"Well, you don't have to worry about the cop anymore. It seems he's met a fate he won't be coming back from. As for the DA, well, he's behind bars as we speak. He won't be any trouble for you, either."

I expected Annie to smile. I expected her to show relief. I expected her to have so very many possible responses.

I didn't expect what I got.

Twenty-four

Being a good guy isn't necessarily what it's supposed to be cracked up to be. You want to get the bad guys. You want to put the criminals behind bars. You want there to be a happy ending for everyone concerned.

That's what it's supposed to be for the good guys.

When all is said and done, I realized the bad guy would go to jail, but this time it didn't make me feel any better. Oh, don't get me wrong; it was the right thing to do. I just didn't like what had to be done. I called Manny and told him to meet me. When I explained why, the other end of the line went quiet. We hung up and I made a few other calls.

I really hate David Cromwell. He's a pompous, arrogant son of a bitch. It seems right for the asshole to be locked up in jail for the rest of his life.

It almost seems poetic.

~ * ~

It had taken the better part of two days for everything to be put together for this remarkably complex case; a case I would never get credit for solving.

Dakota met me for a private conversation at the local restaurant I suggested. Now that more information had come to light, I was glad for the extra time to make sure of what I was doing.

"Hey, Samson," Dakota said affectionately and gave me a hug. I held on to her a shade longer than I should have. She looked in my eyes. I didn't want things to go the way they had to. I wanted things to be simple. I could see that her interpretation was for a different reason. "It's so nice to see you. Where've you been?"

"Just working on a few things. Annie Lee disappeared. I was trying to find her, for one thing."

"Has there been any progress?" she asked, seeming concerned for the girl.

"Some, I think. I should know more any time now."

"You'll keep me posted, I assume?"

"You'll be the first to know. She'll be a key to getting this thing with the DA to be a slam dunk. Anyway, I just wanted to see you and talk to you for a bit. It's been a long time since we've had any *real* time together. I've missed that."

There were no other customers in the restaurant so we had privacy. We sat down at one of the booths in the back corner and she leaned forward and grabbed my hands.

"Are you all right, Adam? Is everything going okay with you and Jill? You seem like the weight of the world is resting on your shoulders."

"Everything's fine at home," I replied. I let her continue holding my hands. "Jill is going crazy with her father and his newest love interest, but we're getting along just fine."

"Then what is it?"

The pause was longer than I wanted it to be. I wasn't feeling good.

"I'm afraid we might have made a mistake," I said finally. "Cromwell may be innocent after all."

She dropped my hands.

"What the hell are you talking about? Everything is working out exactly as you said. Bennett's pinned him as the head guy and the trial is set up for the beginning of next month. What am I missing?"

"Well, just one thing," I said. "I can't seem to find the tie between Cromwell and Ramos. There aren't any conversations I can link between them, so how can Bennett be so definitive about him being the head guy?"

"The point is moot," she replied. "There are enough other details we can use to close that gap. Besides, there's still time for us to get that information. We'll be okay. I'm sure."

"I'm glad you think so. Of course, there is another question I need answered before I can close the book on this."

"What is it?"

I had her attention. She didn't seem to have a clue what was next. I really didn't want to ask her, but the time was now or never.

"How long have you and Bennett been sleeping together?"

"What are you—?"

The door opened and her expression changed from what I thought was anger to an expression of guilt. In walked Manny, with Annie Lee, Deputy Chief Young and two uniformed officers. When DA Cromwell finished the parade, she knew the truth was out.

"It's not what you think," she finished.

"I think it's pretty much exactly what I think, Dakota. Oh, there may be some details you could help me with. But, I think I'll let you discuss them with your attorney before we go there. The only question I have is...why?"

Epilogue

It's official. I'm a moron.

I'm not the kind of person to cherish awards or accolades. For the most part, I'm pretty laid back and unassuming. I did, however, think that by catching a killer, uncovering corrupt cops and identifying and arresting the leader of the ring, I would be awarded a reduction of my suspension and allowed to get back to work.

For reasons yet to be explained, the district attorney, the man I originally arrested, David Cromwell, has seen to it that my suspension is to stay in full force. He even went so far as to convince the chief of police that if I even sniff the inside of the police station—his words, not mine—during the remainder of my suspension, he will see to it that my vacation will be extended another sixty days.

Where's the gratitude? Where's the love?

Like I said...I'm a moron.

~ * ~

As for the why? Well, that falls into the ignorant category. I guess it could be a fringe moron thing, but I'll stick with ignorant.

Dakota wasn't very forthcoming after her arrest. As a matter of fact, she wasn't cooperative at all. Seems she was under the opinion she could somehow slither out of the mess she had made.

I tried to figure everything out. Was it the money? Power? Influence? I didn't know, and after a few days, gave up trying to figure it out.

Bennett finally came clean. He explained that he and Dakota had been having a relationship for some time. When Dakota realized I had put all my eggs in the basket by accusing the DA, she decided the best way to protect herself and Bennett was to have him implicate Cromwell and Ramos as the big wigs and have him take whatever plea deal he could get. The idea was that sometime down the road, Dakota would find him a way to get him out. They could then be together again. It sounded so romantic.

I knew that eventually it would all come together. Bennett had a lot to lose. Now that his get-out-of-jail-free ticket out was no longer available, he was cooperating fully.

On the fourth day after Dakota's arrest, I got a message that she wanted to speak to me. I was told she wanted to confess and maybe get a lighter sentence, but that she would only talk to me.

I wasn't really interested. She had broken my heart and betrayed a trust that would make me question relationships for years to come.

Let's face it, I was pissed.

~ * ~

"I don't care about the confession, Dakota," I said as I entered the small, stark interrogation room. "I already know what you did. You made your bed. Now lie in it."

"I understand, Samson. I figured as much."

"So then, why am I here?"

"To answer your question," Dakota replied, cocking her head to the side and smiling as if she had a special secret that only she knew.

"What question?"

I didn't want to have to go through the whole psychobabble aspects of the case. I was completely convinced about what had happened and who did it. The shrinks could figure the rest out later.

"You asked me why I did it. I figured I owed you that much."

"You owe me a lot more than that."

"I don't have anything more to offer, so it'll have to do."

"Okay, why? Why would you kill, or have killed, someone like Bobbi Marshal? Why would you get in bed with a known criminal like Sheffield? Why would you turn your back on the profession you love? I know that's a lot of whys, but I would really like to know."

"You made me do it, Samson. You destroyed everything that mattered to me when you walked out of my life all those years ago. If you would've loved me like I loved you, none of this would ever have happened."

"What the hell are you talking about? We both knew we weren't good for each other. You know that.

"'We aren't good for each other.' That's what you said back then too. We were perfect, you son of a bitch!"

"You wanted your freedom...fine! You wanted your space...fine. I gave you everything you ever asked for and all I got from you was a wedding invitation. I believed in that old saying: 'If you love someone, let them go. If they return, they're yours forever. If they don't, they never were.' You were supposed to come back to me, Adam. You were supposed to love me. When you didn't, nothing else mattered.

"When I finally figured out you had left me for good, I started drinking and sleeping around. I must have done thirty guys in six months. That is, until I met Joe Bennett. He got me. He understood what I was going through. He made me feel good about myself again.

"What I didn't know was his relationship with Ramos and how deep they were into certain things."

"You mean crime things?"

"Yes, crime things. Ramos set me up. He made it look like Joe was going to go away for a long time if I didn't help him. I loved him, Adam. I thought I would never love again after you. I thought I would die after you left. When Joe came into my life, I thought I had been given a second chance and I couldn't let anything happen to him. I couldn't just let him go to jail. I covered up some things. From then on, Ramos had me.

"I didn't know about his connections. I didn't know Joe was a part of it. I just figured that if I was going to survive, I had to go along.

"Don't you see, Adam? It's your fault. If you would have loved me, I would never have had to do what I did."

"It wasn't my fault, Dakota. You were at the top. You were in charge of it all. You can't sit here and tell me it was all Ramos' fault, either. That's a lie and you know it."

"He *was* at the top, Adam. At least he was until I realized I had no way out. That's when I decided that if this was destiny, I would do everything I could to get out of it what I could. I went to Sheffield Senior and offered my services. I did to Ramos what he did to me. I took from him what he took from me—my freedom to do and be what I wanted. The funny thing is, Sheffield never placed any requirements on me. He never had me doing dirty jobs. He wanted me at the top. He wanted to control things in a way that would be seamless when he wanted things done. And I would have made it if not for his stupid son.

"Sheffield the third came to me and told me what was going on and the problems with Reynolds. He asked for my help. He wanted to keep his grandfather out of it. It wasn't an order, Adam. I know you think it was, but it wasn't. I thought if I did the grandson this one favor, he would see to it, through Senior, that I got elected DA in the next election. With Senior's political connections, I was on my way to the top.

"I just made one mistake."

"Me."

"Yes, you. I didn't know how tight you were with Reynolds. If I had known, I would have killed him and let the girl take the blame. I think it would have been better all around."

Her head dropped and a tear fell down her cheek. I didn't know if it was because of losing the friendship we'd had or because she was going to prison.

"I knew I would have to get out of this mess I had made someday. I just figured I would have more time. I thought Joe and I would have more time."

All of a sudden, I wanted her suffering to stop. I wanted to defend myself. I wanted to make everything better. I wanted everything to go back the way it was before Bobbi Marshall changed all of our lives.

Instead, I left.

Maybe she was right. Maybe I had screwed up her life. If I did, I didn't know it at the time. That's where that ignorance stuff comes in.

On the other hand, maybe I'm just a moron.

~ * ~

Time has passed since all of this went down. I'll be going back to work tomorrow and looking forward to getting back to my routines.

I still feel bad for having to arrest Dakota. For a time in my life, she was the one person I could most feel comfortable around and confide in. I never in a million years would have suspected the changes in her life. I would never have suspected she could turn so cold, so lethal. It just goes to show, you don't always know people as well as you think.

Sam is back at the pool hall, but he's selling the place. He told me he was sorry for the mess he caused, but I'm not so sure about anything with him anymore. He wants my forgiveness for placing me, my family and friends in danger, and I believe he's sincere. I'm just not willing to let it go yet.

The news created by the arrests made headlines all over California. Manny was considered a major player, maybe because I sort of made an anonymous call and told a local reporter about him and how it was really his efforts that saved the day. Anyway, as a result, he landed a large security job and won't have to spend so much time digging in the dirt of creeps and crazies any more.

As an aside, he decided that Margie's talents weren't being utilized to their fullest potential so he made her a partner. It's a major uptick in her income.

Speaking of Margie, she and Stephanie, a.k.a. Lady Shadows, have become an item. Apparently, Margie has no qualms about Stephanie's chosen profession as long as when the day is done, she reverts back to simply being a girlfriend. Whips and chains are prohibited in the bedroom.

How do I know this?

It seems my fascination with koochies has been placed on the endangered species list. Hey, I told you before—I'm a guy! I've been told in no uncertain terms that koochie talk, lesbian fantasy talk, and any other gross and disgusting man-talk is to be hereinafter off limits. The two of them swore that if I continued such banter they would discuss said fantasies with Jill, and that convinced me.

As a reward for being such a good sport, they told me in detail about what it was like being in love with—and in lust with—another beautiful, sexy woman. The details will be embedded in my mind forever.

For weeks afterward, poor Jill never had a chance.

Tootie will always be Tootie: devastated when the girls told him they were off the market and committed to each other. Of course he offered them both the opportunity to let him change their minds. They agreed to think about it.

Bitsy decided she could not take Tootie's wandering eyes and went back to Texas. Tootie decided to stick around. He's rented a little place in the Village and is currently dating three different girls named Mary. All of them, more or less, are an age-appropriate forty-something, all of them are current or ex-models, and all of them are giving the old man whatever he wants, if you know what I mean.

Don't ask me how he manages that, because I don't know.

The man will, from this day forward, *always* be my hero.

Meet L. C. Wright

L. C. Wright turns the story over to the characters from the beginning just to see how they might get into trouble. He believes that each person tells a unique story and it's the author's job to blend those stories together no matter how serious (or absurd) they become. He lives on California mountainside in Carmel Valley, CA with his wife Melissa, their Black Lab, Barney and Little Girl, the precocious cat who rules them all.